He made her fe[el] nervous, as if s[omething] near at hand.

The closer he came, the higher her sense of alert climbed.

Over the pounding of her heart, she could hear the sound of his breathing.

Beneath his slightest touch, her skin quivered, twitching like a cat right before someone stroked its fur.

Through all the wondrous scents of the forest, the trees, bushes and earth, his scent—worn leather, sweat, the oil on his chain mail, the lingering aroma of rosemary—teased at her nose.

And yet she wasn't afraid. The pervading sense of unease didn't frighten her; it was more of a disquieting anticipation than real fear.

She didn't understand how he of all people had so invaded her senses. Elrik of Roul was not just King David's Wolf; he was the man sent to return her to a fate she wished not to face.

Her first instinct should be to run, to find a way to escape. Yet she found herself more than willing, nearly eager to stay close.

DENISE LYNN

The Warrior's Runaway Wife

Recycling programs
for this product may
not exist in your area.

ISBN-13: 978-1-335-52280-1

The Warrior's Runaway Wife

Copyright © 2018 by Denise L. Koch

Printed in U.S.A.

Award-winning author **Denise Lynn** lives in the USA with her husband, son and numerous four-legged "kids." Between the pages of romance novels she has traveled to lands and times filled with brave knights, courageous ladies and never-ending love. Now she can share with others her dream of telling tales of adventure and romance. You can write to her at PO Box 17, Monclova, OH 43542, USA, or visit her website, denise-lynn.com.

Books by Denise Lynn

Harlequin Historical

Falcon's Desire
Falcon's Honor
Falcon's Love
Falcon's Heart
Commanded to His Bed
Bedded by Her Lord
Bedded by the Warrior
The Warrior's Runaway Wife

Warehaven Warriors

Hallowe'en Husbands
"Wedding at Warehaven"
Pregnant by the Warrior
The Warrior's Winter Bride
At the Warrior's Mercy

Visit the Author Profile page
at Harlequin.com for more titles.

For Tom and KM with love.

Prologue

Carlisle Castle—April 1145

The large double doors of the Great Hall groaned open, slowing the fever-pitched conversations to a hushed whispering. Lord Elrik of Roul strode through the open doors, bringing even the whispers to a complete halt.

Rain from the spring storm fell in rivulets from the wolf pelts trimming his full-length mantle. The cape swirled, sending droplets of rainwater to the floor in his wake.

Men and women alike made way, clearing the path ahead of his long strides. The clinking of his linked-mail hauberk and spurs along with the heavy fall of his footsteps were the only sounds echoing in the hall.

The visitors to King David's court stared in fascination at the sight of the fabled man before them. Some were young enough to have grown up hearing stories of the King's Wolves. They'd trembled at the tales told in the dark of night, wondering how much truth lay behind the words, yet not wanting to discover the answer for themselves.

From the unkempt overlong hair, black as night and shot through with silver, to his frowning countenance, the furrowed brow resembling a dark outcrop over his greenish-gold eyes, to the beard covering his lower face, hiding his features, leaving only the thin line of his tightly held mouth visible, made them wonder if he was indeed part-wolf. A barely civilised, not quite human warrior who would think nothing of unleashing the terrors of hell on an unsuspecting prey.

Elrik dropped to a knee at the bottom of the raised dais and bowed his head. He knew what these people thought of him, these weak-kneed courtiers who had rarely, if ever, used the sword belted to their side for anything more than show, and he cared not. As the Lord of Roul, he did what he needed to do to keep his lands, and his family, safe.

Being one of David's Wolves wasn't easy, but then he'd never been blessed with a life of ease so why would this be any different? The one saving grace was that his three brothers made up the rest of his wolf pack and he could trust them with his life.

King David stood. 'Roul, join me.'

Elrik rose and followed the King into the smaller chamber beyond the dais. Once the door closed behind the two of them they were afforded a privacy not available in the Great Hall.

'Thank you for coming so quickly.' David poured two goblets of deep red wine and offered one to Elrik, before settling into a chair.

He accepted the liquid, hoping it would thaw his blood. 'My liege?'

'I apologise for taking you from the comfort of your fires, but I've a need for your particular skill.'

'Who do you need found?' He'd been born with an uncanny ability to track down things lost, whether it be a missing shoe or a person not wishing to be found.

'Avelyn of Brandr.'

Elrik paused before swallowing his wine. In the space

of one heartbeat it all came flooding back. His father had sought to commit treason against King David at the prompting of Galdon, Lord of Brandr Isle. Brandr, named so because of the long, sharp, pointed rocks that stuck out from the northern end of the isle like ready swords, drawn for attack, wasn't enough land for Galdon. Whether the traitor had acted of his own accord, or at the behest of his uncle by marriage and liege, Lord Somerled, the Lord of Argyll, or his maternal grandfather Óláfr, the King of the Isles, was never discovered since Brandr had used his connections to escape punishment. Unlike Elrik's father.

To save his father's life, he and his younger brother Gregor had thrown themselves at King David's feet, begging for mercy. Their plea had been heard and mercy granted—at the cost of nothing more than their souls.

While their father had been confined to Roul Isle, he and Gregor, along with their two younger brothers, when they'd become old enough, had become King David's Wolves. Men tasked with deeds that required secrecy and, at times, the steadfast ruthlessness of a wolf.

He swallowed, then said, 'I wasn't aware Brandr had a daughter.'

'A natural-born daughter.'

Elrik wasn't surprised. Especially since Brandr's mother was conceived out of wedlock. Still, why would King Óláfr's grandson come to the King of Scotland for assistance? More curious, why would Brandr risk coming to King David when the man had once joined forces with those intent on taking the throne from David? Not wanting to dredge up the traitor's history—especially since his own father had been part of that treasonous act—he instead asked, 'And Brandr came to you rather than going to his uncle or grandfather?'

'Yes, it appears that way.'

'Any reason given for keeping them in the dark?'

'A marriage has been arranged between the girl and Sir Bolk, one of Óláfr's minor lords.'

Bolk? 'Surely you don't mean Bolk the elder?'

The King nodded. 'Yes. If I'm counting correctly, this will be his third wife.'

What had the girl's father been thinking to agree to that arrangement? That old, gnarled warlord had outlived the previous two. Obviously, Brandr's daughter had not liked the idea of being number three. 'How long has she been gone?'

'My understanding is that she vanished three weeks ago, just moments before officially meeting the man.'

Elrik set his empty goblet on the table, waving off a re-fill, and asked, 'Any description of the woman?'

'All I was told was that she has night-black hair, ice-blue eyes, fair skin, a well-made form and a temper befitting a daughter of Brandr.'

Excellent. Not only was he required to find the daughter of a warlord whom he considered an enemy of his family, but a king's great-granddaughter who had a three-week head start on him and a headstrong one who most likely desired not to be found.

'Where was she last seen?'

'She ran away from Oban.'

There was little there other than the ruins of an ancient tower fort. 'Any word after that?'

'There were rumours of a black-haired wench in Duff-ield who'd killed a man for trying to stop her from stealing bread. Brandr's men stopped their search there.'

Elrik doubted the rumours held any truth. If the girl was smart enough to run away without being caught thus far, she wasn't going to risk capture by doing anything to foolishly call attention to herself.

However, if she had been spotted in Duffield, this mission could prove a little more difficult, which was why her father's men had stopped their search. Going into England to hunt for the girl was one thing, but heading deeper into the Earl of Derby's lands was another thing altogether. The first Earl of Derby had done much to help King Stephen keep unfriendly forces at bay—it was doubtful the second earl would do any less.

Elrik knew he could find himself at the wrong end of a sword. Which, of course, was why he was being given the task—the Wolves were expendable. If captured, King David wasn't going to offer a ransom—in fact, the King would deny all knowledge of the mission.

So, he needed to make certain he wasn't caught.

The woman was either very strong and brave, or completely lacking in wits. She'd already travelled a far distance for a woman alone. Thankfully, it required no special powers to know she was headed for the southern coast and then on to Normandy, or France.

'You need to find her before she leaves England.'

'Where will Brandr be expecting her return?'

'Not our concern, since his expectations will go unmet. Bring her here to me. Marrying off the eighteen-year-old great-granddaughter of a king to a nearly eighty-year-old minor vassal with no title, or holdings to speak of, seems a little suspicious, made more so by Brandr's request for my assistance.'

Elrik couldn't disagree with that reasoning. 'It is a bit... odd.'

'More than just odd. Considering the man has already proven he cannot be trusted, I can't help but wonder what he is plotting.' David waved a hand, dismissing further discussion. 'Find her, bring her here and do it quickly. Brandr will arrive within the next four weeks. I do not wish his presence for any longer than necessary and I intend to put a halt to his plans before his arrival.'

Elrik's stomach knotted at the last part of the King's statement. Something about David's emotionless, steady tone of voice when he said he intended to put a halt to Brandr's plans was...unsettling. The King already knew what he was going to do—and Elrik wondered if there was more to his involvement than David was willing to divulge at this moment.

For over ten years he'd been the King's Wolf. Not once had he questioned any order he'd been given, not even the ones that had forced him to harden his heart, or turn a deaf ear to those pleading for mercy. But this was different—it was personal. It touched on the very reason he'd sold his soul to the King. 'Why me?'

'The girl had nothing to do with the past.' David's stare darkened. 'At that time, she was but a child and her father hadn't yet claimed her as his daughter.' He paused before leaning forward to add, 'Your father made his choice. He would have done nothing different whether Brandr had been involved or not.'

Elrik disagreed. He'd been there. He'd heard Brandr's rallying speeches against the foreigners King David had put in control of what were considered choice areas of land and seen the effect the man's passionately spoken words had had on the older men gathered in Roul's Great Hall. With nothing but his voice, he'd stirred them into a frenzied desire for revenge.

The striped scars crisscrossing his back were a permanent reminder of the hellish glee Brandr took in seeing punishment meted out to those deemed insubordinate— whether they had been or not. Brandr hadn't applied the lash, but he'd done much to ensure it had been used.

Elrik wasn't about to voice his thoughts to the King.

Brandr was a king's grandson and the nephew of a very powerful lord, while he was nothing more than a traitor's son.

'You will do as ordered, Roul.'

Elrik kept a tight hold on his rage, swallowed the bitterness coating his tongue and nodded. 'Of course, my lord.'

King David leaned back against the chair and tossed him a sack of coins. 'This should cover what you need. I've no men to spare.'

Elrik dropped the smaller sack into the leather pouch secured to the inside of his cloak. The money would come in handy and additional men would only slow him down. 'What need I of any men?'

'Perhaps I failed to mention that Brandr's men found evidence that someone might be hunting the lady. He fears their intention is not to bring her home alive.'

Chapter One

South of Derbyshire, England— one week later

'Open up.' The wooden door to the room rattled. 'I've a ready need for a willing whore.'

Avelyn cringed at the man's request and kept a firm grip on the borrowed dagger she held out before her as she backed away from the locked door of her room. The need to protect herself was from habit since she knew she need only keep quiet and eventually he would move further along the corridor.

Just as they had for the last seven nights, men looking for a willing woman had stopped by to test her door countless times before moving on to find one that would open beneath their touch. So far, she'd been lucky and the thin metal locking bar had held.

There seemed to be a code of honour of sorts, even for this brothel. Apparently, a locked door meant either that the room was already occupied, or the lady wished no company at that moment. To her surprise, the men seemed to abide by that wish.

When silence once again fell in the hallway, she lowered her weapon and breathed. She choked out a strangled laugh at the loudness of her breath. Not even the unceasing rain beating on the roof had drowned out what sounded like a near gasp for life.

Avelyn sat on a stool by the window, staring at the overcast sky. Everything was grey. The sky, the road outside the brothel, even the buildings blended into near nothingness against the unending grey.

She longed to be gone from here, but had let her newfound friend Hannah talk her into waiting yet another day in the hopes the sky would clear even a little. Right now, after nearly eight days of rain, the streams would be so overfilled that the crossings would not be passable, which would only increase the likelihood of being caught.

She hadn't risked her life running away from her father and forthcoming nuptials only to be captured and returned.

Everyone at home had told her that she'd been lucky and how privileged she should have felt to find herself betrothed to one of King Óláfr's warlords. Especially considering the King was not beholden to concern himself with her welfare. Óláfr was her father's grandfather—her great-grandfather—but she was nothing more than a by-blow from a dalliance her father had had with a common servant. King Óláfr was not beholden to see to her future. So, why had he gone to such lengths for her?

Even with the questions plaguing her over the arrangement, when Lord Somerled had first come to Brandr with the news, she had been so excited about the prospect of being married that she'd slipped away to return to her mother's burned-down hut in the village to retrieve a ring her mother had given her on her twelfth birthday. She'd been told it had been her grandmother's wedding band and she'd buried it to keep the ring safe until her own wedding day loomed in hopes that she could convince her husband-to-be to use it as her wedding band.

But those who'd thought her so lucky and privileged had not seen the warlord selected to be her husband. He was old, so ancient that his own sons were older than she. He was wrinkled, his skin ashen. And he had a belly that hung half way to his knees. She couldn't begin to imagine her wedding night.

And when she had tried to reason it out in her mind, it seemed that the only viable options open to her were either death by her own hand, or to run away.

Unwilling to kill herself, she'd chosen to run. However, because her half-brother Osbert was watching her far too closely, she'd bolted quickly, taking with her a small stash of food, her ring, which she'd placed in a small pouch and hung around her neck with a ribbon, and even fewer prospects. There were not many ways for her to make enough money to buy food and none of them seemed welcome.

The food had lasted her only the first two days. On the third night, she'd stolen bread from a cottage window where it had been left on the sill to cool. She'd almost been caught. A man stumbling out of the local inn, barely able to walk a straight line, had seen her swipe the round loaf and took chase. Quicker on her feet, she'd outrun him, only looking back once when she'd heard him shout out in pain as he'd tripped over a tree root. His slurred curses let her know that he'd live, so she'd not stopped.

The next night she'd not been as lucky at finding anything to eat. So, the following evening she'd joined the gathering outside the gates of a castle and waited for the food scraps that would be tossed their way. She'd managed to nab a sodden, hard bread trencher and a couple of pieces of half-eaten fruit, food that would seem like gifts from heaven to her growling stomach.

But she recognised the half-dead stare of hunger from a bedraggled child at her side. It had been a part of her own childhood. Without having to think twice, she placed over half of the trencher, along with the fruit, in the small, shaking hands.

Thus had become her life—a woman alone, on the run, hiding from all who might seek to harm her, or worse, return her to her father. She'd been sick from hunger and exhausted from her non-stop march south. At times, she'd considered giving up her quest for escape. But then an image of the man waiting to become her husband flashed through her mind, lending her enough strength to put one foot in front of the other.

To her relief, she'd managed, for the most part, to avoid others by keeping off the main roads and staying out of town. But one afternoon, while she'd been leaning against a tree bemoaning her fate, an arrow had whizzed right past her nose to pierce the tree trunk, quivering less than a finger's width away.

She'd run wildly through a forest to a narrow, rutted road and kept running until she'd fallen to her knees. Exhausted she'd crawled from the road to hide beneath piles of leaves and underbrush. The sun had been high in the sky when she'd finally woken to find herself hungrier and more tired than she'd been the evening before.

She'd happened into a good-sized town and quickly found the common well in the centre. That was where Hannah had found her—gulping water from the bucket while sobbing like a spineless fool.

The good lady had coaxed the story from her—it hadn't been hard considering her mind was as numb as her body—and she had brought her here, to the brothel above the town's inn where Hannah and a few other women made their living.

So far nobody had tried to talk or force her into plying the same trade. They'd simply given her the use of one of their rented rooms while two of them shared another and brought her food and drink.

Avelyn was more than grateful for their help in her time of need and vowed to herself that she would find a way to repay them some day soon.

Movement in the street below caught her attention. Three men she'd not seen before walked towards the inn, their booted feet splashing muddy water from the puddles on to the hems of their long, hooded mantles.

The tallest of the three looked up as if he knew she watched. Avelyn leaned away from the window, hiding from his searching gaze. Something about him and his companions sent worry skipping along her spine. She shivered as the apprehension settled cold in her belly.

A soft, quick knock on her door drew her away from her troublesome cares. Recognising Hannah's gentle tap, Avelyn rose to cross the small room and open the door to invite her newfound friend inside.

The boisterous sounds from the main room below had been loud, but they grew impossibly louder when she pulled open the door. She'd grown accustomed to the jovial laughter and curses of drunken men, but tonight the tone held a tension-filled undercurrent that had not been present before.

She motioned Hannah inside and quickly closed the door against the troubling voices. From the concerned look on her friend's face, she, too, felt the tense heaviness in the air. 'What is wrong?'

With a roll of her eyes, Hannah headed towards the bed. 'Let us sit.'

Avelyn closed the door, then joined the other woman. The foreboding chill from seeing the strangers still lingered and now turned to icy cold pricks of warning with each step she'd taken.

Again, she asked, 'What is wrong?'

Hannah sighed as she looked around the room before saying, 'You know that Mabel has been unable to be here the last three nights.'

'Yes. She's been at home with a sick child.' Avelyn gasped. 'Did something happen?'

'No. No, the child is getting better. But Edward, a favoured customer of Mabel's, is below and he demands a woman. If it can't be Mabel, it must be someone who looks like her.'

Avelyn frowned. He wanted a whore, what did her looks matter? 'What difference does the woman's looks make to him?'

Hannah patted her arm. 'Not all men come to us for pleasures of the flesh. Some require nothing more than simple human contact, a hug, a kind word, a caress. This man is old and he lost his wife two years ago. Apparently, she had black hair and a slim body in her youth.'

Avelyn closed her eyes. Since the others had often remarked that she and Mabel could be sisters, she knew why Hannah had come to her. But to be certain, she looked at the woman and said, 'What are you asking of me?'

'You are not daft. You know what I'm asking you. I need you to take Mabel's place this night.' Before Avelyn could protest, Hannah quickly added, 'The man is unable to perform, so it is not as if you would need to do anything more than let him hold you.'

'Hold me?' There had to be more to it than that.

'Well, he'd hold you through the night, in bed, unclothed. He will call you Agnes and might require a kiss or two and sometimes he likes to fumble with Mabel's breasts, but I swear that is all.'

That was all? Avelyn blinked. Other than a quick, chaste peck on the cheek, she'd never been kissed by a man before. And she certainly had never let a man see, let alone touch, her naked flesh. What seemed *nothing* to Hannah was far more than what Avelyn had ever done, or wanted to do, with a man not her husband.

Hannah broke the lengthening silence. 'Nobody ever need know and for very little more than your companionship, he will give you enough coins to compensate for what we've provided you.'

The reckoning Avelyn feared might one day come had arrived. She shouldn't have let Hannah convince her to stay until the rain ceased, no matter the logic behind the woman's reasoning.

Now she was faced with paying off a debt and had no means to do so except by surrendering her grandmother's ring, or doing as Hannah requested. She couldn't give up the ring—it was all she had left from her mother.

Avelyn wanted to cry at her lack of options, but forced the useless tears back. As Hannah had said, no one would ever know. As long as even a slender thread of luck remained on her side, she would soon be gone from here— maybe in the morning, if it stopped raining. She could then rush on to Normandy or France and start a new life where nobody knew who she was, or about this night, or that she'd even stayed in this place.

Except, no matter where she ran, one person would know—*she* would know and, somehow, she would have to learn how to live with her shame.

She nodded her agreement, adding, 'If he tries anything other than what you have stated, I will gut him.'

Hannah laughed and patted her arm. 'Rest assured that will not be necessary.'

* * *

From his seat in the far corner of the establishment, Elrik watched and waited for the right moment. Two of his men were situated in different corners of the main room, doing the same as he—listening to the conversations of the others.

Everyone in town seemed to know that the owner of this ale house rented out the upper rooms to women willing to share their favours…for a price.

There'd been talk of new lady, a young one with hair the colour of night who had yet to accept a customer. Several of the men present had wagers on who would be the first.

If his hunch was right, this woman could be the one he sought. The search thus far for Brandr's daughter hadn't been easy—it wasn't as if he could put his nose to the ground like a hound. Instead, snippets of conversations overheard in one place and rumours garnered in another helped to lead him in the right direction. The bits gathered had brought him here.

He was glad he'd changed his mind about travelling alone. His men had come in handy more than once during this search, as what pieces of gossip he missed, they had overheard.

Fulke, one of his men, approached and took a seat on the bench behind Elrik. 'The elderly man who is sitting at the table nearest the fire, where I was, is looking for a black-haired wench for the night. Seems his regular woman isn't available.'

Elrik lifted his tankard to his lips, but didn't drink, instead, he asked softly, 'Are they going to find him another?'

'The woman in green is heading above to see if one is available.'

Elrik turned his full attention to the man Fulke spoke of.

He was old, bony and from the way his hands shook Elrik wondered how he didn't spill most of his drink on himself.

He rose and pretended to shiver, then approached the old man. 'The fire looks inviting. Mind if I join you?'

'Suit yourself. I won't be here long.'

Elrik took a seat and waved the barmaid over. 'Bring me ale and one for my friend here.'

The old man squinted at him. 'Haven't seen you here afore now.'

'Just passing through.'

'Ah. Decided to enjoy a little soft company for the night?'

'Perhaps.'

'What type of wench you looking for?'

Elrik shrugged. 'A lusty red-haired one would be to my liking.'

'Not me.' The man shook his head and a few of the sparse white hairs on his head flopped down over his face. 'I want one like my Agnes. A little thing with black hair and breasts that'll fit in my hand.'

Elrik swallowed his laugh at the man's bawdy talk. 'Is your Agnes at home?' If so, she probably wouldn't be happy to know where her husband was this night.

'No.' A heavy sadness fell over the man, setting his lips to droop and making Elrik feel guilty for having ruined the man's former good mood. 'She's been gone these last two springs now.'

'I am sorry. I meant not to trouble you.'

'No trouble. I come here when missing her gets to be too much to bear.' He leaned over the table and lowered his voice. 'At times just having a woman's arms around me while I sleep helps ease the loss.'

Elrik patted the man's hand before picking up his tankard. 'You cared greatly for her.'

'I loved her, lad. That I did.'

He wasn't going to debate the misguided notion of marital love with the man. 'You should find yourself another wife.'

To Elrik's surprise, the old man stomped a foot and slapped his knee as he howled with laughter. Wiping tears from his eyes, he said between gasps for breath, 'Oh, that's a good one that is. What would I do with a wife at my age?'

'I suppose the same things you did with Agnes.'

'You are younger than you appear, aren't you?' The man reached across the table to throw a half-hearted punch at Elrik's shoulder. 'Trust me, boy, twenty or thirty years from now you'll see things differently.'

Elrik resisted the urge to roll his eyes. 'You misunderstood me. I meant things like sharing a meal, or a conversation around the fire and a soft warm body to lie against in bed. Nothing more.'

'I'd not bring another woman to Agnes's bed. No.'

The woman in the green over-gown came back down the stairs and approached the table. 'Edward, give her but a few moments to get ready and then you can go up. It's the room on the end. Just knock, she'll be waiting.'

The man turned to the others gathered and raised his mug. 'You owe me, boys.'

Elrik knew the man had just won the wager over who would be the first to visit the new woman's room. Too bad he wasn't about to let that happen—at least not until he discovered if this woman was Brandr's daughter or not.

Needing to get upstairs without drawing unwanted attention, he asked the woman in green, 'Any of the ladies free at the moment?'

She looked him up and down and then smiled. 'For someone like you, they'll fight over the honour. Do you have any preferences?'

The old man answered, 'He likes them red-haired and lusty.'

'That settles it then. The second door on the right will be the one you want. She's free right now.'

Elrik rose and shot a glance towards Fulke, giving him the slightest nod in the direction of the stairs. He then took his leave of the old man. 'I trust you'll enjoy your evening.'

'As will you, I'm sure.'

He approached the stairs, pausing by Samuel, his other guard, and gave him the same slight nod towards the stairs. While he was above trying to determine whether this woman was Brandr's daughter or not, his men would make their way closer to the bottom of the stairs. They would then be near at hand if he ran into any trouble.

Elrik took the steps two at a time and quickly traversed the length of the corridor, stopping in front of the last door. Careful to keep his knock soft as an old man might, he tapped on the door.

'Enter.'

He pushed open the door and approached the bed in the dimly lit room. As stiff as a board upon the bed, the young woman had the covers pulled up to her chin. She held fast to the edge of the blankets with a grip that turned her knuckles white. Hair the colour of night was spread out atop the pillow beneath her head. She kept her eyes tightly closed.

This was no experienced whore. It was only a guess, but he was fairly certain he'd just found Brandr's missing daughter. He leaned over the bed and whispered, 'Lady Avelyn, your little adventure is over, get up.'

Her eyes sprang open at the same time her lips parted. He clamped a hand over her mouth. 'Do not force me to carry you from here naked. I doubt your father would approve.'

She shook her head, then wrapped her fingers around his wrist and tugged.

Elrik lifted his hand slightly, giving her room to talk, but keeping his palm close enough to cover any scream should she decide to do so.

'I am not going home.'

Had the appearance of her icy-blue eyes not given her identity away, her comment confirmed his suspicion. His guess had been correct—this was indeed Brandr's daughter. He knelt on the bed and loomed over her. 'The old man you are waiting for will be up here in mere moments. I am not letting you share a bed with him.'

If he did anything that witless, King David would be offering up a special serving of wolf's head—his—on a platter at the next banquet.

'So, either you get up and get dressed or I'll pull you from the bed and dress you myself.'

To his amazement, she hesitated as if debating some third option he'd not given her.

Elrik leaned closer to disabuse her of the idea. 'It is simple. Get up and dressed on your own, or I will see to both myself. Either way, you *are* getting out of that bed and you *are* getting dressed.'

When she narrowed her eyes at him, he had the feeling that she was preparing to argue. Which was something they had no time for at the moment. He grabbed the blankets and tore them from her grasp.

She squeaked and crossed her arms against her chest, trying to cover herself.

'Unless you possess a third breast, you have nothing I've not seen before.' He took hold of her wrists. 'I have no time for your false show of sudden modesty. Get up.'

'I am not a whore.'

He knew she wasn't. She might be Brandr's bastard

daughter, but he knew that until this unfortunate event, she was far too valuable for him not to have kept a tight control over her upbringing. As the man's only daughter, there would have been little opportunity for her to have become a whore. But the fact was that he'd found her in bed, naked, in a known brothel and she was going to debate her position? Elrik pulled her up from the bed. 'We can argue that later. Where are your clothes?'

She nodded towards the window. He released her, pausing to say, 'Do not run and do not scream.'

He then retrieved a chemise and tunic from a bench beneath the window. Pushing the clothing against her chest, he ordered, 'Get dressed.'

Instead of doing as he bid, she stood there, holding the clothing, and stared at him. 'I am not going with you.'

A twinge of tension started behind his eyes. He hadn't wanted this mission to begin with. However, he was certain that if he didn't deliver her to King David, his lands and life would be in grave danger.

His temples throbbed. David should have sent one of his younger brothers on this task. Either one—Rory or Edan— would have been a better choice than him. At least they had the patience and temperament to deal with women in a much kinder and gentler manner than he.

His deceased wife had taught him well that women were untrustworthy liars and good for only one thing—the getting of children—and, as in Muriel's case, sometimes not even that.

Elrik jerked the clothes out of her hands. After gathering the skirt of the chemise in his hands, he dropped it over her head. Keeping his attention directed at the fabric beneath his fingers instead of the pale smoothness of her skin, or the dips and swells of her comely body, he tugged the chemise down to cover her.

He then did the same with her tunic, leaving the laces hanging, before pushing her down on to the bed to squat before her and drag the stockings over her feet and legs, then slipped on a pair of soft boots.

Elrik placed his hands on her knees. 'I like this no more than you. But I am charged with taking you to Carlisle. You can argue this arranged marriage of yours with King David.'

She shook her head and crossed her arms before her as if the action would grant her some type of protection.

'I warn you, Lady Avelyn, I have little patience for childish behaviour from anyone but children. It will go better for you if you come willingly as an adult ready to calmly debate this marriage arrangement, rather than being dropped at King David's feet like an unwilling prisoner. I promise you the King will be less likely to entertain the complaints of a prisoner.'

When she remained seated and did nothing other than look away, he added, 'I will not ignore my orders, nor will I fail to execute them. You can get up and come with me of your own accord, or I can carry you like a sack of grain.'

That warning got her attention. She stared at him. 'You wouldn't dare.'

In no mood for further delay, Elrik stood up and before she could determine what he was about to do, he hauled her up over his shoulder.

'All right.' She pounded her fists on his back. 'You have proved your point. Put me down.'

He set her on her feet and turned her to face the door. 'We are leaving. Now.'

Avelyn refused to budge. 'I owe them for my keep.'

Elrik rubbed the bridge of his nose in an attempt to ease the still-growing tension, then reached inside his mantle for the coins King David had given him. Without counting them, he tossed the sack on the bed. 'That will more than cover the roof over your head and food.' He pushed her forward. 'Now go.'

'No. Wait.'

'Wait?'

She rushed to a small table in the far corner of the room, picked up a small pouch and slipped the ribbon dangling from it over her head. After tucking the pouch inside the neck of her gown, she came back to him.

'Anything else?'

'No.'

He waved towards the door. 'Then go.'

'You are just going to walk out of here with me?'

'That is the plan, yes.'

'And you don't expect anyone to question or stop you from doing so?'

He would like to see them try such an act, it might provide him with an opportunity to release some of the tightness burning along the muscles of his neck and shoulders. 'Why would anyone do so? Do you belong to anyone here?'

'No.'

'Have you entered into some sort of dubious agreement with anyone?'

'No.'

'Then I do not see what reason they would have to stop me.'

'They don't know you.'

Elrik blinked. 'They obviously don't know you either.'

'I have been here over a week. They know me.'

If that were true, she would not now be in this position. It was doubtful that she would still be under this roof. 'Oh, so you told them you were Lord Brandr's daughter and that you'd run away from a marriage arranged by your great-grandfather King Óláfr?'

She hesitated. 'No.'

'Would you like to tell them? We can go below and once I get everyone's attention you can then make your announcement. Of course, I won't be responsible for any who decide to take you captive and hold you for ransom—or think to return you to your father for some sort of reward—or worse, marry you himself with the assumption that there will be something worthwhile to gain.'

She shot him a look that threatened to skewer him on the spot before opening the door and marching stiffly out into the corridor.

Chapter Two

Avelyn fisted her hands at her side. The last few days she'd started to believe that she'd managed to escape her fate and would not be found.

Instead, once again she learned the uselessness of fanciful hopes, wishes and luck.

How had this oaf found her? She'd expected her father to send men after her, but she'd thought they would be his men, someone she knew or someone who was at least familiar.

Apparently, her father had gone to King David for assistance instead of to his grandfather, King Óláfr, or even to his uncle and liege, Lord Somerled.

Why?

Perhaps he didn't want them to learn that she'd run away rather than wed the man they'd chosen as her husband.

And now this…this stranger thought he was going to take her to King David like an errant child? She frowned as yet another hopeful thought drifted into her mind. Was it possible that her father had dragged the Scots King into this because he'd had a change of heart and had found the ancient warlord chosen as her husband to be unsuitable?

It was doubtful, but she clung to that thought as it would

be the only slender thread of sanity available to her. However, her fanciful wishes did little to explain the identity of this man.

From what she could tell, he was strongly built—the long, fur-lined mantle covered him from shoulder to ankle, so she couldn't see the shape of his body—but he'd easily lifted her over his shoulder with one arm. Yet, at the same time, his attempt to dress her hadn't been overly harsh, fumbling perhaps, as if unused to the task, but not cruel.

And his touch, when it had rested on her knees as he'd tried to reason with her, had been warm. Had she not been distraught over being found she could have easily fallen into the comfort that warmth had conveyed.

His eyes were green, flecked with gold. His hair was nearly as black as hers, but his was shot through with silvery strands that made it impossible to know his age.

But he wasn't old. Older than she was, but not ancient like the man she'd been betrothed to wed.

'Who are you?' she asked over her shoulder.

He did nothing but grunt and poke a finger into her back to prod her along the corridor towards the stairs.

Just as they reached the top of the stairs they met an old man. She could only assume this was Edward, the old man Hannah had coerced her into sharing a bed with. He was most likely headed to her room. Avelyn wondered how her unwanted *rescuer* would deal with this event.

Edward looked from her to the man behind her, a frown of puzzlement creasing his already lined face. 'This is not the red-haired wench.'

'No. It isn't.'

'This is my woman. I paid for her.'

'How much?'

'What does the amount matter to you?' Edward reached for her, adding, 'I paid. She is mine.'

'It matters greatly to me because she is my wife.' The man looped an arm about her waist and pulled her close. 'And because we have three hungry children at home who would be grateful for the coin their mother could deliver.'

Wife? Home? Three hungry children?

Struck mute by his outrageous lies, Avelyn could only stare blindly ahead. She wasn't completely lacking in wits. He had spouted the lies in an attempt to leave the inn without incident. She wished he'd have devised something less demeaning to her.

'If the amount is right, I might be willing to allow her to go with you. Provided, of course, that I stand guard over the two of you to ensure no harm comes to the mother of my children.'

Avelyn narrowed her eyes, then turned her head to glare up at him. She didn't know him well enough to decipher the quick look he gave her, but she was fairly certain it had been a silent warning to keep quiet—a warning she planned to ignore.

She jutted an elbow into his gut and turned her attention to Edward. 'That is not the reason he wishes to watch.'

Her rescuer's fingers tightened against her waist, but she forged ahead, determined to make him feel as foolish and embarrassed as he'd made her feel. 'Oh, no, his rutting leaves behind nothing memorable except children and he wishes to see if he can learn anything.'

The man's soft hiss gave her enough satisfaction to stop her own outrageous claims.

Edward stepped aside, shaking his head vigorously as he waved them towards the stairs. 'No. No. Please, go. I will find another.'

Without wasting any time, the man moved his hand from her waist to wrap his fingers around her wrist before rushing her to the steps. Halfway down he muttered, 'Woman, you need have care with your words.'

'My words?' She kept her voice just as low as he had. 'You made me look and feel like a whore.'

He once again tightened his hold. 'You did that to yourself.'

Avelyn tried to tug free. 'I did no such thing.'

'My mistake. I could have sworn I found you in bed, naked, waiting for a man to join you for the night.'

She couldn't very well deny what he'd found upon entering her room. However, it wasn't quite what he'd assumed. 'Nothing was going to happen.'

Their discussion stopped as they reached the bottom of the stairs where two men waited, but she wasn't about to let this end her explanation for long. Avelyn hung back, uncertain what these men wanted. But her rescuer walked past them, saying, 'Let's be on our way.'

She was relieved to discover they were his men since both looked as dark and dangerous as he. The two fell into step behind her and they all exited the establishment.

The cold rain pelting against her face did nothing to cool her ire. He'd called her a whore—accused her of things that would enrage her father should even a hint of such a rumour reach his ears.

Not willing to spend another heartbeat in this man's hold, Avelyn jerked her arm free and marched quickly ahead.

Heavy footsteps stomping in the mud behind her warned that he wasn't letting her out of his sight. She knew she'd be unable to escape, especially right now, while they were on foot. But she didn't have to endure his company.

She glared at him over her shoulder. 'Leave me alone.'

'I will gladly do so once I deliver you to King David.'

He again captured her wrist with strong fingers, then pulled her about to face him.

The two men stopped alongside, only to be ordered, 'Retrieve the horses and meet us near the well.'

The crestfallen looks on their faces might have been laughable at another time. But right now she didn't care that their desire for listening had been thwarted. The things she wanted to say to this man did not need an audience that would make her the object of gossip.

Once they were on their way, she looked up at the man who'd quickly made himself an irritant in her life. 'Release me.'

To her surprise, he did. She stepped back, putting a little space between them. 'I am not a whore.'

His lazy, bored glance from the sky back down to her did not endear him to her in the slightest. In fact, his silent display of derision only made her want to fly into a rage. Instead, she fisted her hands at her side and repeated, 'I am not a whore.'

'I wouldn't expect Lord Brandr's daughter to be one. Although, finding you as I did would have made it easy for another to have come to that conclusion.'

The arrogant half-smile on his face was her undoing. Everything she had suffered these last weeks—the hunger and thirst, the fear, the cold dampness—all roiled to the fore serving to ignite her rage. Avelyn raised her arm to strike the smug expression from his face.

His arm shot out as fast as a loosened arrow and he grasped her forearm, warning, 'I wouldn't do that if I were you.' He pulled her against his chest. 'I am not beholden to your father, nor to you. I will not meekly endure your abuse no matter how angry you become.'

Avelyn lowered her head, wishing she could simply disappear as quickly as her rage had at the deep tone of his voice. What was wrong with her to make her act like such a simpleton, such a fool?

At her lingering silence, he said, 'Your anger is misplaced. I have done you no harm, nor have I wronged you.'

'I know. I am sorry and apologise. It's just that…'

She stopped speaking and closed her eyes, unable to find the words she sought and not wanting to say anything more to a man not known to her.

He released her and with a finger beneath her chin lifted her head. 'What? It's just that what?'

She opened her eyes and met his gaze. He didn't appear angry or out of sorts. Just curious, as if what she'd been about to say mattered. 'It's just that I don't wish to wed Sir Bolk.'

He laughed softly and lowered his hand. 'I can understand that. I wouldn't want to marry him either.'

How could she not laugh at his ridiculous comment? However, knowing he was taking her back to do just that— marry Sir Bolk—tempered her humour.

Avelyn sighed and stepped away from the comfort she'd found pressed against his chest. 'Yes, well, while neither of us wishes to marry my great-grandfather's warlord, I will soon be forced to do so.' She shivered at the thought of sharing a life and a bed with the man.

'Then you have two or three days to find a reason that will convince King David to intervene on your behalf.'

'I am nothing more than a piece of property. Anything I say will fall on deaf ears.'

'Ah, perhaps you have forgotten, property has value.'

That was true. Property did have value. But that value was determined by men who had little, if any, concern for her or for anything she might want for her future. A future she hadn't thought about in what seemed ages.

Her wants were no different than any other woman's. She

wanted a husband, home and children. But she had little faith in the love that troubadours sang about—it seemed a rather fleeting and useless emotion. Something more solid seemed a better choice—caring, friendship, sharing, a partnership of sorts were all things she would prefer over some elusive feeling that served only to leave one suffering the relentless pain of loss.

Her mother had pined for her love every day until the last. Even on her death bed, she'd wanted nothing more than the touch of his lips against hers one more time. At fourteen years old Avelyn had come to the harsh realisation that this love her mother craved was never going to come to her bedside—at least not while she lived. After her mother had died, she'd vowed never to allow herself to be trapped so neatly by a man's pretty words.

No matter how sweetly spoken, they were false and meaningless.

But that didn't mean she did not want a husband. She simply wanted one who would honestly care for her and her alone. One who was nearer her own age, so they could grow old together. One strong enough to protect her if need be and lustful enough to give her children.

One not unlike the man before her.

Avelyn gasped softly. What devil had put that notion in her head?

She took another step backwards, wanting to put more than an arm's length of distance between them.

'Avelyn? Lady Avelyn?'

From the sharper tone of his voice and the quizzical way his brows were drawn closer together, he had asked her a question. One she'd missed while her unruly mind was off wandering places it shouldn't go.

'What?'

'I asked why Sir Bolk had been chosen.'

She shook her head. 'I have no idea. It isn't as if they included me in making their decision.'

'You have a brain, otherwise you would not have got this far on your own. So, think about it. Why would they have chosen such an elderly man and why would he have agreed?'

'Well, of course he agreed. What man in their right mind would naysay their King?'

'You obviously don't know Sir Bolk. Not even the King could sway him if he wasn't agreeable to the arrangement.'

'No, I don't know him. Nor do I wish to.'

'He must have seen some advantage to the wedding.'

'Other than trying to outlive a third wife?'

'I doubt if that would happen. However, he would go to his death bed as son-in-law to Brandr and great-grandson-in-law to King Óláfr. Everything of value he possessed at that moment would go to—'

'My father!' she interjected, cutting off his words. 'Including me.' She staggered a couple of steps back, shocked by the realisation that her father and great-grandfather were even more underhanded than she could have imagined.

'Then they would have the opportunity to marry you off once again.'

Even though Bolk's possessions were meagre, they would all pass to her father. Avelyn wanted to scream. Instead, she narrowed her eyes and asked, 'Do you think King David would go against my family?'

'If given a good enough reason to do so.'

'You said I have two or three days to devise one?'

'That is about how long it will take to reach Carlisle.'

She stepped forward and reached out to place a hand on his arm. 'Then, my good sir…' she pulled her hand back '…what is your name?'

'Roul. Lord Elrik of Roul.'

Avelyn burst out laughing. When she was able to gain control of herself, she wiped the tears from her eyes and shook her head. 'Of course you are. It only makes perfect sense that King David sent his Wolf to sniff out and retrieve King Óláfr's lowly prey.'

He frowned down at her. 'I fail to see the humour.'

'That is because you are not in my place. I am nothing but a defenceless dove. You are a wolf. It seems out of place that they would send such a skilled hunter to track down so meek a prey.'

He offered her his arm and then turned to escort her to the men and horses waiting near the well. 'It is impossible to know ahead of time how dangerous a prey might prove to be.'

'Yes, that is true. You had no way of knowing if this dove hid fangs inside her beak.'

He nodded in agreement. 'Or perhaps talons worthy of any eagle.'

Once they reached the others, Elrik paused to ask, 'Can you ride?'

Avelyn could count the times she'd been on the back of a horse on one hand—two fingers in truth. But the alternative was obvious—she'd be forced to share his mount and that would place her too close to him for comfort. She shrugged. 'Not well, but I'll manage.'

He lifted a brow, but said nothing. Instead, he removed his long mantle and slung it over her shoulders. While securing the pin to hold the cloak in place and tucking her hair inside the hood, he said, 'This will keep you from getting any wetter than you already are.'

'What about you? It will do little good for you to catch a chill.'

'I won't get sick from a little rain.'

She looked up at the animal next to her and, even though it was the smallest of the lot, she wondered how she was going to scramble up on something that tall. Before she could ask, Elrik wrapped both hands round her waist and lifted her up on to the saddle.

Avelyn swung a leg over to the other side and tucked the long edges of his cloak beneath her legs. She took a deep breath before taking the offered reins in her hands, then stated, 'I am ready.'

She could only hope her words sounded more confident to him than they had to her own ears.

'You will be fine.' He patted her knee before mounting his own horse.

By the time they stopped a few hours later, the rain had ceased and now the clouds had begun to part allowing the stars to twinkle against the darkening sky.

Avelyn shivered on her log seat before the fire and barely tasted the food in her mouth. She was tired and stiff from riding. Her hands ached from holding on to the reins so tightly the entire time and her thighs burned from clamping them against the saddle in an attempt not to fall.

Her rescuer, Lord Elrik, had said nothing, but she'd felt him watching her the entire time and had feared that at any moment he was going to pluck her from her horse and plop her in front of him on his. She had to admit that there had been a couple of times when she'd not have argued with that arrangement. Times when they'd ridden too fast, or when the road beneath the horse's hooves seemed to rise too steeply as they'd climbed a hill.

To her amazement, she'd managed. But right now, she was most thankful to be planted firmly on solid ground. Her only desire was to curl into a ball and give over to the beckoning sleep teasing at her sluggish mind.

Elrik leaned against a tree and watched Avelyn sway and then quickly jerk upright as she stopped herself from falling asleep right there on the log. It was obvious the woman was exhausted. It'd been more obvious that riding a horse was not something she'd been taught.

They'd lost a few hours due to her inexperience and that was something he couldn't afford to let happen tomorrow. She wasn't going to be pleased, but they needed to make up some time and would only be able to do so if she rode with him.

The thought of holding her before him, his arms around her, his chest a platform for her back, didn't seem as unappealing as he might have expected. Granted, she would argue and put up a fuss at first, but she would soon become accustomed to the feel of his body against hers. After all, it wasn't as if they would be doing anything unseemly.

He groaned softly at the image that thought had conjured.

Elrik shook the vision from his mind. What was wrong with him? Had a comely body and pretty face made him suddenly lose the ability to reason? She was Brandr's daughter. Hadn't that family already caused him enough trouble?

Besides, a woman was the last thing he needed in his life—no matter how attractive he'd found her. Experience had taught him that women were not worth the time, expense or heartache they brought along with them.

Hadn't Muriel given him enough grief to last two lifetimes?

No. Holding her in front of him would not do. He needed to come up with some other way of keeping her securely on the horse.

Avelyn swayed on her seat again, but caught herself with a jerk that brought her upright once again.

When she once again swayed on the log, she'd been slower to jerk herself awake.

Elrik pushed away from the tree, knowing that this next sway would not be stopped as successfully. He caught her in his arms a heartbeat before she hit the ground.

Cradling her against his chest, he carried her to the makeshift pallet spread out not too far from the warmth of the fire and placed her on the blanket. Without waking, she instantly rolled on to her side, curling into a relaxed ball with a hand beneath her cheek.

He grabbed his mantle, which, after it had been dried by the fire, had been laid alongside the pallet, and covered her with the fur-lined garment. After tucking the edges tightly around her, he rose and stared at a wayward ebony lock of hair resting against the paleness of her cheek.

He had to give Brandr credit for one thing at least. The man could be a traitorous viper at the best of times, but he had produced a very lovely daughter.

Elrik joined his men near the fire.

Just as he stretched his legs out to get comfortable, Fulke asked, 'How are you going to deliver her to King David if she falls from her horse and breaks her neck first?'

Not one to let a question go without comment, Samuel said, 'It isn't her neck we should be worried about. At the rate we are travelling, it'll be our own necks in danger.'

Sometimes, like now when complaining seemed the current activity of choice, Elrik had to remind himself that these were more than just childhood friends, they were his two best men—they could both sleep in the saddle while still retaining control of their horses, both were handy with a blade be it a sword or a dagger and both men would always protect his back if the need arose. So, enduring their complaints was usually bearable.

This was not one of those nights. 'The pace will pick up tomorrow and she'll not break her neck.'

When Samuel opened his mouth, Elrik glared at him. The dark look gained him the result he'd desired—the man closed his mouth without saying another word.

Chapter Three

To Avelyn's relief, she'd slept well on the hardness of the ground. It was more like her old pallet at her mother's than the over-soft, lumpy mattress in her shared chamber at her father's keep. For the first time in what seemed ages, she'd awakened feeling rested, although a bit stiff, and ready to continue their journey.

She did wish, however, they could do so on foot instead of on the back of a horse.

Well aware that her wish would not be considered, she studied the horse being led in her direction. It was the one she'd ridden yesterday, the smallest of the four, but as far as she was concerned the only difference size made was in the distance to the ground—the fall would still hurt as much.

What did catch her attention was the saddle. The one she'd used yesterday—with the shorter pommel and cantle—had been placed on Roul's animal, while his saddle, with the high front and back meant to help keep him seated during a battle, was on her horse. Lashed to the inside of both the pommel and the cantle was a rolled-up blanket.

That wasn't the only difference. The stirrups had been cinched higher so that she'd be riding with her knees slightly bent, instead of hanging straight down, and a lead string had been secured to the reins.

Roul held his hand out. 'Come, we need to make up for lost time.'

She hesitantly took a step forward and grasped his hand.

The fingers closing around hers were warm and a smile curved up the corners of his mouth, lending Avelyn a small amount of courage as she joined him alongside the horse.

He stroked his free hand the length of the animal's nose. 'I didn't properly introduce you yesterday as I should have. Avelyn, this is Little Lady and she's helped train more guards than I can count.'

'You brought her along to train a guard?'

With his fingers still woven between hers, he raised their hands to the horse's head. 'No. I was uncertain if the runaway I sought could ride or not.'

He stroked the animal's neck with their entwined hands. 'And since I've discovered that she cannot, I am giving Little Lady here a task she is well suited to perform.'

From the way the animal eyed her, Avelyn got the impression she was not exactly a welcome task.

Roul nudged her shoulder with his. 'Relax. She's never bitten or thrown anyone.'

Under her breath, Avelyn muttered, 'Yet.'

His laugh let her know that her comment had been heard.

It wasn't until he grasped the lead string with one hand and rested the other hand on her shoulder that she noticed she was stroking the horse alone—his hand no longer covered hers. Avelyn frowned.

How had he managed that without her knowledge?

From the solid wall of warmth at her back she knew that while he might have released her hand and moved behind her while she'd remained unaware, he'd stayed close enough to prevent anything from happening. She stiffened her spine.

He lightly squeezed her shoulder. 'I'll be this close for the entire journey. Nothing is going to harm you.'

She wasn't certain what bothered her more—the heated breath rushing against her ear, his nearness that made her feel protected yet threatened at the same time, his words promising her she'd come to no harm, or the sudden realisation that he wasn't going to give her any chance to escape.

'Ready?'

As much as she wanted to tell him no, she knew they weren't going to stand here for ever. 'I suppose.'

'Up with you.' He lifted her on to the saddle before she could change her mind and handed her the reins. 'Lady will follow my horse's lead. You need do nothing to guide her.'

He adjusted the roll of blankets behind her, wedging it tighter between her body and the cantle, then did the same with the roll in front. 'These should keep you from sliding around on the saddle. If you feel unsteady, hang on to the pommel.'

After checking the length of the stirrups, he rested a hand on her knee and looked up, assuring her, 'You will be fine. Just try to relax.'

Through the layers of her tunic and chemise, she felt the warmth of his touch. *And he wanted her to relax?* She nodded. 'I shall try.'

Elrik mounted his horse and tucked the end of the lead string behind his belt. Since Little Lady would follow along without baulking, he knew he didn't need to keep a tight hold on her lead.

Once they were on the road, his men split up, Fulke in front and Samuel behind. With them guarding the road, Elrik was better able to keep his attention on Avelyn.

Even though they were moving faster than they had yes-

terday, her rigid back and near-white knuckles from gripping the reins so tightly made him wonder how long she'd
be able to keep up this pace.

Elrik rarely remained at King David's court longer than
absolutely necessary. The times he had tarried overlong,
he'd discovered that few, if any, of the men and women in
attendance wanted anything to do with David's Wolf.

However, he had been called to court often enough to
notice the actions and manners of the people there and he'd
seen enough women of substance on horseback to realise
that learning to ride was normal for them. So, Lady Avelyn's lack of skill confused him.

'How is it that you never learned to ride a horse?'

Without taking her stare from the spot between her
horse's ears, she asked in return, 'Even if I'd have had a
need to learn, where would I have found a suitable horse?'

'In your father's stable?'

The laugh that escaped her lips was more bitter than
pleasant. 'My father did not acknowledge my existence
until after my mother died.'

'I thought—'

'The same thing everyone else thinks,' she interrupted
whatever he'd been about to say. 'That I was born and raised
in my father's keep. An assumption that couldn't be more
wrong.'

Elrik knew she was the man's natural-born daughter
conceived outside his marriage. Still, she was an important enough possession to have been raised at his keep and
taught the ways of nobility. Since Brandr had been more
concerned with removing King David's rule over the land,
perhaps he hadn't been aware of her birth. 'Did he know
about you?'

'My mother said that he did. She'd been a servant in
his keep, but when it was discovered she carried the lord's

child, the steward banished her from the keep.' She paused, frowning a moment, then said, 'Mother had been certain the order came from the lord or lady, yet he seemed shocked when he discovered me in our hut after her funeral. Perhaps he hadn't issued the order.'

Elrik shook his head, wondering what he'd been thinking to have started such a personal conversation about things that were none of his concern, but curiosity prompted him to push forward, asking, 'What do you mean he discovered you?'

'I still don't know why he came that day.' Her voice was barely above a whisper as if she were talking to herself. 'She'd pined for him for as long as I can remember. His name was the one on her lips when she took her last breath. But her prayers and wishes had gone unanswered. Not once in the fourteen years since I'd been born had he come to our home. Not until after her body was covered with dirt.'

'And that's when he came for you?'

'Came for me?' She looked up at him and shook her head. 'No. I think he came to make certain my mother was truly gone.'

'And instead, he found you?'

'Only by accident. I'd been sitting in a corner eating my last crust of bread when he entered with two of his guards. They stopped me when I tried bolting to safety. I thought they were going to kill me from the way they were excitedly shoving me back and forth, daring each other to be the first to take a taste, but after staring at me for a few moments he ordered the guards to release me.'

Elrik doubted if their intent had been to *kill* her. 'So, he did recognise you?'

'He said I looked like his mother, the late Lady Avelyn. That's when I realised I'd not been named for my mother's mother, but for his. Which obviously shocked him, because he paled upon learning my name.'

'No one had ever told you that?'

'When my mother said I was named for my grand-mother, I always thought she'd meant her mother. So, both he and I were rather surprised.'

She laughed at the memory and, this time, her laughter was lighter, not quite as bitter as it had been earlier. Since she seemed a bit more relaxed than she had when they had first started out, Elrik wanted to keep her talking, so he asked, 'Did he then move you to the keep?'

Again, she shook her head. 'Not that day. He had one of his men gather some food from the village for me and vowed to return in a day or so.'

It was difficult to imagine Brandr leaving a fourteen-year-old girl to fend for herself even for just a day or two, especially one who he knew was his natural-born daughter. Old enough to take as a wife—or simply use as one—she'd been left unguarded and alone. Perhaps that was what he had hoped would happen—it would have taken away his responsibility for her care.

Elrik glanced at Avelyn and noticed that she'd released her death grip on the reins and had rested one hand atop the pommel.

'To my surprise, he did return.'

Since Brandr had shown no previous interest in her or her mother, Elrik could understand her surprise.

'He and his men terrified the whole village when they loaded me and my few possessions into a cart before torch-ing the hut.'

This time, the stiffening of her body and clenching of her hands had nothing to do with fear of the horse, but ob-vious anger at Brandr's actions.

Elrik asked, 'Did he give any reason for setting fire to what could have provided another with shelter?'

'He'd claimed it was so I had no place to ever return to. But from the way he tore through my mother's things first, I believed he'd been looking for something and, when he couldn't find it, burned the hut to ensure no one else would either.'

'What could your mother have had that was so valuable to him?'

'While I suspect he was looking for a gold ring, I never cared enough to ask.' Avelyn shrugged. 'All I knew was that he'd destroyed the only home I'd ever known.'

He'd always considered Brandr to be heartless, but he'd never imagined the man to be so devious and petty. It would have made more sense to thoroughly search the hut again instead of torching it. Destroying an enemy's property during battle was one thing, but to destroy what was essentially his own property out of frustration or spite was not only thoughtless and short-sighted, it showed a complete lack of concern for his villagers—the very people whose welfare was his responsibility.

Noticing the sad downturn of her lips, Elrik drew her attention back to her suspicions. 'A gold ring?'

'For my twelfth birthday, my mother gave me a gold ring, stating it had been my grandmother's wedding band and that I was to keep it safe at all costs.'

'And did you?'

'I buried it beneath the floor under my pallet.'

Of course the man hadn't thought of digging up the hard-packed floor. 'That was good thinking for one so young.'

'No, not really. I knew the ring was of value from the markings on it and burying it like a treasure was all I could think of doing.'

'Markings?'

'Yes.' She reached inside the neck of her gown, tugged out the small pouch and handed him the ring, saying, 'I don't know what they mean.'

Elrik inspected the piece of jewellery. The ring was not a wedding band. He narrowed his gaze and glanced at her before looking back at the gold seal ring. She couldn't read. Had her father seen to anything that might have benefitted his daughter? If not, then why hadn't his grandfather done so?

She might have been born to a servant, but she was a lord's daughter, more importantly the great-granddaughter of a king. There were things she needed to know how to do in order to be able to run a keep successfully, otherwise she would have to always rely on her husband, or trust the people in her service and neither were the best options. It would be far too easy for someone to take advantage of her.

He held the top of the ring out for her to see. 'This is the letter "A" over the top of your great-grandfather's seal. Your grandmother would have used it to put her official wax mark on any missives she'd sent.' He turned the ring. 'The roses on the side are simply for decoration.'

She frowned. 'Why would my mother say it was a wedding band?'

'Perhaps she'd been told it was and didn't know any different.'

'Why would she have it in the first place?'

Elrik handed the ring back to her. 'I can only guess that your father gave it to her for some reason.' It could have been a token of his affection, or payment for services rendered, but he kept those thoughts to himself.

While once again securing the ring in its pouch tucked safely beneath the neck of her gown, she asked, 'I can neither read, nor write, so why would she have placed so much importance on keeping it safe when she gave it to me?'

'Lady Avelyn, it is a way for you to prove your relationship to your family if need be. Your mother was looking out for your future in the only way she could.'

'Oh.' Her eyes widened. 'Oh! Maybe this is what my father was looking for when he tore apart my mother's home.'

'Most likely.' Although why Brandr would need any proof of his identity was a mystery he had no desire to unravel.

'He could have just asked. There was no reason to destroy my home.'

Elrik had no reply to her comment as there was no good reason for his actions. A few moments of silence passed when he felt her watching him and when he turned his focus back to her, she asked, 'Have I ruined your high regard for Lord Brandr?'

Fulke turned to look over his shoulder at her question until Elrik's hard glare made him once again face forward. Not willing to divulge his hatred of her father, he answered her innocent question as non-committally as possible, 'Fear not. My regard for Brandr has never been high.'

'Yet you are returning me to him.'

He reminded her, 'I am taking you to King David.'

'Who will then hand me back over to the tender care of my father.'

The disdain in her voice prompted him to ask, 'Your life with him has not been better than it was before?'

Avelyn looked at him, wondering if she'd already told him far too much. Instead of telling him that life with her father had been much harder than she'd expected, she said, 'I learned more in the four years at his keep than I did in the fourteen years with my mother.'

It wasn't a lie, she *had* learned more—much more about the ways of men and the lies they told.

'I imagine it wasn't easy to leave the life you'd known behind.'

'No, but other people would disagree with you. There were many at my father's keep who believed the life I had before was not worth living. They didn't understand how being brought to Brandr could prove a hardship for me. The simple truth was that I had nowhere else to go.' She would have rather been left alone living in her mother's home.

'How did you find yourself betrothed to Bolk?'

'I suppose the same as any unwed woman—my family arranged it. From what Lord Somerled claimed when he arrived with the news, my great-grandfather arranged it all.'

She looked up at him. From the bland expression on his face, she knew he wasn't interested in anything about her, but had likely been seeking to draw her fear away from being on the back of a horse. His tactic had worked, but it was time to learn what she could about him.

'Enough about me. What was your childhood like?'

At first, he stiffened and she feared he would say nothing. She'd spent four years living with people who spoke to her only when they absolutely had to do so. These last days spent with Hannah had been a rare blessing as the women were all more than happy to converse. She didn't look forward to a return of the silence.

When she could stand the quiet no longer, she said, 'Please, my lord, I do not ask that you betray any secrets, I want only to hear the sound of another's voice.'

Finally, he sighed, then said, 'My childhood was likely not much different than yours. But my three brothers and I grew up with our father as our mother died in childbirth.'

'The baby survived?'

'Yes. Two of the women in the village had given birth about the same time, so they cared for Rory along with Edan who was about one in addition to their own.'

That made sense to her since it wasn't unusual for the women in her village to band together and help each other in time of need. Besides, how would his father have cared for an infant by himself? She couldn't imagine her father even bothering to attempt the task. He would have been more likely to set the baby outside the castle walls to await its certain death than to assume any responsibility for its well-being.

'How old were you and your other brother?'

'I was nine, so Gregor would have been six.'

At nine he was still a child. 'How did your father cope with two young boys and his other duties?'

Roul laughed before answering, 'He didn't. He saw to his duties while I kept Gregor and myself out of trouble as much as possible.'

The guard behind them snorted. Without turning around, Roul responded, 'I did a fairly good job of it, except for the times *other* boys got us embroiled in childish pranks.'

His men were quick to interject. 'Like raiding the roost for eggs to toss from trees at people passing by?'

The one in front of them added, 'Or getting mud all over the clean laundry?'

Avelyn couldn't help but laugh. When this subsided, she said, 'So the lord's boys weren't much different than those from the village?'

'Probably worse, since we had no one at home to mete out punishment for our pranks,' he admitted, then added, 'Like the whipping these two took when one passer-by was Samuel's father.' He hitched a thumb over his shoulder to the guard riding behind them, before he nodded towards the guard in front of them and said, 'And Fulke's mother was the head laundress.'

'Sadly, the pranks ended shortly after that,' Samuel said.

'Why is that?'

'Because their parents...' Roul nodded towards both men before continuing '...suggested to my father that Gregor and I needed some tasks to keep us from having idle hands during the day. So, we had lessons with the priest in the morning and spent our afternoons split between the stables where we learned how to care for and ride horses and the bailey learning how to fight.'

Fulke added, 'We didn't exactly get off lightly either. The two of us were banished to the shipyard and wharf until we were old enough to handle a weapon.'

'What did you do then?' Avelyn asked.

'Trained hard to get into Roul's guard.'

She looked at Elrik, who shook his head. 'Not mine— my father's.'

'Oh. I thought all men owed service to their lord.'

'Well, yes, but on Roul, as long as we aren't under attack—or the threat of attack—their service is only mandatory a couple of weeks a year. We need the men working at the shipyard and docks in addition to the keep. But even those who choose to employ their services at the keep aren't necessarily qualified to join the guard.'

She frowned in confusion and leaned back against the blanket-padded cantle. 'I'm afraid I don't understand.'

'While every keep needs to be guarded at all times, the normal day-to-day responsibilities can be supplemented with men who aren't always there. For example, right now Henry is on gate duty for the next two weeks. He'll eat and sleep in the guard quarters at night, so that he's available any time day or night. When his two weeks are completed he'll return to his own home, wife, family and his normal routine at the docks.'

'But he's not a guard?'

'No. He is on guard duty.' Elrik drew in a breath and

frowned, before explaining further, 'Where Samuel here is a guard and is never off duty. He will take his turns at guard duty wherever he is assigned, but if I or my brothers need him for another task that's where he will go.'

She glanced over her shoulder at Samuel. 'And you do this by choice?'

The man nodded.

Elrik leaned over to whisper, 'He is no good with tools, so he's useless at the shipyard and he likes to drink too much to be left to his own devices at the dock.'

As Elrik sat back up, Samuel cleared his throat and then said, 'But I am good with a sword and this way I don't have to cook, do my own laundry, find my own place to live and the pay is reasonable, so I've no complaints with my lot.'

Without turning around Fulke added, 'And sometimes the task that takes us away from Roul is easy, making it far more preferable than gate duty.'

'Gate duty is hard?'

'Boring!' both men answered at the same time.

'What made you choose these two for this task?' she asked Elrik.

'Simple. Whenever I've need of men I trust without question, these two are first on my very short list. Since the three of us grew up together we can communicate many things without words. I know that when Fulke stiffens in his saddle that something questionable is ahead, or when Samuel hisses beneath his breath danger lurks nearby. I know without ordering and without a doubt that they will guard my back.'

'And we trust Elrik to return us to Roul in one piece.' Samuel said.

Ahead of them, Fulke nodded in agreement.

'So, the three of you are…friends?'

Elrik shrugged. 'I suppose you could say that.'

'Perhaps,' Fulke said while looking over his shoulder. 'But I am not tucking either of you into bed tonight.'

Samuel snorted before blowing a loud smacking kiss towards the other man.

'Enough.' Elrik ordered. 'As evidenced by their behaviour we are more like brothers than friends. Even so, at times, someone has to be in charge.'

Avelyn nodded. 'Yes, I can see where some order at times might be needed. Do you think that someone in charge might order a break soon?'

Samuel stretched, then yawned. 'Now there's an order that would be welcome.'

Elrik looked up at the sky and, from the slight widening of his eyes, seemed surprised to discover the sun had already passed its cenit to begin its descent. He motioned towards a clearing just ahead. 'We've ridden longer than I'd thought. We'll stop here to eat and stretch.'

Fulke and Samuel rode ahead. When Avelyn and Elrik arrived at the clearing a few moments later, the men had already started to unpack a leather sack of food.

Elrik dismounted and, after removing the padding, he assisted her from the horse. The moment her feet hit the ground, Avelyn's legs wobbled and she stumbled against him, clinging to his shoulders to regain her footing.

His arms closed around her easily, as if they had done so countless times to support her and hold her close. 'Take a moment.'

The deep huskiness of his voice caught her attention. She looked up at the face so near hers. The hardness of the chest she rested against, the warmth of his embrace and his heavily lidded gaze warned her that taking a moment would not be wise. A shiver raced down her spine, leaving her less steady on her feet than she'd been a heartbeat before.

Avelyn gasped softly and tore her stare from his. She

pulled away, forcing her legs to hold her upright, and lowered her hands from his shoulders. 'I am fine now. Thank you.'

'You are far from fine.' His voice had lost all traces of any warmth. In fact, he sounded decidedly angry. He took her arm and led her towards a log. 'Sit down before you end up face first in the dirt.'

She pulled free of his grasp and then took a seat. 'You create such a lovely vision of me.'

'You could have said something earlier about being stiff and tired.'

Why was he now being so contrary? 'Yes, I could have and then you would have complained about me slowing you down.'

'I need to get you to King David quickly.'

'Oh, yes, so he can hand me over to wed Sir Bolk.' She stared up at him and quirked a brow. 'Perhaps I should suggest that you would be a better mate for the ogre than I. Do you think your King might agree with me?'

'Is that your attempt at humour?'

'No.' She shook her head. 'I am quite serious. It seems to me that the two of you might have much in common.'

'Such as?'

'Surliness, impatience and arrogance to begin with. If you give me but a moment, I am certain I can find more things you share.'

A muffled snort from one of the men let her know that they were paying close attention to this conversation. She didn't care.

'Arrogance?'

'Yes, you heard me correctly. Arrogance.'

His threatening glare deepened, but Avelyn refused to let it intimidate her. She held his dark stare with what she hoped was a threatening glare of her own.

Chapter Four

Elrik knew he was directing his frustration towards her unfairly. He wasn't angry with her in the least, simply frustrated. And he had no explanation why just holding her close in his embrace for a few short heartbeats had left him so…wanting.

Countless times since leaving King David, he'd reminded himself that the King was right—she had played no part in the harm her father had brought to the Roul family. She was not to blame and in fairness he could not take his hatred for Brandr out on her.

Yet, a small, tiny part of his mind warned that he did not know this woman and had no idea how much of her father's evilness had been passed to her. While it could be none, it could also be a great deal. There hadn't been enough time for him to decide.

Now, if his mind could just convince the rest of him that she was not to be trusted. It had been years since any woman had had this type of effect on him and he wasn't sure why. However, as confused as he was by his own reaction, hers left him just as surprised.

Instead of quietly accepting his change in mood, like most people did, she'd raised her eyebrows as if judging him, only to find him lacking and had then given him a taste of her own temper.

Complaining would only make him appear foolish since he did deserve it.

He found her reaction to his change of mood…interesting. Had he snarled at one of his men, in the same manner, they would have said nothing before giving him a wide berth.

Yet here this little bit of a woman who barely reached his shoulders glared at him and intentionally taunted him in a manner that made him wonder how many times she'd poked a stick at a beehive in her past.

Elrik felt his lips twitch and knew that without clenching his jaw he would soon find himself grinning like a fool. Unable to summon the will to stop himself, he laughed in surrender as he took a seat next to her on the log. 'Since I would rather kill Bolk than look at him, I do not think we would be a good match.'

Avelyn reached down to pick up a twig. While flicking off the bark with her fingernail, she asked, 'How do you think I feel?'

'I fully understand your position, but what can I do about it?'

'You know King David.' She poked his arm with the twig. The tiny stick slipped easily between the links of his chainmail. 'You could help me devise a plan he might find acceptable.'

'I hate to lower your overblown opinion of my relationship with the King, but I do not know him well enough to know what he would or wouldn't find acceptable.'

She shrugged. 'Maybe not, but you've been to his court and are surely more familiar with the things he values than I.' Once again, she poked him before adding, 'Besides, you are a man, so you could tell me what things might be of more value to another male.'

'You noticed that, did you?' He snatched the twig out of her hand and tossed it away. 'First off, poking a man is not the way into his heart.'

'Who said I was looking for a way into anyone's heart? I've seen the pain caused by love and wish nothing to do with it or any other tender emotion.'

Elrik frowned at her admission. 'I thought that's what all girls dreamed of finding one day—a husband who would shower them with love and kisses.'

'I would think it obvious that I am no longer a girl. I'd much rather have a husband willing to be my friend and consider me worth treating fairly than one who would shower me with pretty words and sweet kisses one moment only to forget my existence the next.'

From the determined tone of her voice, he could only assume she spoke her true feelings on the matter. Since he had pulled her naked from a bed, of course, he was well aware she was no longer a girl and, while her wishes seemed reasonable to him, they would never find fruition—not for a king's great-granddaughter, not even a bastard one. 'Do you realise how impossible that will be for you?'

'Why?' She looked up at him. 'Why will it be so impossible for me?'

'Lady Avelyn, surely you must know your value. You can't have been so protected, so kept in the dark, that you know nothing about how much you can bring to your family's coffers.'

Her focus turned to the ground at her feet. 'I am nothing but a servant's shamefully begotten spawn.'

Something in the sadness of her voice and the slight, barely perceptible tremor of her chin touched him deeply, making him feel guilty for something not his doing and filling him with a need to convince her of her value. While the unfamiliar emotions pricking inside his chest deserved some thought, the young woman sitting beside him needed his attention more.

'Lady Avelyn…' Elrik reached out and lifted her chin with the tips of his fingers, coaxing her to look at him. 'Avelyn, you are not to blame for what your mother and Brandr did. She might have only been a servant in his keep, but no matter the circumstances of your birth, you are a lord's daughter and a king's great-granddaughter, nothing can change that.'

When she tried to turn her head away, he slid his palm to her cheek to keep her focus on him. 'I know not who made you feel this shame, or lack of worth, but they were wrong to do so.'

She rose, bringing an abrupt halt to this conversation. 'I am famished.'

As much as he wanted to, Elrik wasn't going to push the issue—it was none of his concern.

He stood up, saying, 'Then we should get you something to eat.'

They joined Fulke and Samuel who had unpacked a meagre fare atop a boulder. Samuel waved a hand towards the food. 'It is nothing grand, but there's plenty for all of us.'

Avelyn picked up a wrinkled apple and took a bite. After swallowing it, she said, 'The food here suits me far better than anything you might consider grand.'

Fulke tore off a piece of bread from the dark round loaf and handed it to her. 'I doubt you would find any of this at your father's table.'

Samuel inspected the small wheel of cheese before slicing off a few slivers, which he also gave to her. 'Surely Lord Brandr's table provides better food than what we can offer.'

Avelyn took the cheese while shaking her head. 'Since I always made certain to eat with the cook and helpers in the kitchen, I am afraid I wouldn't know what was served in the hall.'

Fulke offered her a good-sized portion of smoked fish, nearly bumping into Samuel in his haste.

Elrik watched his two men vie for the opportunity to wait on her. Their actions were so out of character that he nearly choked on the piece of bread he was eating.

If he had to guess at their reason for such gallantry, he'd say they had overheard the conversation he'd been trying to have with Avelyn and were going out of their way to be more than kind to a woman who'd apparently experienced little kindness in her short life.

Since he found nothing amiss with their actions, he saw no reason to stop them and slowly backed away from the boulder to watch from a distance.

Avelyn's soft laugh at something Samuel said made him smile. He was grateful his men were showing her such attention instead of ignoring her as they normally would. From what he'd seen and heard, the lady deserved a few light-hearted moments before she would once again be back in the cold embrace of her family.

From King David's description, Elrik had believed Avelyn to be lovely yet headstrong. She was indeed quite lovely, but he'd yet to witness much that could be considered overly headstrong. Oh, yes, she'd been defiant when he'd discovered her at the inn, but that had been expected since he was unknown to her. She would have been foolish not to have questioned him. And he'd experienced a small flare of her temper when he'd taken his frustration out on her a short while ago.

But he'd seen no overt stubbornness or any action that could be considered headstrong or wilful, quite the opposite, actually. Even though it was obvious she'd had no experience riding a horse, she'd not complained once yesterday. Nor had she given any argument when he'd essentially tied her into the saddle like a child today. She'd simply accepted the fact that she had no choice in the matter of riding the horse and had made the best of what had to be an uncomfortable situation.

And when he'd suggested she argue her future with King David, she'd not whined or complained. As far as he could tell she had given it some thought, otherwise she'd not have asked him for a man's opinion on what might be considered valuable.

No. This was not some simple-minded woman who would argue for the sake of arguing. She might not have been raised in her father's keep and had yet to learn courtly manners, but she was not lacking in wits. She stood up for herself. And she knew what she wanted, along with what she didn't want.

In a way it was a shame she was so connected to Brandr. He was not someone Elrik wished to be related to in any manner, otherwise, he might be half-tempted to offer for her himself.

Elrik shook his head in an attempt to clear that ludicrous thought from his mind. Things like a wife and family were for other men, not him. But sometimes…times like this when he let his guard down and his musings drew him once again into wondering what if…he had to remind himself of that simple fact.

A hand rested gently on his arm, startling him away from his odd thoughts. 'What are you thinking about so intently?'

He looked down at her and asked, 'Did you get enough to eat?'

'More than enough, thank you.' Avelyn laughed. 'I had

to walk away before the two of them fed me enough for four meals.'

'They were simply being kind.'

She let her touch fall away from his arm. 'I know that. I wasn't complaining.'

Elrik closed his eyes for a moment at the feeling of loss, then he reached out to draw a fingertip along her cheek. 'I apologise. I know you weren't complaining.'

She tightly clasped her hands before her and lowered her gaze. 'We should be getting back on the road.'

'In a bit.' He covered her hands with one of his own and tugged gently. 'Come, sit with me for a few moments.'

At her nod, he pulled a fallen log to rest at the base of a tree. 'Here, you can rest against the tree.'

When she settled on to the log, he took a seat on the ground next to her legs, pulled off his helmet and then unlaced and pushed back the chainmail covering his head. The breeze rushed against his damp hair, drawing a sigh of relief from him.

Samuel and Fulke paused to stare at him a moment before they finished packing the food away. Once finished, both men took up a position at opposite ends of the entrance to the small clearing.

Avelyn nodded towards the men, asking, 'Do they expect trouble?'

Elrik shook his head. 'No. But this ensures that if any threat should occur, I'll know in advance.'

'Ah. So, they see to your safety when you aren't.'

'That's what they are here for, yes.'

'But aren't they more than just your guards?'

'Of course they are. But when there is a task to be done, they do it without having to be told.'

'Oh.'

'Oh?' The tone of her voice seemed filled with censure. 'Do you have some quarrel with this?'

'No. I just…it just seems… I don't know…'

'Of course you know, otherwise you wouldn't have said anything to begin with. What do you wish to say?'

'If you are taking time to rest, don't they require the same?'

Samuel turned to look at them. Close enough to have heard her question, he answered, 'Lord Elrik guarded the camp most of the night while we slept, my lady. We have no argument if he takes some rest now.'

Avelyn sighed heavily. 'Well, don't I sound like a lack-witted fool?'

'Not at all.' Elrik bumped her leg with his shoulder. 'You wouldn't know if you didn't ask.'

'This would never happen with my father.'

'What wouldn't happen? Sitting on a log?'

She returned his bump by bouncing her leg against his shoulder. 'He does not treat his men in the same manner as you do yours.'

'That's because they aren't his childhood companions. He came of age in King Henry's court, where I grew up on Roul Isle far away from any king or court.'

'So, how did you end up being King David's Wolf?'

Elrik paused. What could he tell her about her father's involvement without upsetting her, or making her question his explanation?

Nothing.

The two of them would soon part ways; there was no need to tell her anything. So, he chose to keep it brief.

'Not pleased with the new laws placed upon them, nor with the newly installed lords, my father and some of the other men thought they could battle their King without any repercussion for their act of treason. My brothers and I are paying for our father's mistaken thinking.'

'What happened to him? Did the King take his life?'

'No.' Elrik shrugged. 'Gregor and I were old enough to offer ourselves in his place. Our father was confined to Roul Isle and died in his own bed.'

'While you and your brothers spend the rest of your lives in service to the King?'

'Or until he decides to release us from our duty.'

'That must be a terrible way to live.'

He looked over his shoulder at her. 'Why do you say that?'

'Instead of having your own life, you are at the beck and call of another.'

'Isn't everyone at somebody's beck and call? Every man answers to their overlord, just like every woman answers to her guardian, be it husband, father or protector. How is my situation any different?'

'But you have been forced to do things that make people afraid of you.'

'Are you afraid of me?' He rested a hand on her knee. 'I don't feel you trembling beneath my touch, nor do I see you pulling away in fear.'

She laughed. 'That's different.'

'How so?'

'You've given me no reason to fear you.'

'I've given very few people reason to fear me, yet they do.'

She frowned. 'Are the tales told of King David's Wolf true?'

He ignored Samuel and Fulke's snorts of amusement to ask, 'Which ones?'

Avelyn nodded towards the two men. 'Well, from their response, I suppose I should ask if any of the tales are true.'

'No.'

'Then why do you let them exist?'

'Exist? I've done more than just let them exist, I've fed them, nurtured them, letting them grow beyond the believable.'

'Why would you do such a thing?'

'Because the rumours keep people away. The tales keep me from having to explain myself. And because in all honesty, the fearsome reputation of King David's Wolves keeps all of us safer.'

'Safer?'

'If you believed someone was heartless, merciless and bloodthirsty, would you recklessly attack, or even provoke, that person, or would you think twice about doing so?'

'Since I would think long and hard about such an action, I suppose your reasoning makes sense.'

'Good. Just don't share that knowledge with anyone.'

She toyed with a lock of hair at the nape of his neck. 'I should be jealous.' Her voice had been little more than a whisper, as if she'd been speaking to herself.

Elrik briefly closed his eyes at the shiver rippling down his spine, before asking just as softly, 'Why?'

She twirled the lock around her finger before releasing it with a sigh. 'Your hair curls so nicely.'

He frowned at another shiver as her fingertips brushed against his neck. The sound of muffled choking as Samuel and Fulke fought desperately not to laugh reminded him that they were not alone.

Elrik reached up to stay her hand. 'Lady Avelyn, we should be getting back on the road.'

That wasn't what he'd wanted to say. He'd been torn between ordering her to stop the distracting touch and asking her to continue. Since his men were close at hand, he couldn't decide. The safest course of action seemed to be avoidance. That would be more easily accomplished if they were once again travelling.

Thankfully she didn't argue or question his abrupt change of mind. Instead, she quietly waited while he once again donned the mailed head covering and helmet before helping her mount her waiting horse.

Once she was again secured between the rolls of padding on the saddle, she reached down and touched his shoulder. 'I apologise if I said, or did, anything unseemly.'

'You did nothing.'

She jerked her hand away, making him feel foolish for using such a gruff tone. Elrik covered her hand, now resting on the pommel, with one of his and moved closer until his chest rested against her leg. 'Lady Avelyn, I would like nothing more than to spend the day enjoying your company.' He nodded towards his men, who were both pacing their horses on the road, apparently anxious to get underway. 'But I would prefer to do so without such an avid audience.'

Without looking at him, she nodded. Then her lips curved into a small smile and she turned to stare at him, a look of surprise on her face as if she'd just now understood his words. 'Oh!'

She curled her fingers around his to squeeze lightly. 'Thank you for saying such a kind thing.'

Elrik stepped away, letting their hands fall apart. What he'd said wasn't out of *kindness*. He truly wanted to spend some time alone with her.

Unfortunately, he wasn't at all certain why he felt that way.

Normally he avoided women, going out of his way to do so at times. They were a complication he wished not to deal with in his life.

And any involvement with this particular woman would

be more of a complication than others. Besides, whether she agreed or not, she was currently betrothed to another.

He looked at her and fought the sudden urge to reach up and draw her closer to him for a kiss. No amount of logic, no reasonable argument over right and wrong, could shake his desire.

He cleared his throat, an act that did nothing to help clear his mind. 'I speak only the truth, Lady Avelyn. But we both have some place else we must go.'

She nodded. The smile disappeared from her face. 'Ah, yes. We need to make haste to King David's court.'

Elrik ignored the traces of sadness and anger in her voice. There was nothing he could do to change his orders, or her waiting fate. That very lack of ability chafed. Even though he answered to King David, not being in control of a situation was not normal. In this instance, that lack of control set him oddly on edge.

'We should go.'

At her nod, he moved away to mount his own horse and motioned the men forward.

Chapter Five

When they made camp for the night, the light of day was beginning to fade. Fulke took care of the horses while Samuel started a fire in the centre of the small clearing.

Avelyn hesitated when Elrik reached up to help her dismount. Unwilling to chance a repeat of earlier in the day when she'd needed his support, she made certain to stretch her legs before accepting his assistance.

It wasn't that she didn't like the feel of his touch or his arms around her—she did—far too much.

This last couple of hours riding had given her time to consider the strange rush of feelings Elrik's nearness created.

He made her feel shy, uncertain and nervous as though some unseen danger was near at hand. The closer he came, the higher her sense of alert climbed.

Over the pounding of her heart roaring in her ears, she could hear the sound of his breathing.

Beneath his slightest touch, her skin quivered, twitching like a cat right before someone stroked its fur.

Through all the wondrous scents of the forest—the trees, bushes and earth—his scent—worn leather, sweat, the oil on his chainmail, the lingering aroma of rosemary—teased at her nose.

Yet she wasn't afraid. The pervading sense of unease didn't frighten her—it was more of a disquieting anticipation than real fear.

She didn't understand how he of all people had so invaded her senses. Elrik of Roul was not just King David's Wolf, he was the man sent to return her to a fate she wished not to face.

Her first instinct should be to run, to find a way to escape. Yet she found herself more than willing, nearly eager to stay close and discover the reason for her anticipation.

'Lady Avelyn?'

His question broke through the riotous thoughts chasing each other around her mind.

'I'm sorry.' She blinked to clear her head and gazed down at him. Placing her hands on his shoulders to accept his assistance, she said, 'I meant not to keep you waiting.'

He laughed, his breath rushing warm against her cheek as he lowered her to the ground. 'Now it is my turn to ask, what are you thinking about so intently?'

She'd asked him that exact question when they'd stopped earlier. *Had his thoughts then taken the same direction as hers had just now?*

Avelyn laughed softly at her odd thoughts, before answering, 'Nothing of any importance.'

She lowered her hands from his shoulders and straightened out the skirt of her tunic while stepping away. 'Although, I could have been thinking about food.'

He held out his arm. 'Then we should see to it that you eat.'

Avelyn placed her hand on his forearm, accepting his offer to guide her safely over the uneven ground.

'But I will need to make certain the men don't feed you four meals' worth of food.'

She smiled. So, he did remember having nearly this

same conversation earlier. That made her strangely happy. It wasn't as if the conversation had been of anything important. It had been small and insignificant, yet he'd remembered.

Elrik paused in front of a log and shook his head. 'One of these times I would like to lead you to a better seat than a fallen tree trunk.'

'I would like that, too.' She sat down. 'But for now, this is fine.' She waved at the growing fire. 'Soon it will be quite warm, making this spot more than just convenient.'

'Oh, yes, almost as good as a comfortable and safe castle hall.'

The disdain in his tone was unmistakable. 'My lord, I am truly comfortable.' She stretched out her legs and wiggled her feet before nodding towards his men to ask, 'And what woman would not feel safe in the company of the King's Wolf and two of his most trusted men?'

Elrik countered, 'Without a full contingent of armed guards, no woman should feel safe out on the road.'

She understood what he meant. Ever since this war between Stephen and Matilda started, thieves and murderers roamed the roads unfettered by law or morals of any kind. Those who normally upheld the law in the areas near their keep were occupied elsewhere with their duty to their chosen liege.

However, Avelyn hadn't spent her entire life protected by guards or safe behind the walls of her father's keep. 'You forget I am not like the women of court. There were no guards in the village where I grew up. Thieves were a part of everyday life. If you didn't learn to protect things you valued, you would soon find them missing.'

'You had no reeve? Nobody in charge of upholding order?'

'No. The reeve cared only that the villagers showed up

to work in the fields. He never ventured out to our village. Since our little gathering of huts was the furthest away from the keep, we were left mostly on our own.'

'And when something dire happened?'

'You mean like murder?' At his nod, she said, 'Rather than wait for the lord to hold court, the men took care of the law themselves. Once when I was a child, a stranger came into the village and killed the blacksmith's wife. The next morning his body was found hanged from a tree at the entrance to the village. There was never another murder.'

Samuel snorted. 'That would be enough to deter me.'

Elrik's glare sent his man back to the task of setting out the food. He then reminded her, 'You are no longer living in the village and need to become accustomed to your current life.'

'As what? The lord's natural-born daughter, or King Óláfr's great-granddaughter?' Avelyn laughed at the last thought. 'I am only related to the King for as long as he holds on to his crown. He could have it taken away at any moment.'

'Which is why you are so important. Your marriage will bring him more men to help keep him safe.'

'Not many. Besides, while he is safe and warm, I will suffer under Bolk's care. It does not seem like a fair deal to me.'

'Fairness is not a consideration.'

'Oh, yes, I nearly forgot, I am but a possession to be used at my family's discretion.' She drew up her legs and rested her forearms on her knees, leaning forward to ask, 'Where was my family during the winters of my childhood when every night was a battle against freezing to death? Where were they the days my stomach cramped in pain from the lack of food? It seems to me that I owe them nothing—least of all my entire future.'

'It is called life, Lady Avelyn, and whether I agree with you or not makes no difference.'

'So, you do agree with me?'

He shook his head. 'You are not going to draw me into an argument over right and wrong. Your future is not up to me.'

'Oh, my lord, I don't need to draw you into an argument. You have already made your opinion known.' He was returning her to her father—and Bolk—so she was well aware of where he stood on this matter. 'I am simply asking if I am wrong to think this way.'

'Make room.' He waved her over on the log and sat next to her. 'It would be easier for you if you accepted what was going to happen without dwelling on a different outcome.'

'I cannot just accept Bolk without question. If I am the possession of a king and his grandson, surely I am worthy of someone other than a minor warlord.'

'That's where you need to begin your discussion with King David. What are you worth, Lady Avelyn?'

'Someone younger than Bolk?'

'Many people marry someone far from their own age. Why should you not do the same?'

Had he lost his ability to reason? 'Isn't it obvious?'

'Not to the King it won't be. This will be your only chance to sway him. And trust me, King David isn't going to care if you find your husband desirable or not.'

She felt the flush heat her cheeks. Desire for the man hadn't entered her mind. She'd been talking about the two of them having nothing in common. Bolk was an ancient warlord, while she was a servant's daughter who knew nothing about his world.

When she remained silent, Elrik continued. 'This marriage will not be about your satisfaction with the man chosen as your husband. It is about the wealth or power he can bring, that is all.'

'Wealth or power? Bolk has neither. He arrived at Brandr Keep with half-a-dozen poorly armed guards and a gold chest little bigger than my hand.'

'That may be true, but he has something your family wants. And you are the means of gaining it.'

'And my safety, happiness or, as you said, satisfaction is of no consequence.'

'No.'

Avelyn knew that whether she desired the man or not made little difference to anyone—however, physical desire did have one benefit others might consider. She asked, 'Having more men gives the King more wealth and power, does it not?'

He nodded. 'Yes.'

'Then my husband's ability to get me with child, creating more subjects for the King, should count for something.'

Elrik looked at her, his brows raised and asked, 'What makes you so certain Bolk is not able to do so? You do realise a man's age has little to do with his ability of getting you with child?'

No, that was something she hadn't realised. Her stomach seemed to turn over at the thought of sharing that man's bed. She frowned while desperately seeking any answer. Finally, instead of answering his question, she asked, 'How old is his youngest child?'

Elrik smiled, then said, 'Twenty-seven, I think.'

'And Bolk's last wife died how long ago?'

'It has been less than a year.'

'How old was she at the time?'

'I am not certain, but she couldn't have been much over thirty yet.'

'If I am correctly remembering what I'd overheard, she

was sixteen years old when they wed and in all their years of marriage she never had a child.'

'It is possible she was barren.'

Once again Avelyn frowned. 'You are making this difficult.'

'That is my intent. Since this is not a matter to be taken lightly, King David will make it more difficult.'

'Oh!' She turned to face him more fully. 'Did Bolk dally with other women?'

'Dally?' Elrik laughed. 'Several and not all of them willing.'

Avelyn was shocked to learn that her family thought nothing of marrying her off to such a base man. 'Did any of them have his child?'

'No.'

'It is doubtful every woman of his acquaintance was unable to conceive.'

'But possible.'

She narrowed her eyes. 'Doubtful.'

He shrugged. 'I'll grant that your argument holds weight, but it's going to take more than questioning his ability to sire children to sway the King to your side.'

Avelyn sighed. 'I can think of nothing else.'

Elrik nodded towards the food. 'Perhaps something to eat will help you.'

Her stomach growled in response, drawing a laugh from him before he stood and pulled her to her feet. 'Come on, up.'

Elrik fought back a yawn as he stretched out on his makeshift pallet at the edge of the fire's flickering light. It had been a long day on the road and now with a full stomach all he wanted was to fall asleep. Samuel and Fulke would see to the camp and guard duty until he relieved them later.

However, the woman lying on her back atop the pallet next to him, staring up at the sky through a break in the canopy of tree branches overhead, kept darting glances at him.

Even though it was not yet nightfall, he'd hoped to retire soon so they could get an early start in the morning. Apparently, this day's travel hadn't made her tired enough to seek slumber. Finally, he asked, 'What keeps you from sleep?'

She sighed and then rolled on to her side to face him. 'Other than strength and wealth, of which I possess neither, what does a man value?'

'Sleep.' He regretted his response the second it left his mouth. Before she could turn away, he apologised. 'I'm sorry. I meant not to be so abrupt.'

When she moved to roll over, he snagged her hand. Curling his fingers around her wrist, he held her in place. 'Honesty, soft words, a warm and comfortable place to lay our head, an ear to listen, a well-managed abode.'

'So, basically, you want a servant who will see to all your needs, share your bed and offer no complaint?'

He blinked. 'Is that what you heard me say?'

'Not in so many words but, yes. Do your servants not see to the making of your bed and fire for warmth in your chamber? Do they not listen to your complaints without argument? Do they not see to every aspect of your keep?'

'Well, yes, but a wife's touch would add much.'

'Such as?'

He never should have started this conversation. 'Was there anything special your mother used to do or make for you that seemed different when another did or made the same thing?'

She frowned a few moments before saying, 'Yes. When

she tucked me into my pallet at night she sang to me and stroked back my hair before kissing my forehead. But after she got sick, Mistress Berta would simply send me to bed with little more than a wave to shoo me away.'

Her comparison was a little more drastic than what he'd meant, but it would do. 'It's the same difference between a servant's touch and a wife's.'

'How so?'

Elrik feared she'd ask for a more detailed explanation. It wasn't as if he'd had much experience in the matter as his wife had never cared about his wants or needs enough to offer anything that could have been considered a gentle touch. In truth, he'd only given voice to wishes that he'd once taken to heart.

'The servant does their job—it is nothing more than a task to complete before moving on to the next task. But when a wife does, or sees, to the same task she's interested in more than simply finishing the chore at hand. Usually, she wants her husband, or children, to be happy, comfortable with what was done with them in mind.'

'Usually?'

Since he had no intention of discussing his former wife, he shrugged in response.

'While I understand what you are saying, I do not see how that will help me sway King David.'

'I simply answered your question. I've truly no idea how you can use that information to your advantage. I can only tell you that King David possesses a soft spot for women. He has great regard for his mother and still, after nearly fifteen years, speaks highly of his dearly departed wife.'

Avelyn frowned. 'It is something I can think about over the next day or two.'

He cleared his throat. 'Since we covered so much ground today, we should arrive at Carlisle before sunset tomorrow.'

'What?' She bolted upright, repeating in a higher-pitched tone, 'What?'

'Is that a problem? I thought you would be relieved to have all of this over and done with.'

After tossing her cover aside, she grasped the skirt of her tunic. 'In this?' Her hands flew to her hair. 'Looking as though I just left the fields?'

'The King knows you've been on the road. He isn't going to expect you to arrive dressed for court.'

'Being dressed for court isn't a consideration since I do not own any clothing so fine. What matters is that I smell as bad as you and your men. I am filthy. My hair is a nest even a rat would avoid.'

'Are you saying we stink?'

Wrinkling her nose, she nodded. 'Horribly.'

Unable to stop himself, he laughed.

She crossed her arms against her stomach and glared at him. 'I am glad you find this so amusing.'

'I had no idea that you were so vain, Lady Avelyn.'

'Vanity has nothing to do with my concern. I am going to beg for my future and it will be a little difficult to claim any worth if I am covered in grime.'

She had a point. 'We can stop in the village before Carlisle. There is an inn there and I'm sure I can procure a chamber for your use. I might not be able to obtain a bath, but surely they'll supply water. I have soap and a comb you can use. I am also certain the innkeeper, or a serving maid, will know where clean, serviceable clothing can be found.'

'I have no coin to purchase clothing or for the use of a chamber.'

'The cost will not be so great that I cannot afford the expense.'

'But I have no way of repaying you.'

He waved away her worry. 'I do not expect you to do so.'

She shook her head. 'Since you are not related to me, nor betrothed or wed to me, it would be inappropriate.'

Inappropriate? It wasn't as if he'd suggested they do anything unseemly. 'I think you worry far too much.'

'No. If anything I worry not enough. I may be inexperienced in the ways of court, but I do understand how gossip grows and spreads. You would be seen as my…my protector…my keeper. And I would be seen as your woman.' She sighed heavily before continuing. 'While I may find you attractive, I do not wish to be known as your woman. It would make finding a suitable husband more difficult. If I did find someone, once he heard the rumours it is doubtful he would wish to take another man's cast-off to wife.'

'Procuring clean garments to casting you off is quite a long jump.'

'Not when it comes to gossip.'

'Lady Avelyn, I am fairly certain that your conversation with the King will prove more gossip-worthy than who supplied your clothing. A king's great-granddaughter running away from a marriage, then returning only to cry assistance from another king to avoid the marriage, is not an everyday occurrence.'

'Don't you see? That is precisely what will make every detail open for speculation and gossip.'

Elrik frowned. The only thing that would calm her worries and allow him to get some sleep was to work out how she could pay for it herself.

At a loss as how to accomplish that, he shrugged. 'Let me purchase something from you.'

'What? I have nothing of any value.'

'A bauble, a ribbon, something. I don't know.' He glanced at her, noticing her frown and pursed lips, then said without thinking first, 'A kiss, perhaps.'

Her eyes widened briefly before she leaned towards

him. 'Since I have no baubles, nor ribbons, a kiss will have to do.'

He leaned away, surprised that she'd taken his offhanded suggestion seriously. She was overly worried about possible gossip at court, but not worried about kissing a man she barely knew?

She dipped her head and looked at him through her eyelashes. 'It is all I have. I trust you not to seek anything more than a kiss.'

Her breath brushing warm against his lips left him wondering how they'd come so close to each other when he didn't remember moving. His fingers slid easily through her hair as he cupped the back of her head. 'You don't have to do this.'

She shifted on her knees to lean against him. 'Oh, but I do.'

Elrik groaned at her breathy whisper. Sleep was not going to be an option this night. 'Avelyn, this is a mistake.'

'Are you afraid?'

He heard the teasing lilt of her voice, but it settled in his mind as more of a challenge than anything else. Gathering her closer, he asked, 'Of what?'

'A dove.'

'A defenceless little dove?' Although at the moment he was the one feeling rather defenceless.

She curled her fingers into the fabric of his shirt. 'One with fangs.'

Elrik covered her lips with his.

He had already guessed that curiosity had prompted her to be so bold, so her startled flinch wasn't unexpected. However, the sudden catch in the pit of his stomach was more than just unexpected, it was downright disconcerting.

But more disconcerting was her extended pause. After her initial flinch of surprise, she seemed to quickly become…distracted. His original plan had been to chastely kiss her lips, fully expecting that would be enough to satisfy her curiosity. But he'd tarried over-long and her lack of response brought those plans to a crossroads.

Did he end this kiss, leaving her to think poorly of the act? Or, did he veer off his chosen path—a safe path—and recklessly change her opinion?

When had he ever trod the safe path?

Elrik lifted his head, leaving barely enough room between them for a breath of air to escape, and asked, 'Not quite what you expected, little dove?'

The second she parted her lips to reply, he captured her open mouth beneath his. Threading his fingers through her hair, he tightened them against the back of her head, tilting it slightly before sweeping his tongue across hers.

Chapter Six

Avelyn gasped at the stroking touch, thankful for the tightness of his arm around her, preventing her from falling to the blankets beneath them.

She was more thankful that he'd changed his kiss into something that dispelled the disappointment that had been building.

His first touch hadn't been at all what she'd expected from a man's kiss. From what she'd overheard the other girls talking about in her father's kitchens, she'd been certain the act would prove so much…more. She'd foolishly worried that her expectations had been too high.

But this…this was far better than what she'd expected or what she could have hoped. It wasn't just a kiss. There was nothing gentle or soothing about this kiss. He wasn't cruel, but he silently demanded that she respond, that she follow his lead. She willingly did so, knowing that she couldn't have ignored the demand had she wanted to do so.

It was as if he were claiming her and it sent heated shivers clear down to her toes. He did nothing more than hold her impossibly close and kiss her, yet every speck of her flesh tingled with longing. A virgin she might be, but Avelyn knew what her body longed to experience and it was all she could do not to beg him to—

The distinct snap of a twig in the forest broke through the haze of desire swirling around her. Instantly, Elrik pushed her to the ground, covering her with his body right before she heard the twang of a bowstring being released and the whoosh of an arrow flying no more than inches above them to thud into the trunk of a tree right behind them.

'Find him!' Elrik shouted at his already moving men as they crashed deeper into the darkening forest.

'Not again.' Avelyn groaned at the thought of once again being forced to flee someone seeking to kill her.

'What do you mean, *not again*?' Elrik pushed off of her and rose. Standing over her, he asked, 'This has happened before?'

Light from the fire flickered across his face. If his brusque tone hadn't alerted her to his irritation, the hard frown narrowing his eyes to glittering slits would have made it clear.

She looked away, nodding. 'Yes.'

'When?'

'A few days after I set off on my own.'

Avelyn flinched at the nearly growled curses escaping his mouth before he asked, 'And you didn't think that important enough to mention?'

Now she understood why people feared him. There was no leniency in his tone, nor in his cold gaze or unyielding stance. This was not the same man who mere heartbeats ago kissed her until her senses swirled. He reminded her of the men at her father's keep, the ones who thought nothing of quelling their anger by using their fists on someone weaker and smaller. She'd found herself on the receiving end of their ire a time or two and now, to her horror, her lower lip quivered, but knowing better than to ignore his question, she shakily answered, 'No, I never—'

'Stop!' His shout cut off her reply. When she turned away, hoping to avoid what could possibly be the strongest fists she'd ever encountered, he reached down to grasp her hand and pulled her to her feet. 'Don't you dare think to appease me with tears, it will only make things worse.'

'I was not trying to… I would never…' She paused to catch her breath and swiped a hand across her damp cheeks. 'I am not crying.'

'Good.' He stroked a thumb beneath her eyes. Instead of making any comment about the tears he'd wiped away, he said, 'Now tell me what happened. From the beginning.'

She blinked at his now mild tone. That was it? His tirade was over? No blows, no slaps or further shouting? She looked up at him, warily meeting his stare.

He shook his head and sighed. 'Because I encounter it so often, it is easy for me to recognise fear on another's face. I know not what you have experienced at your father's keep, but I do know Brandr and his men.' He placed a hand over his heart. 'Avelyn, I swear to you neither I, nor my men, will ever bring you harm.'

Unable to find the words to express her uncertainty, or relief, she could only nod her acceptance of his vow. Besides, if they were less than a day's ride from King David, he would be rid of her soon. She frowned at the twinge of pain that thought caused.

Elrik waved towards the log they'd sat on earlier. 'Come, sit and tell me what has happened since you left your father's protection.'

Once seated, she began. 'I didn't take enough food with me, so I ran through my supplies in the first two days.'

'How did you eat after that?'

'I think it was the third evening when I saw a few loaves

of bread cooling in a cottage window and I stole the smallest one.' She shrugged away her guilt. 'Some drunken sot tried to stop me, but he tripped over a rut in the road, so I got away.'

'That's probably the man they say you killed in Duffield.'

'No!' Avelyn jumped to her feet. 'No, I killed no one. He was still cursing at me after he landed on the ground. I swear he was alive.'

Elrik pulled her back down on to the log. 'I didn't think you did.'

Images of the murderer who'd been caught and punished at her childhood village flashed through her mind, making a tremor of dread flash down her spine. 'Why would you think that when you have only known me a few days? How will I convince anyone of my innocence? Dear Lord, what will they do to me?'

'Hush. You worry for nothing. Logic says it wasn't you. Why would anyone trying to escape her family kill a man over a loaf of bread when it would needlessly draw attention? You don't seem to be that foolish.'

Another thought crossed her mind. 'Even had I killed someone, how would anyone have known it was me?'

Elrik chuckled. 'You didn't believe your father would allow you to escape without sending someone to bring you back, did you? They followed you into England before Brandr went to King David for assistance.'

After giving her a few moments to mull over his explanation, he prompted, 'What happened after that?'

Avelyn sighed. 'The next day I wasn't as lucky. But the following afternoon I joined the others at the castle gates waiting for scraps.'

'Which castle?'

She shrugged. 'A big one?'

Instead of chastising her for not knowing, he asked, 'Did any of the others comment about your presence?'

'No. The village was so large that I doubt if any could say who lived there or who didn't.'

'Likely it was the Earl of Derby's keep.'

'Perhaps. If so, someone needs to tell him to take better care of his people. The child I gave most of my share to looked as though she hadn't eaten in days.'

'I'll be sure to tell him, the next time we meet in battle.'

His mocking comment gave her pause. 'Are we in enemy lands?'

'You have been in King Stephen's domain since you stole that loaf of bread. Did you not take that into consideration when you decided to travel south?'

'No.' She honestly hadn't. 'I knew I had to watch out for thieves and murderers, so I kept off the main roads. But other than that concern, I wanted only to reach the coast, so I gave it little thought.'

'You should consider yourself lucky.'

'Not in the least. After all, I did get caught.'

'Yes, you did. At great risk to myself, I might add.'

She glanced up at him to gauge his mood and caught the twitch of his lips. He was teasing her. 'You needn't have put yourself in such a dangerous situation, not for a mere woman.'

'More than just a mere woman.' He nudged her shoulder. 'A king's great-granddaughter.'

'Oh, yes.' Avelyn waved her hand in the air with a flourish, as if to brush off her lapse in memory. 'I forgot.'

'What happened after you begged at the gates?'

'I found an unguarded, falling down and blessedly empty stable to spend the night in and started out again the next morning. That afternoon I was resting against a tree when an arrow landed a hairsbreadth from my nose in the trunk. It sent me running until I could run no more. After that, I found my way to the village inn where you found me.'

Elrik frowned. 'Brandr's archers wouldn't have missed twice.'

'So, who is it, then, if not one of my father's men?'

'All I know is that King David hinted at someone seeking to bring you harm.'

Avelyn swallowed the lump of fear forming in her throat. 'You mean my death.'

'It would serve no purpose for your father to have you killed. He would stand to lose much.'

'Then who?' It wasn't as if anyone could profit from her demise.

Elrik shrugged. 'Bolk, perhaps.'

'Bolk!' Shock that he would try such a thing caused her tone to rise.

Elrik looked at her, one eyebrow hitched up in question. 'And now you are insulted that the man you wish not to wed might not want you either?'

'No. That isn't what I find surprising. I would be pleased should he not wish to make me his wife. But to kill me rather than cancel whatever agreement he has with my family is a little drastic.'

'You have no way of knowing how much it might cost him to do so. Perhaps having you meet an unfortunate end might prove less costly. Or maybe it isn't Bolk. It could be someone who wants their own connection to the man and considers you nothing but an obstacle who needs to be removed.'

She hadn't wanted to rush to King David's court, but now it might be the best option for her safety. 'Do you think that if King David can be persuaded to set aside this marriage that whoever is after me will give up their chase?'

'There is no way of telling. But you can't rely on King David's decision being in your favour.'

Her heart sank at the thought of still being forced to wed Bolk. Especially after she'd gone through so much to escape the marriage. 'Well, then I suppose I will have to find a way to convince him.'

The stomp of booted feet as the men returned to the clearing put a halt to their discussion. Unfortunately, they were alone.

Elrik rose, asking the obvious, 'He got away?'

'Yes,' Samuel answered.

Fulke added, 'There's more than one. We found a spot further up the road where three or four horses had rested, probably in readiness to escape.'

Elrik glanced up at the stars starting to dot the sky. 'It is too late to try following them. Be on alert in case they double back.'

Instead of both taking up their earlier positions along the edge of the road, the men split up. Samuel went to the back of the clearing, patrolling along the edge of the woods, while Fulke returned to his position along the road.

Elrik looked down at her. 'You might want to get some sleep. We leave at the first light of day.'

His suggestion worked like some odd spell, because all at once exhaustion settled over her. Avelyn yawned as she rose to return to her bed of blankets. 'And you?'

He followed her to the makeshift pallets. Pulling his bed roll closer to hers, he answered, 'Will be right here.'

But instead of stretching out beneath the covers as she did, he sat up on his bed watching, his gaze sweeping every inch of the trees and bushes surrounding the clearing.

Did he expect her would-be murderer to return? *What if they did?*

Avelyn rolled over to face out towards the clearing.

Would she be lucky enough to avoid their arrow a third time?

She pulled the cover over her head. While she wished not to wed Bolk, she didn't wish to escape her fate by dying.

Not yet.

There was too much left to discover, too many other things she wanted to experience.

Even though these last thirty or so days and nights had been fraught with danger and hunger, they had been wondrous.

She'd never been on her own, or away from home by herself before and she rather enjoyed the freedom. To walk alongside rushing streams, take her boots and stockings off to splash her bare feet in the icy water without anyone admonishing her to behave like a lady, made her feel like a carefree child once again.

Even her time with Hannah and the others at the inn had been an experience to cherish. Strangers had offered her not just shelter from the unending rain, but food and companionship.

Her father would consider the women nothing but whores beneath his contempt. His own actions would have no place in his opinion.

She, on the other hand, had found them to be kind and more compassionate than anyone she knew under her father's roof. They reminded her of the women from her childhood village—doing what they had to do to see to the welfare of their families.

She saw no shame in their actions, not when the coin gained went to put food in the bellies of their children.

How could that be considered sinful? Would it not have been more of a crime to let the children starve?

Unable to breathe easily in the close confines under her

cover, Avelyn pulled it off her head and once again rolled over to study Elrik.

A flush raced up her neck to heat her cheeks. Had she not run away, she would not have experienced her first kiss. And, oh, what an experience that had turned out to be.

No, those after her could not be allowed to succeed—she wanted to know a man's touch before she died.

She studied the line of his stubble-covered jaw. Intent on the task of guarding her, the hard, immobile planes of his face appeared carved in stone.

She quelled the sudden urge to soothe the hardness from his jawline, to run a fingertip over the fullness of his lower lip, to trace the barely perceptible crookedness of his nose and to smooth away the deep frown line between his dark brows.

More desperately, she fought to quell the desire for him to provide her first experience of a man's touch.

With a choked breath she pulled the covers off her shoulders. His gaze swept the clearing once more and came to rest on her before hiking his brows up into an unspoken question.

Avelyn wondered if a stroke of his hand would feel as hot.

'Elrik?'

He shook his head. 'No.'

No? Did he possess the ability to read her mind? 'I haven't asked you anything.'

His lips twitched up into a half-smile. 'It requires no magical power to know what thoughts tease your mind. The night air is cool.' He paused to nod at her. 'Yet you've thrown your cover aside. The heaviness in your gaze is not from lack of sleep and, if I am not mistaken, the shimmer covering your forehead is not from a fever.'

He again shook his head. 'No, Avelyn. Go to sleep.'

'But…' She let her complaint trail off, uncertain what to say. He wasn't wrong, she did long for him, for his touch, his kiss, for things she'd only heard about and not yet tasted herself.

He rose and stepped close to crouch down beside her. 'Don't misunderstand me.' He traced one fingertip along her cheek. 'I would like nothing more than to gather you close and spend the night discovering all of your secrets. But, Avelyn, you are not mine and I will not use you in such a manner.' Elrik pulled the cover back up to her chin and tucked it down around her shoulders. 'Go to sleep and leave these thoughts alone, save them for another time, another man.'

From his position at the edge of the road, Elrik glanced up at the sky. Daylight was beginning to break through the thinning clouds. Soon it would be light enough to start out on the last leg of their journey. Tonight they would all be sleeping in a bed instead of on the hard ground. Even a pallet in the hall at King David's court would provide more comfort than they'd found these last several nights. He wondered at his strange longing for comfort—either he was getting old, or he needed to get as far away from Avelyn as quickly as possible.

Just being around her was making him long for things he'd given no thought to for more years than he could remember.

Odd things, like the comfort of a bed. He turned to look at her. And even odder things, like the gentle voice, the soft touch that only a woman could offer.

Elrik groaned. Yes, it was most definitely time to hand her over to King David. Why then did the thought of doing so make him ache with loss?

He slapped at a non-existent spot of dirt on his thigh, before heading across the clearing to shake her shoulder.

'Avelyn, wake up.'

She bolted upright. 'What!'

Laughing at her surprise, he motioned towards the sky. 'It's time to get up.'

'But I just fell asleep.'

That wasn't quite true, she'd fallen into a fitful slumber nearly the moment he'd bid her to go to sleep. Although, from the amount of tossing and turning she'd done all night, she probably felt as if she'd slept mere moments. 'I am sure you feel that way, but it is nearly daylight.'

Other than a quick nod, she gave no comment, a sign that she was either upset with his refusal last night or embarrassed by her desire. Either way it made no difference as by day's end they would not be alone in each other's company, they would be surrounded by a court drowning in curiosity.

It took little time to break their fast, see to morning necessities and clear camp. Samuel and Fulke worked quickly, seemingly as eager to end this journey as he. The only one in their party who tended to linger was Avelyn and, while he understood her reluctance to make haste, every moment out in the open put her in danger.

Elrik secured the rolled-up bedding to her saddle and held out his hand. 'Come, we need to be on our way.'

She stared at him a few moments, a question furrowing her brow, but finally accepted his assistance on to the saddle without saying a word.

Once he was certain she was secure, he paused and looked up at her, waiting silently for her to meet his gaze before saying, 'I truly wish things could be different between us, but they can't. I am not sorry to have met you, or to have kissed you, Avelyn. I am only sorry that I have upset you by doing so.'

She tentatively reached out, before sighing, then cupping his cheek. 'You have nothing to be sorry for. I only wish there were many more miles between here and King David, that is all.'

He couldn't resist turning his head into her touch and placing a kiss against her palm. Then, regretfully, stepped away to mount his own horse.

Elrik led the group from the clearing. They rode in a tight formation, Samuel and Fulke guarding not just his back, but also Avelyn's. Nothing was going to happen to her while in his care. He and his men would be more vigilant now that he knew just how closely danger lurked.

It took a little while, but eventually Avelyn's distress eased, letting her appreciate the warmth of the sun upon her face, the light breeze ruffling her hair and the company of the men riding in front and behind her.

Samuel and Fulke talked quietly of nothing important between them. Unimportant to her—things like needing a good bath, or getting the time to clean their armour.

Wondering how far it was to the village, she called out, 'Lord Elrik?'

Apparently startled by the more formal address, he glanced briefly over his shoulder at her.

Avelyn laughed at his expression, then explained, 'I thought I should be more formal now, so I don't accidentally give those at court any morsel to gossip about.'

Fulke chortled. 'Lady Avelyn, rest assured, they will find something with or without you providing any morsels.'

She frowned and looked down at the bed rolls tied to keep her on the saddle. Tapping the one before her, said, 'These will have to go before we reach the castle.'

Elrik nodded. 'Before we get to the village, we'll stop and remove them.'

'How much further is the village?'

He glanced up towards the sun. 'Not much longer—before midday.'

It took her only a quick glance to realise midday would soon be upon them. 'So, very soon.'

'Yes.'

She pulled back on the reins of her horse. 'Then we should stop now.'

Elrik's sigh would have been humorous had she not sensed his sullen mood. Shouldn't *she* be the one disquieted by the coming end of this journey?

He didn't argue; instead he, too, stopped and dismounted. The other men followed suit. After handing his reins to Samuel, Elrik came to her side and wrapped his hands around her waist.

Unbidden, a soft gasp escaped her lips at his touch. He closed his eyes and hesitated a heartbeat before looking up at her to ask, 'Ready?'

No. She wasn't ready for what was about to come. But nothing could change what awaited her, so she nodded and allowed him to assist her from the saddle.

He unlaced the bed rolls, tossed them to Fulke, ordering, 'Switch the saddles.'

Avelyn agreed—his high-cantle saddle would appear out of place on her smaller horse. Besides, if they were attacked, his battle saddle would be wasted on her.

When the bed rolls were stowed and the saddles switched, Avelyn managed to scramble up on Little Lady without help. Elrik adjusted the stirrup for her and paused to whisper something in the horse's ear before getting back on his own steed.

Even though they'd reached the village about an hour later, Avelyn felt as if she'd been on horseback for days.

She slid to the ground and would have fallen had Elrik not been right there.

'Steady.' He grasped her arms, saying, 'Take a moment.'

'Thank you,' she whispered, amazed at the sudden shyness once again overtaking her. She felt as if everyone in the busy village had stopped to stare at her—a woman travelling alone with three men.

Elrik released her and stepped back. 'Stay here with Samuel and Fulke.'

The two men drew closer, while Elrik disappeared inside the inn.

He exited the inn in a matter of moments and, halfway back to her side, stopped to glare at the crowd gathering.

Elrik had expected to draw attention since he and his men were known in the village. But from the way Avelyn appeared to shrink between Samuel and Fulke the gathering was making her uneasy.

He picked out one of the men familiar to him. 'Something you wish to know, Timothy?'

The village's blacksmith nodded towards Avelyn. 'Be that her?'

There was no point in trying to put the gossips off the scent of what had to be the tale of the season thus far. 'Yes.'

He scanned the nodding faces. Their tongues were already wagging. To give them something else to dwell on he said, 'We are in need of a suitable garment for court.'

An older woman instantly stepped forward. 'I have just the thing. It might not be as fancy as some, but it is nicely made.'

'Thank you. Have it delivered here quickly.'

He held his hand out towards Avelyn. 'My lady, a room is ready for your use.'

She hesitated, looking from the still-lingering crowd to

him a couple of times. Then she straightened her spine before stepping forward.

While her first footstep seemed confident, her chin was tipped down, giving the appearance of an obedient child. Elrik caught her gaze and lifted his own head. She apparently understood his unspoken order and lifted her chin.

The woman who walked from between the horses to come to a stop before him looked every inch the lady she would soon become. Beneath the grime and dirt of the road, her bearing would do her great-grandfather proud.

And just that quickly Elrik felt a sharp sense of loss, making him wonder how he'd so easily become infatuated with a woman—not just any woman, but with Brandr's daughter. Soon his feelings for her would no longer matter, as she'd not be in his company, and this unwanted sense of loss would quickly fade.

He lowered his arm and stepped aside to motion her towards the inn. 'After you, my lady.'

Her bewildered gaze searched his face. He knew she didn't understand the lack of warmth in his tone. She would never understand his sudden withdrawal. But at the moment it was the kindest thing he could think of doing for the both of them.

She turned away and he followed her into the inn with his men on his heels.

Ever ready with his tongue, Fulke said, 'Never seen such a dolt afore now.'

Elrik wanted to turn around and throw a well-aimed fist into Fulke's teeth, but that would only lend truth to the man's words. So, instead, he ignored the comment.

A mistake, because it prompted Samuel to add, 'Could be fear.'

'Enough.' Without turning around Elrik nearly growled the order.

Thankfully both men saw fit to cease their unwanted comments.

Once above stairs, Elrik used the key the innkeeper had provided to unlock a door at the far end of the hall. 'Lady Avelyn.'

He stopped just inside the doorway to do a quick survey of the chamber. Certain she had everything she required— water, soap, towels and a comb—he said, 'Your clothing will be here soon. If there is anything else you require, we will be right outside the door.'

Avelyn took a step towards him. 'Elrik…'

His name, spoken in such a soft, pleading tone, and the shimmer in her gaze sent him rushing backwards into the hallway where he quickly closed the solid door between them.

With his back resting against the closed door, he took a breath, then he took another less shaking one.

Fulke, to his left, cursed. Samuel, on his right, softly said, 'Just breathe, Elrik, just breathe.'

He hadn't felt this angry, or this lost, since the day he'd given his life in exchange for his father's. That was the only and the last time he'd raged—and shed tears over the loss of something he'd never have, but couldn't change.

He'd only given away his soul that day.

Both these men had been with him then, too. They'd been at his back when he'd prostrated himself, along with his brother, at King David's feet to beg mercy for a foolish old man's act of treason. Without arguing, giving excuses, or even placing the rightful blame on Brandr for their father's act, they'd both pledged their lives in exchange for his.

Since that day he'd not begged, nor had he prostrated himself at anyone's feet—he wasn't about to do either now.

He swallowed hard and nearly smiled at the obvious sound of two heavy sighs echoing on either side of him.

If these emotions buffeting him were love, he wanted no part of it. There was no room in his life for this uncertainty—or this weakness. Were they to be attacked right this minute not only was his life in great peril, so were the lives of his men. One split second of indecision could cost him all.

King David's Wolf had not the time nor place for this distraction. Perhaps some day, when his service was completed—if that day ever came—he would find a woman to take as a wife. Someone malleable. Someone who didn't befuddle his mind in such a disturbing manner.

But not now and never this woman.

Footsteps coming up the stairs caught his attention. His hand fell to rest atop the sword hanging from his side.

'Oh, my lord. I meant not to startle you.' The older woman from the village arrived with two young girls, arms laden with clothing, behind her. 'I hope you don't mind, but I couldn't decide which tunic would find favour with your lady, so I brought a couple for her to choose from.'

He stood aside and let the woman and her helpers into the chamber. Avelyn's abrupt squeak of surprise told him she probably wasn't clothed enough for him to enter, so he simply said, 'Your clothes have arrived.' And quickly closed the door.

After what seemed hours, the door once again opened and the older women, with her helpers, exited the chamber. Elrik followed them below to settle the sum for what she'd provided. When he returned above stairs, the door to the chamber was still open. Both Samuel and Fulke shrugged before nodding towards the opening.

Wondering what was keeping her, Elrik walked into the chamber and came to a rocking halt.

To say she was lovely would have been a grave injustice to beauty. In his eyes, she was the most beautiful woman he'd ever seen.

The dark blue, nearly black tunic was slashed on both sides down to the middle of her hips and was laced so tightly that no curve or dip was left to his imagination. The plain darkness of the garment was broken at the neck and hem edges with a thin line of brilliant needlework. A snowy white chemise peeked through the lacings at her sides. They had combed her inky-dark hair until it shimmered about her shoulders, a thin silver circlet held the tresses in place.

She glanced away, staring down at her toes a second, before lifting her gaze back to his. 'Elrik?'

Her throaty one-word question threatened to steal away what little control he still possessed. Like the sirens spoken of in tales of old, he was drawn to her.

He longed to close the distance between them, take her to the waiting bed, strip off her finery and claim her as his—fiercely, as a wolf in the wild claims its mate.

These urges washing over him had nothing to do with such a weak emotion as love. This was lust. Pure unadulterated lust.

And thankfully, no matter how strong the urge, he could control lust. That knowledge lent a measure of calm to his previous worries.

She swished the skirt of her tunic back and forth. 'Am I presentable?'

'Very.' Even in her clothing made from coarse wool she would outshine the other women in the court.

She dropped her hold on the skirt to smooth her hands over her stomach. 'This isn't too plain?'

'Are you fishing for compliments, Avelyn?'

She nodded and then smiled. Her smile seemed to light up the chamber.

He wasn't about to tell her that while she might be the best-dressed lady at her father's court, in King David's she would be seen as plain. He'd not hurt her feelings in such a manner. Besides, from this minute forward, she would always be the standard by which he measured beauty.

Elrik stepped forward and took one of her hands in his. 'Aye, my lady. Your loveliness will put the other women to shame.'

That much was true. Amongst the brightly coloured tunics and dazzling jewels, she would shine brighter.

He tucked her hand into the crook of his arm and grabbed her small satchel. 'Is there anything else you need?'

'No.' She glanced around the chamber. 'Everything I own is already packed away.'

Elrik nodded towards the door. 'Then let us be on our way.'

Chapter Seven

Avelyn tried not to stare at the people crowding the courtyard, but there were so many of them that everywhere she
sent her focus she encountered yet another curious on-
looker. Had the entire area turned out to see what was
going to happen to her? She looked down at her feet, it was
the only place free of other faces.

Elrik lifted her hand to place it on his arm as they as-
cended to the walkway leading into the castle. 'Chin up.
It is almost over. Don't give them the satisfaction of seeing your fear.'

She stiffened her spine at his words. 'I am not afraid.'

To her surprise the area near the double doors leading
into the Great Hall was less crowded. She breathed a sigh
of relief.

Elrik pulled her off to the side. 'Listen to me, Avelyn.
Remember, show no fear. Do not grovel or cry. King David
has a soft spot for women, but he has no patience for tears.'

She looked up at him. 'Thankfully nobody can see that
my legs are already shaking.'

His half-smile felt so safe, so familiar that it was all she
could do not to lean against his chest for support.

'Speak plainly. Do not mince your words. When he asks

what you desire, tell him exactly what you want—not what you don't want.'

Avelyn held back a laugh. If she told the King exactly what she wanted right this moment, Elrik would be horrified. She wanted him. If she had to wed someone, she wished it could be him.

She closed her eyes against the sudden urge to sob. Now was not the time. Later tonight she could cry into her pillow with none the wiser.

Avelyn nodded. 'I promise to remember all you have told me, Elrik.'

When he turned to lead her into the castle, she pressed her fingers into his forearm, stopping him. 'You will be there?'

'For as long as I am permitted, yes.'

She couldn't ask for more.

Just before shoving through the doors, he glanced down at her. 'Breathe.'

Not realising that she'd been holding her breath, Avelyn sucked a shaking gasp of air and laughed at herself.

The second Elrik pushed open the double doors, the noise that had been drifting through the solid doors ceased.

Every pair of eyes in the Great Hall turned to look at her.

Avelyn felt her legs go weak and did her best to remain upright. There were so many people and she didn't recognise any of them.

The only evidence Elrik gave of noticing her near stumble was the tightening of his arm—giving her the support she needed to stay on her feet.

The crowd of people seemed to part before them, leaving an open path the length of the hall. Did these people fear him so greatly? If so, they were foolish to be afraid of such an honourable man.

She kept her gaze straight ahead, focused on the raised dais at the far end of the hall.

It helped her to ignore the obvious—she was grossly under-dressed for this gathering. If Elrik had lied to spare her feelings, he'd not done her any favours. These women wore brightly coloured overgowns that seemed to shimmer with jewels, making her look like a peasant out of her element.

Yet it would have been impossible not to notice the attention of the men. She felt, rather than saw, the measuring stares.

Once again Elrik tightened his arm beneath her fingers. Had he, too, seen the looks? Now that there were other women present, did he find her lacking in comparison?

She wanted to look up at him to judge his mood, but her gaze caught sight of her father sitting at the King's table and suddenly the only thing she wanted to do was to run from the Great Hall and keep running until there was at least an ocean between them.

Without turning his head, Elrik whispered softly, 'He can't naysay the King. Focus on David.'

How would that be better? The King was going to do the same as her father—give her to a man not of her choosing.

Like so many times before, she wished her mother was still alive. At least then she'd never have been forced to leave her village and she would be marrying someone she knew.

The warmth beneath her fingertips reminded her that if her life had taken such a different turn of events she would never have met Elrik. Never would have seen the dark desire in his gaze, or experienced the thrill of his kiss. As much as she wished not to wed Bolk she wasn't willing to give up her memories of the days with Elrik—those memories were all she would have in the long weeks, months and years ahead.

As they neared the dais, Elrik lowered his arm, leaving her to stand on her own. King David rose and motioned for her father to join him. He then addressed Elrik. 'Roul, join us.'

She and Elrik followed her father and the King into a small chamber behind the dais. Once inside, King David sat before a table strewn with books and documents. Her father stood to the right of the table, facing her and Elrik.

The King picked up a rolled scroll and tapped it against his free hand while pinning her with a hard stare. 'What do you have to say for all the trouble you have caused?'

Avelyn clasped her hands before her. 'While I truly apologise for the trouble to others, I do not regret my actions.'

Her father gasped, his face red with rage, and took a step towards her.

Elrik moved forward placing himself directly between her and her father, preventing her father from reaching her. Avelyn held her breath as the two stared at each other. To her amazed relief, her father dropped his gaze and took a step back. Remaining immobile for a heartbeat longer, Elrik then stepped back to her side.

King David's eyes widened slightly at the silent exchange between the two men, but made no comment. Instead he once again spoke to her. 'You understand that you have no say in who you marry?'

'Yes, my lord, but—'

He raised a hand to cut her off. 'You will wed where it best benefits your father and me.'

'But—'

Again, he cut off her words. 'Bolk brings your father a few men, a small plot of land and gold, which in turn benefits me. A marriage to him further binds your family and Bolk's not just to me, but also to King Óláfr.'

Avelyn nodded. Yes, she'd been told that at least a time or two the last few days.

'However…' The King paused, giving Avelyn hope that perhaps he wasn't as in agreement with this marriage as she'd feared. She held her breath while he continued. 'There are other concerns.'

'Concerns!' her father near shouted, before turning to look at the King and asking, 'What concerns have you with my daughter's marriage?'

King David gave her father a glare. 'It seems rather convenient to wed such a young woman to such an old man. It makes me wonder if perhaps Bolk's demise is not already in the planning stages. After all, if someone of his age were to perish shortly after the wedding, who would question his passing? And in such an unfortunate event, who then would gain possession of his men and wealth, little as it is?'

Her father blustered and stuttered in a manner that made it look as though the King spoke the truth.

She could not let his scheming pass without comment. Anger that she was truly nothing more to him than a means to gain ill-gotten wealth emboldened her to ask, 'What would you do with me then, Father? Find me another old man to wed?'

He spun around, ordering, 'Shut your mouth, girl!' He made no attempt to approach her, but she saw his meaty hand clench, then unclench and knew that had Elrik not been there as a barrier that he would have used his fist on her whether the King saw it or not.

'Yes, well, perhaps there is someone else more suitable as a husband for your daughter.' A smile played at King David's lips as he added, 'Someone younger, with more land, men and gold. Perhaps someone in possession of a title more suited to a king's great-granddaughter.'

The hope that had been building in her heart died quickly. Who did King David plan to marry her off to? He was well aware that she knew no titled lord, meaning nothing was going to change. She would still be wed to a complete stranger and her father would still gain a measure of wealth from the marriage. Avelyn couldn't decide which bothered her more—her loss, or her father's gain.

Before she could make the determination, King David turned his gaze to her. 'Is there anyone you might wish to wed?'

She knew only one man who might fit her idea of what she wanted from a husband. Only one man who might possibly—some day—be a companion worth sharing a home and a bed.

Avelyn glanced sidelong at Elrik, remembering his words to tell the King exactly what she wanted. At her prolonged silence, he met her gaze and his eyes widened as if he'd seen something terrifying to behold.

Had he guessed her thoughts? Was the mere idea of marrying her so horrific to him?

A heavy sadness fell over her. In a few short days, she'd come to trust and care for Elrik of Roul and the knowledge that he didn't feel the same made her heart ache in a way her mother's death never had.

She lowered her gaze to hide the moist heat filling her eyes. Finally, when she was certain her dismay would not be heard in her voice, she softly answered the King, 'I know of no willing man who I wish to wed.'

'Roul.' The King called for Elrik's attention. He tapped the scroll he'd been holding on the edge of the table and then extended it. 'Before it once again slips my mind, this is for you.'

Elrik took the scroll and glanced at the wax seal before he frowned at the King. 'What is this?'

'That is one of your two final acts for me as my Wolf. Your uncle in Normandy died without issue and without a wife. The county of Roul has now been bestowed upon you with my niece's blessing. She and Lord Geoffrey expect your arrival.'

'My uncle in Normandy?' Elrik appeared baffled.

'You weren't aware that your family held land in Normandy?'

'Well, yes, but that was years ago, long before I was born.'

'No, I speak of now.'

Elrik frowned, then said, 'I vaguely remember my father mention something once in passing, but I paid little attention, thinking the claim was due to far more drink than normal.'

King David leaned forward as if ready to tell a story. 'On his deathbed, your grandfather bade your father and his brother to fight for possession of Roul. Your father lost.'

Avelyn's father laughed. 'Not surprising.'

'Shut your mouth, old man.'

While Elrik's menacingly deep tone startled her, it was the obvious hatred etched on his face as he glared at her father that caught her off guard. She got the impression that this dark glare was not simply because of her father's comment, but rather from some long-held dislike. Did they know each other? Had they confronted each other at some point in the past? If so, over what?

'Enough.' King David's order was short and effective. Both her father and Elrik visibly relaxed their stances.

The King continued his tale of Roul. 'Your father was banished from Roul and as far as I can tell never had any further contact with his family in Normandy.'

Elrik asked, 'How did he end up with Roul Isle?'

'Through service rendered to King Henry. A deal was struck between my brother and King Henry for possession of the isle.'

'And now you are saying that my…uncle has died?'

'Without issue, yes.'

A slide of Elrik's thumb broke the seal, then he opened and read the document. A soft curse escaped his lips before he looked back up at the King. 'You knew this before sending me on this mission.'

King David nodded. 'Yes, I did. Are you not going to ask what the second task is that you need to complete to end your service for me?'

Elrik rolled his shoulders. 'I almost fear to ask.'

King David swung his focus back to Avelyn. She got the impression from the broadening smile on his mouth that he was enjoying himself immensely. 'I have a husband already chosen for you.'

She saw Elrik visibly stiffen.

'Lord Brandr, as a great-granddaughter of King Óláfr your daughter needs to wed someone with a worthy title. And she will. At first light of day tomorrow.'

Without pausing to acknowledge her shocked gasp, her father shouted, 'No!'

King David's brows rose. 'No?'

'She is not suited to be the wife of anything more than a minor warlord, or perhaps a guard.' He narrowed his eyes and spread his arms, hands out as if pleading for understanding. 'We cannot even prove she is my daughter. That is why she was promised to Bolk.'

Avelyn's breath caught in her chest. He was now going to deny her? After tearing her from her mother's home and forcing her to live in his keep?

Elrik leaned over to whisper in her ear. 'The ring, Avelyn.'

Before she could produce the ring, her father added, 'We may find Bolk beneath us, but he is the best she will ever do.'

With that, she pulled the small pouch out from beneath the neck of her gown. 'How dare you.' Her hands shook as she fished the ring free of the sack and handed it to King David. 'My mother gave me this, telling me to keep it safe as it belonged to my grandmother.'

'You had it!' Brandr's face reddened as he turned to the King. 'Her mother stole that from me. That is why she was released from my service. I demand it be returned to my family.'

'You lie.' Avelyn gritted her teeth to keep herself from screaming in rage.

Elrik looked down at her before turning his attention to King David. 'I assume the person you have in mind as her husband is me.'

'Unless you are willing to forfeit your title, lands, Roul Isle and your family's freedom for the rest of your life, yes.'

Elrik grimaced, but reached down to take her hand. 'As Lady Avelyn is now my betrothed, I can assure you that it doesn't require much inspection of that ring to realise it proves her relationship to King Óláfr.'

King David held the ring to the light and turned it around, inspecting it closely. He then looked at Brandr. 'I think you are correct. The ring should be in the possession of your family.'

Avelyn felt as if the floor beneath her feet moved. She swayed against Elrik. Everything she believed about herself and her family was wrong. While she would be relieved not to be related to Brandr, would Elrik care that he was being told to take the hand of a servant's bastard as his wife, or would he convince the King to retract his decision?

'Avelyn.'

She glanced up at him and saw him nod towards the King.

Slowly turning her head, she saw that King David held the ring out towards her. 'This is yours. And your mother was correct, you need to keep it safe.'

He then swung his attention back to her father. 'To ease your mind, I will have documents drawn up that attest to her parentage.'

'My grandfather will hear of this.'

The King laughed. 'Your grandfather has already heard of this since I sent him word the moment you left my hall.' David reached out and retrieved a sheet of parchment from the table before him. 'As a matter of fact, he has already replied to my suggestion that Lady Avelyn be joined with the house of Roul. Lord Somerled, your uncle, brought word yesterday.'

'I care not what word my uncle brought to you. I will not have it. I'll not have the son of a traitor attached to my family.'

Elrik released her hand and stepped towards her father. 'Traitor? If anyone was the traitor, it was not my father. You intentionally found the oldest, weakest and easiest-to-sway lords you could, those who would listen to a viper's words without debate, sucking in every lie, every tale as if it were the truth. You talked them into going against their King and who paid the price? Not you or yours.'

Avelyn backed away from the two men. No wonder Elrik had looked as though he hated her father—he did. Would that hatred spread to her, also?

To her shock, her father laughed before saying, 'It is not my fault your father was among the weak. Tell me, Roul, does the fact that you grovelled for his worthless life still rest heavily on your soul, or do the scars you bear because of your own weakness still burn?'

Elrik drew his arm back. King David shouted, 'Guards!'

And before Elrik could land the second hit into her father's face, four men burst into the small chamber and forcibly separated the two men.

To her shame, Avelyn gained a measure of satisfaction at seeing the blood drip from her father's split lip while Elrik's face bore no new marks.

Elrik shook off the guards' hold. 'Let me go. I am done.'

Her father did the same.

'Are the two of you finished now?'

Neither man responded to the King's question, but Erik glared at her father.

King David waved the guards from the chamber. 'If anyone is interested, King Óláfr is satisfied with the arrangements I made in Roul's stead.'

Avelyn couldn't tear her stare away from the King. She'd been right earlier about his smile—he *was* enjoying himself. The sparkle in his eyes let her know that he seemed to be deriving great pleasure from playing with the lives of those under his rule.

His voice deep and hard, Elrik asked, 'A word?'

The King nodded. 'Brandr, escort your daughter to the hall.'

Avelyn shivered—once out of the King's sight, her father would make her pay dearly for so ruining his plans. Her knees trembled. She knew nothing of this castle, where would she run? Where could she hide to avoid his wrath?

'No!' Elrik's shout seemed to echo in the smallness of the chamber. 'My men wait outside this door,' he added in a less forceful tone.

When King David waved a hand giving him permission to speak to Samuel and Fulke, Avelyn nearly fainted with relief. Elrik might not be pleased with this arrangement, but at least he was not going to throw her into her father's not-so-tender care. For that she was grateful.

In less than a few heartbeats Elrik returned with his men. While neither of them looked pleased, Samuel offered his arm, 'Lady Avelyn, will you come with us?'

He'd offered her a choice she wasn't about to refuse. Placing a hand on his forearm, she nodded, whispering, 'Thank you.'

Before she could take a step towards the door, her father grabbed her shoulder. 'You are still in my care.'

The hiss of a sword being drawn from a wooden scabbard caught everyone's attention. 'Remove your hand from my betrothed or I will gladly remove it from your arm.'

Avelyn gasped at the deadly coldness in Elrik's voice and looked over her shoulder to stare at him. For a moment she feared he would take her father's life right then and there. But the certain promise in his words and the unholy gleam in his narrowed eyes made her father release her.

Elrik barely met her stare, but when he briefly glanced her way, he lifted his chin, once again silently ordering her to stand tall. She stiffened her spine and then looked up at Samuel. 'Shall we?'

Her father stormed around them and angrily rushed from the chamber.

She and Samuel exited the small room with Fulke right behind them.

The second the door to the chamber closed, King David asked, 'What needs to be discussed?'

'Why me? Why Brandr's daughter?' He suspected the answer had something to do with the treason committed years ago, but wanted to know what that connection was now.

'Simple. It is time Brandr paid for his part in the treason your father committed. But, it is also a way to help silence the new rumblings of treason.'

'New rumblings?' Elrik had heard nothing.

'It seems the beginnings of discontent are stirring in Somerled's court and I wanted them stopped as much as King Óláfr does. We thought perhaps tying the two of you together might help put an end to the stirrings for a time.'

Elrik understood the reasoning. Not only were they uniting the two families who'd been the most involved the last time, but they were doing so with two people who were prized to their respective liege for one reason or another.

'You are not pleased?'

'To once again have a wife? No. You knew I had no desire for another wife. But in all honesty, if I am to have one, I would have chosen the same.'

That much was true. He'd wondered at his attraction to this woman and had convinced himself that once they parted ways, he would forget her. Who had he been trying to fool? He wouldn't have forgotten her—at least not easily. And as much as he told himself that when the time did come for him to wed he would choose a meek, biddable woman, he knew that for the lie it was. What would he do with someone meek and biddable? What would she do with him? The first time he lost his temper the woman would either faint, or be frightened to death.

That was something he didn't worry about with Avelyn. He was certain that if he lost his temper with her, she would hand him back a good measure of her own temper in return.

'Do you care for her, Roul?'

It was too soon to know. 'I find her attractive. Desirable. There is…something…between us. Perhaps in time I may come to care for her and she for me.'

'Good. I had hoped as much. But what then is this need for a private word?'

'While the choice is acceptable, you couldn't have chosen a worse time.' Elrik ran a hand through his hair, trying to calm his tone. Finally, he said, 'From what Lord Geoffrey wrote, there is a heated battle for possession of Roul lands between multiple neighbouring lords. He has ordered me to leave tomorrow for Normandy to fight and claim oversight of Roul Keep.'

'Yes, I know this.'

'Then you also know I cannot take Avelyn with me. Not into what could turn out to be a long-drawn-out battle.'

'True.'

'Then why wed on the morrow? Why not wait until all has been settled with Roul Keep?'

The King shrugged. 'I had thought of that. But then I also thought of the difficulty between you and Lord Brandr and chose not to give him the slightest opportunity to spirit Lady Avelyn away with the intention of wedding her to someone else just out of spite.'

Knowing Brandr, that was exactly what the man would do. 'But I cannot leave her here for that same reason.'

'She will be wed.'

'Do you truly think he will care? Once away from here, he will no longer be under your rule. He will do as he pleases.'

'Other than marrying her later, what do you suggest be done?'

Elrik narrowed his eyes in thought a moment, then smiled. 'Send her to Roul Isle. Rory and Edan are more than capable of seeing to her safety.'

The King nodded. 'I can do that. In fact, I will order them here to escort her to the isle. However, do you think she will be willing to do this?'

Elrik's smile faded. 'No.'

'Will she not do as you order?'

'I am not certain.' Somehow, he had the awful feeling that Avelyn would only do as he ordered if she agreed with the order. Otherwise, who was to say what might happen? She'd already run away once because of a king's order. Would she do any less if she disagreed with him? Unfortunately, he did not possess the leisure of time to discover how she would react.

David waved towards a chair across the table. 'Perhaps a little subterfuge might be in order. Sit. Let us discuss what might be done to ensure her safety.'

When the door to the chamber closed behind them an eerie quiet fell over the Great Hall and once again Avelyn felt every pair of eyes focused on her.

Fulke, with one hand resting on the hilt of his sword, came to her other side.

She wondered if either man knew how much comfort their protection provided. She briefly tightened her fingertips on Samuel's arm and looked from him to Fulke. 'I thank you.'

Fulke drew his brows together to scare off a young man who'd thought to approach her, then asked, 'For what?'

She couldn't hold back a small laugh at his frightening visage. 'For so willingly providing me with your protection.'

'Did you think we'd leave you to fend off these dogs alone?'

'I know not what I thought, but I am extremely grateful for the Wolves at my side.'

Samuel leaned down slightly to say, 'Little one, you are the lady of this pack. We will protect you with our lives.'

Uncertain whether to laugh or cry, Avelyn found herself suddenly doing both.

'You dolt. Look at what you've done,' Fulke chastised Samuel.

His concern only made her more emotional, although Samuel's hissed curse made her chuckle. 'I am fine. Truly, nothing is amiss. I have simply found this day a bit taxing, forgive me.'

Samuel steered them towards the side of the Great Hall where it was less crowded around the few remaining tables. She sat down on a bench, then asked, 'Do you think it possible to get something to drink?'

Both men headed off—each in a different direction—only to return quickly. Samuel carried two ewers and had four goblets tucked behind his sword belt. Fulke held a wooden platter piled high with food.

As Samuel filled three goblets with wine, Fulke set the platter before her on the table. 'If nothing looks appealing, I can find something that might suit better.'

She looked at the food, knowing it would feed a small village for days. Meat and turnips smothered in a dark sauce, bread—light and dark—fruit, three different kinds of cheese and a variety of sweets overfilled the platter.

She glanced from one man to the other, asking, 'Should I be worried about your plans for me once you've fattened me up?'

His expression darkly serious, Fulke answered, 'Winter is hard on Roul.'

Samuel with the same foreboding expression added, 'One as young as you should provide a quite tender meal or two.'

Avelyn burst out laughing loud enough to gain the attention of those gathered several feet away. She wiped the tears of laughter from her eyes and shook her head. 'I suppose I deserved that for asking such a silly question.'

Both men smiled at her before suddenly stiffening to attention.

'What is so amusing?'

She jumped at Elrik's question. While the men had somehow sensed his approach, she hadn't.

He stood across the table from her and did not appear pleased in the least. From his drawn-together brows, lines creasing his forehead and hard, unsmiling mouth she assumed his discussion with the King had not pleased him.

'The two of you need to make ready to leave.' When neither man moved, he nearly growled, 'Now.'

'Elrik, they've not eaten.' Avelyn waved at the platter. 'And I don't require all of this.'

He plucked an apple and chunk of cheese from the pile before handing the platter to Samuel and an ewer to Fulke. 'Go.'

He waited until the men left before sitting on the bench across the table from her. Instead of saying anything he pulled out his dagger and started cutting the apple—slowly, methodically into thin slices.

When she could stand his silence no longer, Avelyn reached out to wrap her fingers around his wrist. 'Elrik, did King David say something to offend you?'

'Offend me?' He shook off her hold and resumed slicing the rest of the apple. Finally, when he'd finished and she was near to screaming, he placed the dagger on the table. 'Other than order me to wed, no.'

She knew he hadn't been pleased with the order, but he'd raised no objection. Why now did he seem angry? 'Did I do something to offend you?'

'Besides making it clear to King David that I was the only man you wished to wed, not at all.'

'You told me to tell him what I wanted, not what I didn't want.'

'Did I not also tell you that there could be nothing between us?'

Avelyn felt her shoulders sag and she couldn't find the will to summon enough strength to do anything more than let them sink, along with her already waning courage.

'Yes,' she answered softly.

'Yet, knowing how I felt about taking a wife, you still found it acceptable to make him aware of your feelings on the matter.'

Was he insinuating that she'd somehow arranged this behind his back? This had been the King's doing, not hers. 'I didn't—'

He cut her off with a hard, cold glare that made her shiver.

'You have your wish, Avelyn. We will be wed as soon as the sun breaks in the dawn sky. And then I am leaving. You will remain here.'

'Alone?'

Elrik made a show of surveying the Great Hall, before he turned back to face her. 'Not at all.'

She didn't know any of these people. There could be thousands of them crowding the castle and she would still be alone.

'But—'

Again, he silenced her with that Roul glare meant to frighten, or warn off, others. He'd had years to perfect that glare and she was not immune to the fear it instilled. 'You have no need to worry about your father. The King has already sent guards to escort him back to his keep.'

To stop their trembling, she folded her hands together on top of the table. 'Thank you.'

Elrik covered her clasped hands with one of his. His

gentle hold belied his anger, leaving her more confused than afraid. 'The only thing I want to hear from your lips are the words *I will* when the priest asks if you accept me as your husband. Do you understand me?'

She nodded. He released her, adding, 'Then we will be done with each other. King David promised to send word to my brothers to come and get you. They should be here in a few days. I've left instructions for your care in my absence.'

He'd essentially just ordered her to keep her mouth shut, but she had to know—had to ask, 'How long will you be gone?'

'For as long as it takes to gain full control of Roul. It could be years, or a lifetime.'

His words left her awash in misery and hopelessness. Her dreams of sharing a life with her husband had been shattered by his answer. She could end up spending the rest of her life alone. Barren. No husband. No children. No future. No life.

Avelyn bit her lower lip to keep it from quivering. Once the sharp pain had stilled her fears somewhat, she said, 'But—'

His icy laugh cut off her words. 'What? You thought there would be a wedding night? Or that one day soon we would begin years of wedded bliss?'

Yes, she had thought those things, but she wasn't about to admit those childish hopes to him. Instead she remained silent and stared down at the table.

'You should have thought a little harder before deciding to let King David know you wanted a wolf for a husband.'

In her defence, she'd said nothing of the kind to the King.

'A wolf chooses its own mate and I'd chosen to remain alone, unwed. I've no need of another wife. No desire to be responsible for another woman, least of all a king's great-granddaughter.'

He'd been married before? What had happened to his first wife?

'Avelyn, in case you haven't realised it yet, you would have been better off wed to Bolk. At least he had no reason to mistrust you, or your family.'

'Mistrust?' Now she was thoroughly confused. 'I have done nothing to prove myself disloyal.'

'I will warn you once, and only once. If you ever give me reason to think you have betrayed me, I will make you wish we had never met. Do you understand me?'

All she could do was nod. She understood his threat, but not the reason behind it.

'For now, the only thing you have gained is the protection my name and title can offer, a home with my brothers for as long as they'll have you and the peace of being left alone.'

If he'd said those things to offer some sort of odd comfort, he was mistaken. She found no comfort in the idea of being left alone—for ever.

Avelyn knew that if she fought to stop the threatening tears they would only escape as a gasping sob that everyone within earshot would hear. So, she didn't try. Instead, she let the silent tears drip on to the table.

With a soft curse, spoken in a tone that, like his touch, didn't match the anger he'd been displaying, Elrik rose. He briefly extended a hand to wipe a tear from her cheek, before pulling it back, turning around and leaving her.

Frozen in place, Avelyn closed her eyes. Confused by his angry words and gentle touch, both on her hand and just now against her cheek, she didn't know what to think, or what to do. If he truly did leave her, how would she find any purpose in the future?

'Lady Avelyn?'

She opened her eyes to find an older woman standing

alongside the table. 'The King sent me to escort you to your chamber.'

Avelyn followed the woman across the hall, desperately trying to ignore the pitying looks from the others. It didn't matter if they pitied her for her coming marriage to the King's Wolf, or because of the obvious way Elrik had abruptly left her alone. Either way, she didn't want their pity—it only served to make her feel worse.

Chapter Eight

Once inside an upper chamber befitting any visiting royal, Avelyn waited silently until the woman left and closed the door behind her. She sat on the edge of the large, curtained bed to stare morosely at the wall where a finely stitched wall hanging depicting a hunting scene filled her with understanding for how the quarry felt—lost and frightened.

Could this day possibly get any worse?

Not only had she once again enraged her father, but King David's order that she wed Elrik had apparently enraged her husband-to-be also. Was she to go from one home where she was neither wanted nor welcome to another with the same harsh coldness?

Why did it seem that everything she did not want from life was what she was given? The one thing she truly feared was being alone and that was exactly how she would live out her days. Alone and unwanted.

She had so longed to marry a man who might one day come to consider her a friend, a confidant, a partner in life. Instead, she was to be wed to a man who obviously despised her.

Avelyn sighed, knowing her thoughts were running wild because she felt sorry for herself. Yet, she couldn't begin to sort through all the sadness and dark fancies buffeting her to find one single good thought that could carry her through the coming days.

A knock at her door interrupted the seemingly unending sorrow besetting her.

'Enter.'

The woman who had just led her up to this chamber came in. 'My lady, forgive me, but King David requests your presence in the Great Hall for the evening meal.'

Oh, yes, the day *could* get worse. Instead of being left alone to wallow in her own despair, she was to join a hall filled with people she didn't know and who, from the looks they'd given her, pitied her more than anything else.

'Please, could you tell the King I do not feel well and wish only to seek some sleep this night?' It wasn't a lie, her head throbbed and stomach churned. Food was the last thing she wanted.

'No, she can't.'

She flinched at the sound of Elrik's voice. He entered the chamber and dismissed the maid before closing the door and then came to stand before her, ordering, 'Get up and get dressed.'

'I am dressed.' She knew he'd seen the tunic spread out on the end of the bed. From the jewels sewn along the sleeve and hem edges, the King had likely supplied the finery. While it was a nice gesture, she had no intention of wearing anything other than the tunic she currently wore. It might be considered poor in comparison to what the other women wore, but at least she had paid for this overgown. Unfortunately, the cost of that kiss had been higher than she ever could have imagined.

'You are going to wear that?'

'I paid dearly for this gown and as it is the only clothing I own, yes, I am wearing this.'

To her amazement, he didn't argue. He nodded. 'Then you are ready.'

'No.'

'No?' The deep frown creased his forehead. 'You can't tell King David, no.'

'I feel ill.'

He reached down and grasped her wrist. 'As do I.'

She knew what he meant—he was offhandedly saying he was sick about the idea of marrying her. 'You need not go out of your way to make me feel worse than I already do. Just go, Elrik. Go.'

He rubbed a hand across his eyes. 'Avelyn, that is not what I meant.'

'Yes, you did. You just didn't mean to say it aloud.' She pulled away from his hold and rose to cross the chamber to stand by the window opening.

'It has been a long day for all involved.' He didn't sound angry, his voice filled more with frustration than rage. 'Let me escort you to the evening meal. It will go far in stopping the tongues from wagging.'

'Now you think to be kind? Why? What do you care? You won't be here.'

'But you will. And while I may not want a wife—'

'*May not?* You made it perfectly clear you do not want *me* as your wife.'

He ignored her statement and continued, 'That choice has been taken from me. I do not want you to be without the protection my name can offer.'

'So, you want to parade me around before everyone so there is little doubt I belong to King David's Wolf?'

'Yes.'

Avelyn stared at him. 'You cannot be serious.'

'Very.'

'And once you leave, how will this help me?'

'Tongues will still wag, but it will be done behind your back, not to your face. By the time any of the craven fools below summon the courage to say anything directly to you, my brothers will be here and that flimsy courage will vanish.'

What he said made some sort of odd sense. That didn't mean she wanted to spend any time in his company.

'I cannot bear more of their pity. Why can you not understand that?'

He joined her at the window. 'And why can you not understand they only pity you because you permit them to do so? Instead of showing them how sad and upset you are, act as if this is what you want. Their pity will be wasted on one who doesn't need it.'

'I am not good at hiding what I think or feel.'

'I never noticed.'

She huffed at his outright lie.

'It is easy, Avelyn. You do it like this.'

He turned his face away for a moment and, when he once again looked at her, she gasped at the dark shimmer in his half-closed eyes, the softness of his lips curved into the one-sided smile she'd come to know. He reached out to draw her close for a kiss.

For a moment, for one breathtaking, mind-robbing heartbeat or two, she believed he wanted her, desired her.

The truth quickly won out and she broke the kiss to look up at him. Once again, the hard line of his mouth had chased away the smile.

She pushed free of his hold. 'I don't think I can do that.'

He tucked her hand into the bend of his arm and moved towards the door. 'Then you need to learn how quickly. Make believe it is just the two of us back out on the road.'

Yet again, he was giving her no choice in the matter. Whether she wanted to or not, she was going to have to try to do her best. It was going to be crowded and loud in the Great Hall, the distraction might help her do as he asked. She took a breath and said, 'I can try.'

Nearing the bottom of the steps, Elrik softly said, 'Chin up. Smile. And breathe.'

She glanced up at him, surprised to see him break out into a pathetic grin. Avelyn leaned against his arm. 'That is truly awful. How about if you glare and I'll smile. That would seem more normal.'

'That depends. Let me see your fake smile.'

She crossed her eyes, wrinkled her nose and parted her lips wide.

Elrik burst into laughter, drawing attention to their entrance.

He quickly swallowed his mirth and leaned his head down to whisper, 'Perfect. That will stop them from pitying *you*.'

Thankful that she had made him laugh, she smoothed out her features. 'Instead, they will pity the poor beleaguered wolf.'

'And rightly so.'

This was all she had wanted. He didn't need to ever fall in love with her. She had no trust in love, or any declaration of tender emotions, they were without merit and as useless as shredded cloth. All she ever wanted was someone to talk with, laugh with, jest with. Someone, who at the end of the day, still wanted to share her company. Someone who could trust her without reservation.

Elrik lowered his arm and placed a hand at the small of her back to guide her through the crowd. The heat of his touch, even through the layers of her clothing, set her heart to flutter. She barely noticed the people she smiled at, or those who nodded at her and Elrik.

What she did notice, other than the confusion flooding

her body, was that Samuel and Fulke tracked their movements. Even though the two men remained close to the wall, they kept pace with her and Elrik as they made their way around the Great Hall, never more than a few strides away.

His men were loyal and extremely watchful in the crowded hall. They spoke to no one and ignored the women who were brave enough to approach the Wolf's guards. Instead, their attention was focused on her and Elrik at all times.

Samuel winked at her and she blushed at having been caught watching them so closely. Fulke said something that had the two men laughing.

'Stop distracting the men. They are here for our protection, not for your amusement.'

She looked down at her feet and muttered, 'I am sorry.'

Elrik slid his hand across her back to rest at the side of her waist and tightened his fingers to pull her closer. 'Up. Look up.'

When she forced her gaze up from the floor, he said, 'I wasn't complaining, Avelyn. They wink at you, you blush, they laugh—what do you think the people who witnessed that interaction will assume?'

'That I am too familiar with your men.'

'It will make it difficult for any here to take our marriage seriously if you are flirting with other men the night before the ceremony'

'I never—' His hand tightened, reminding her to lower her voice. In a softer tone, she said, 'That was never my intent.'

'I know that. But the others here expect you to act besotted with your husband-to-be.'

She stared up at him to see if he was serious, or teasing her. Unable to determine anything from his bland expression, she asked, 'And how am I to do that? Would you like me to fawn over you? Press little kisses against your cheek? Shall I simper and blush prettily at every word that leaves your lips?'

'It would be a start.'

'You, my lord, have lost the ability to reason. Not one person here who witnessed our earlier conversation in this hall would believe for one heartbeat that I was besotted with King David's Wolf.'

She raised her hand to tug at the fingers pressed tightly against her side. 'Let me go.'

He guided her towards the high table, releasing her only when the King waved them over to join him.

Helping her on to a chair, he leaned down to whisper against her ear, 'Only a fool would expect you to simper and fawn. I am no fool.'

She closed her eyes. He had not been serious. Would she ever learn how to judge his moods? Then she realised that it would make no difference since they would be living apart.

Elrik sat between her and King David. He looked at her and sighed before asking, 'Now what has you sad?'

She forced a small smile to her lips. 'Nothing. A moment's lapse is all.'

His answering snort let her know that he didn't believe her.

She reached past the trencher she shared with Elrik to pick up a goblet filled with wine and took a long sip. Unused to drinking wine that was not well watered, she swallowed hard, hoping she didn't embarrass herself by choking.

After her third swallow, she set the goblet down. Elrik's hard stare seemed to bore through her and, for once, she found she didn't care.

Avelyn returned his stare, daring him to say anything. He didn't utter a word, simply raised his brows before turning to talk to the King.

She finished off the remaining wine in the goblet and turned her attention to the trencher. Nothing looked appealing. But when a serving maid refilled her goblet, she leaned back in her chair, the goblet in her hand, and stared out at the others gathered in the hall.

The families with daughters of a marriageable age were easy to pick out. The parents talked with the men seated around them while, for the most part, the young ladies sulked. Avelyn didn't blame them in the least. Their parents were acting as if the girls weren't even there.

The older women on the hunt for a husband were even easier to spot. Nobody talked for them, they did it for themselves. One overly friendly woman made it a point to lean so close to the man she spoke with that her ample breasts rested on his arm. The man didn't seem to mind and Avelyn idly wondered if the woman would be spending the night alone in her bed as she would.

A stranger sat down next to her. 'My lady, I wanted to come and wish you good luck with your coming marriage.'

'What an odd thing to say.' She looked at him, trying not to frown.

He was young, closer to her age than Elrik's. And from the unblemished skin on his face and hands, he was as yet untested by any battle. What good would he be in the face of danger?

'Not odd at all.' He took an ewer from a passing maid and poured himself a goblet full of wine before raising the vessel in her direction. 'Would you care for some?'

She shook her head. 'Thank you, no. I have yet to finish what I have.'

'As I said, not odd. Is it not good manners to wish the new couple well?' He leaned closer to add, 'The bride especially.'

Avelyn found herself leaning back, towards Elrik as if

instinctively seeking his protection. The young man wasn't threatening her, but he made her uncomfortable enough to hope Elrik was paying attention.

Without a break in his conversation with King David, Elrik slung his arm over the back of her chair, his hand dangled near her ear, the heat of his fingertips brushing against her neck.

She knew it was his way of silently declaring his possession of her. Right now, she didn't care. Because it was also his way of offering her the protection she'd sought.

At any other time, she would have made some excuse to walk away from this conversation and the young man who'd started it. But the knowledge that nothing and nobody was going to harm her this night gave her enough courage to ask the man, 'Why especially the bride?'

He shrugged and took a long swallow of his wine. 'In this case it should be obvious.'

What was he insinuating? 'Not to me it isn't.'

His glance briefly flew past her chair. She didn't need to look to know that Samuel and Fulke had drawn closer.

'While it is common for brides of standing to be sold to the highest-ranking noble, you are quite different, are you not?'

Did this fool realise he was putting his life in danger? Did he think Elrik was deaf? Or perhaps not listening? She knew full well he was paying very close attention by the way his fingers brushed against her neck every time the young man opened his mouth.

She turned slightly in her chair, not so much to face the man talking, but to press more of her body against Elrik. To her relief, he didn't pull away, instead he lowered his arm from the back of the chair to rest across her shoulders.

'Tell me, why am I so different?'

The man looked from Elrik's hand caressing her shoulder, to her. 'Do you not find it odd that someone who has only recently come to the court's attention has been fed to the Wolves?'

He was baiting her. On purpose. Avelyn couldn't have stopped herself from laughing had she tried. When she regained control of herself, she wiped the tears from her eyes and studied the man. 'Who are you? Nobody with half a wit would speak so to me when I am obviously surrounded by those Wolves, unless they were known to the pack.'

Fulke stepped to the back of her chair. 'My sister's oldest son, Richard.'

The young man finished off his wine and set the goblet down with a sigh before he rose. 'Uncle.'

Fulke cuffed him on the shoulder.

He looked beyond Fulke to nod. 'Sir Samuel.'

Samuel grunted in reply.

He then nodded to her, saying, 'My lady, I do wish you well.'

He turned his attention to Elrik. 'My lord.'

Elrik asked, 'What are you doing so far from Roul Isle?'

'King David requested the presence of Edan, Rory or someone who could act in their stead. Since they seem to have recently received a royal order for more ships, they sent me. Little did I know it would be to witness your marriage.'

Elrik glanced at the King before bringing his attention back to the conversation. 'Yes. A surprising turn of events to *some* of us.'

Richard looked back at her. 'I apologise, my lady. I couldn't possibly resist teasing the newest Wolf. Although I didn't expect you to catch on so quickly.'

'It didn't take a great deal of thought to realise you were insulting not me, but my husband-to-be and his men, yet not one of them showed any concern.'

Elrik laughed and patted her shoulder before withdrawing his arm. The loss of his warmth left her cold and strangely disappointed.

After Richard took his leave to drag his uncle and Samuel off for a more private conversation, Avelyn turned back around on her chair to face the table. Not knowing what to do with herself, she picked up her goblet and finished off the wine.

'Are you going to eat?'

She once again surveyed the food on the trencher. 'No. I am not hungry.'

'I could have Fulke and Samuel find you something that might appeal to you more.'

She laughed softly and shook her head. 'I doubt King David would appreciate them emptying the castle of food just to find me the right apple, or hunk of bread.'

'Avelyn, you have not eaten since this morning.'

'I will not starve by missing one day of food.'

'Perhaps not. But there is no reason for you to do so any more.'

She placed a hand on his forearm. 'I know that. And I appreciate your concern. But I am truly not hungry in the least.'

'If you change your mind, let me know.'

'I will.' She leaned closer and lowered her voice. 'Why is everyone staring at us?'

'They have been.'

'I know. But I've done nothing to draw attention to myself.'

King David leaned forward to join their conversation. 'I wouldn't say you've done nothing. First off you sought protection instinctively from a man most people fear. Like a wolf in the wild you went straight to the pack leader for protection and he offered it without hesitation. You do realise every eye was upon you when you leaned against your betrothed, don't you?'

She shook her head. Actually, she'd been too focused on Richard to notice the others.

'Then, you burst forth with a very unladylike laugh that Elrik here found amusing when he should have been aghast at your indecent action.'

'Indecent?'

'Lady Avelyn, you are at court. Have you not noticed it is a very solemn event?'

She looked down at the table.

Elrik leaned over to whisper, 'He is teasing you.'

'Oh.'

With a pointed look, King David drew her attention to her hand resting on Elrik's arm. 'And here you are now, blithely petting a wolf as if it were an everyday occurrence.'

She looked at her hand and noticed that he was right. She was absently stroking her fingertips in circles on his forearm.

Avelyn lowered her arm and placed her hand in her lap. 'So, if I just sit here and do nothing, say nothing, will they turn their attention to another for amusement?'

'It isn't for amusement.' King David shook his head. 'It is curiosity, and you will find it every day, everywhere you go for a very long time, Lady Avelyn. No matter what you do, or don't do, people will wonder who this woman is with enough bravery to become the Wolf's wife. They will study you, watch you and they will wonder how one so small and seemingly weak ended up in this terrible position.'

What nobody truly understood was that she didn't find the idea of marrying Elrik terrible. It didn't require a great deal of bravery. What was going to take a strength of character that she didn't possess would be living without him— living alone.

Avelyn swallowed hard against the cry of denial threatening to escape, then looked at Elrik. 'I find myself needing to seek my bed.'

He nodded and rose to lead her from the Great Hall.

Outside the door to her chamber, she paused to look up at him. Uncertain what to say, she asked, 'I will see you in the morning?'

'Yes.'

She nodded. Of course she would see him in the morning; they were to be wed at first light.

He touched her cheek. 'Avelyn, do not make this hard for yourself.'

'Hard for myself? You are the one who has made this hard. And then on top of knowing that I am expected to live without the husband I am to wed, I learn that for some reason I do not understand he apparently expects me to betray him in some manner.' She looked away a moment, then clenched her hands at her side and stared up at him. 'This is hard only because of you.'

'Avelyn...' His words trailed off and he looked down at her silently.

Unwilling to continue this one-sided conversation, she pushed open the door to her chamber, and whispered, 'Goodnight, Elrik.'

Once inside, Avelyn gasped for breath. The only thing she had ever hoped for was to not be alone.

She threw herself across the bed and closed her eyes against the heaviness of her heart. *Why did it have to be this way?*

Chapter Nine

Morning came far too quickly.

Avelyn had spent the night sitting on a cushioned chair near the window, staring at the sky. She'd prayed for morning not to arrive. She had hoped for some miracle that would keep the sun from rising.

But as the stars faded one by one in the ever-lightening sky, she knew her useless prayers and hopes had been in vain.

It was a sorry state of affairs—unlike most women, she was going to marry a man she wished to wed. Yet, how many of those other women went to their marriage ceremony knowing there would be no wedding night, no husband to truly make her his wife?

She rose slowly, trying to stretch the stiffness from her body before once again donning the dark blue gown she'd worn yesterday. She ran a comb through the tangles in her hair and left it to hang about her shoulders.

Her gaze fell on a tunic still spread out on the end of the bed. Had circumstances been different, she might have gladly donned the elaborate gown. But this ceremony was nothing she wanted to celebrate. She clenched her jaw to hold back a curse at what was to come, vowing not to cry. Not to shed a single tear.

Lost in her own world of loss and despair, the loud pounding at her door startled her. Avelyn wiped her cheeks dry and shook out her tunic before calling, 'Enter.'

The door opened to reveal Elrik standing in the doorway. He had changed into a dark blue, near-black surcoat that matched the colour of the overgown she still wore. Surprised, Avelyn glanced up at his face. And while the wolf-like glare still marred his features, something was different in his eyes. They lacked the coldness that had been evident yesterday.

He said nothing, simply glanced at the tunic spread across the bed, to her and then, as if against his will, the corners of his mouth twitched slightly before he hardened the line of his lips and offered her his arm.

Avelyn frowned, wishing she knew him better and wishing more that she was able to read his thoughts the way he could hers. When he extended his arm, she placed a hand on his forearm, willing to let him lead her to the ceremony that would join them as husband and wife, and end their contact with each other.

Somehow, she had to find a way to accept what she'd been given. She knew that eventually she would discover a way past this pain of rejection to seek out her own future and whatever it would bring. Her train of thought brought her an unexpected sense of peace and she found the tightness in her chest and the tenseness of her shoulders finally relaxing.

Elrik must have sensed it, too, because he glanced down at her before escorting her across the Great Hall to a narrow passageway that led to the King's private chapel.

To her relief, Samuel and Fulke were present. They'd both donned black with silver-trimmed tabards over their armour. She was thankful for the sense of security that would have been missing had they not been in attendance.

Along with Richard and the woman who'd led her to the chamber yesterday, King David and his priest were the only other people there.

Without any further discussion, the priest asked, 'Who gives this woman?'

Both Samuel and Fulke stepped forward at the same time, gaining a frown from Elrik. When he remained silent, they stated in unison, 'We do.'

The King and his priest exchanged a brief look before the priest nodded his acceptance of their declaration.

The remainder of the ceremony was just as brief, Elrik took her as his wife and she accepted him as her husband. But when it came time for the priest to bless the rings, she reached for the pouch hanging around her neck and gasped in dismay. The only thought she'd given to a wedding ring was her grandmother's ring that she'd always wanted her husband to place on to her finger, mistakenly thinking it'd been a wedding ring. Not once had she given any thought to a ring for him.

Elrik reached out and dropped two golden bands in the priest's palm for the blessing. Avelyn lowered her arm and couldn't help but wonder if those rings had belonged to him and his former wife. But when he slipped the ring on her finger, he whispered, 'They were my parents' rings.'

She stared at the plain gold band now adorning the finger on her left hand. It should have bound them together, but it felt more like a yoke of possession than anything else. A sad reminder of what she would never have.

With an effort, Avelyn swallowed those thoughts, refusing to dwell on what she could not change.

When the ceremony ended with him placing a quick kiss on her forehead, Elrik signed some documents which he then handed to the King. In return, King David handed him two rolled-up documents. Elrik quickly scanned both, before rerolling them and handing one to Richard and another to her, stating, 'This is for my brothers. See that you give it to them upon their arrival.'

She was surprised to hear that his brothers would still be arriving. 'I thought Richard was here in their stead.'

'For the ceremony only. Rory and Edan will arrive soon to escort you to Roul Isle.'

'Oh.' She didn't bother trying to hide the sadness in her voice. Why? Who would care?

With a heavy sigh, he frowned at King David. 'Enough.'

Elrik took her hand and led her from the chapel down the narrow corridor to the far end. He traversed the distance with such purpose that she nearly had to run to keep up with him.

Once at the end of the hallway, he spun her around and backed her into a small alcove. 'Avelyn, there is little time, so listen to me.'

Her back pressed against the hard, cold stone in a corner of the alcove, she tipped her head to look up at him, but not enough light broke the darkness to enable her to clearly see his face.

The palm of his hand was warm where it rested against the side of her neck, his fingers gentle where they softly stroked her skin. But she knew his touch could contradict his mood and wanted desperately to see if his eyes glinted with anger, or his lips flattened with rage.

He pulled her close to him, enveloping her in his embrace, crushing the document he'd just given her between them. His breath rushed against her cheek. 'Avelyn, I am not angry with you. Nor am I angry about marrying you.'

She gasped softly at his admission. 'But—'

'Hush.' He kissed her words away until she relaxed against his chest. 'I am angry only that there is no time for us. We should have wed later, after all was settled and we would have had the leisure of time to get to know each other as husband and wife. That is all I discussed with the King—waiting. There was no discussion about not marrying you. I simply wanted to wait. But now, I must leave, there is no choice. I cannot naysay the Empress, or her husband, not even for my new wife.'

Her knees threatened to fold with relief. 'Then why—?'

He hushed her again, to explain, 'We thought if I angered you, that you would not care if I left you alone. That you would welcome my absence long enough for me to complete my tasks in Normandy.'

'I know not who this *we* might be, but you were wrong.'

'I understand that now. King David and I have been sorely mistaken in this. I tried, but it is obvious that I succeeded only in upsetting you instead of firing your rage. I meant not to do that. It was foolish and wrong of me to play such a game when we don't know each other well enough to be able to judge the other's intent.'

'Your touch.'

His lips against her forehead moved as he asked, 'What?'

'Even if your eyes glinted with anger, your lips were flattened into a hard line, or your voice was cold and curt, when you covered my hand with yours and you wiped away a tear from my cheek, your touch was gentle.'

He laughed softly. 'I will work on that.'

She clung to his shoulders. 'No, please don't.'

'Kiss me, Avelyn. Promise that you will wait for me.'

'Always.' Just before he covered her lips with his, she added in a whisper, 'I swear, Elrik, I will always be true.'

His kiss was gentle, filled not with desire, but more of a hope, a promise for tomorrow. He would think her witless, but her wolf's kiss was sweet, so much so that it brought tears to her eyes when he finally broke their contact.

Without releasing her, he said, 'I must go.'

She smiled at the roughness of his voice and his lingering embrace. 'I know.'

'The most important thing to me is that you are safe. Do you understand? That is why I cannot take you into battle with me and why I want you safely installed on Roul Isle. I cannot let worry for you distract me from what I must do.'

'I am the Wolf's wife, of course I will be safe.'

With nothing more than another chaste kiss on her forehead, he left her standing in the dark alcove.

King David's voice broke through the sorrow threatening to swamp her. 'Come, Lady Avelyn.'

When she stepped out of the alcove and into the corridor, he said, 'I may have been wrong about Elrik's ability to execute this mummery, but I was not wrong about this marriage.'

She couldn't argue, because even though she was distraught that they'd wasted this last day for no good reason, she was thankful for what he'd done regarding their marriage.

The older woman led her back up to the chamber and then left her to make do on her own. Avelyn crossed the room to stare out through the narrow window opening. From there she could see the courtyard and watched Elrik, Samuel and Fulke mount their horses. Elrik grabbed the reins to Little Lady and glanced up towards her. He raised his arm in a gesture of farewell before he led them through the gates and out of her sight.

She felt tears fill her eyes and sucked in a deep breath to help quell the pain building in her chest.

She glanced again out of the window towards the road that had taken Elrik from her and was surprised to see six men quickly gather in the courtyard, mount their horses and then follow after her husband and his men. One man turned in his saddle to glance furtively back at the castle.

Avelyn's breath caught in her throat.

No.

Osbert was trailing Elrik to the ship. What devilry was her half-brother up to now? Nothing he did was ever for anyone's benefit but his own.

Her blood ran cold. Elrik had worried about *her* being safe? He had no idea what sort of danger he could be in with Osbert around.

Even as a child he had been a tyrant, teasing and tormenting anyone smaller or weaker.

She'd known him only as the lord's son, before her father had moved her to the keep. Osbert and his companions would come into the village when they were hungry for their brand of cruel amusement.

As the ringleader of the group of ruffians, he was loud, boastful and the cruellest of all. He thought nothing of taking old Duncan's cane and breaking it, after having beat the elderly man with it first.

A skilled liar, Osbert had accused her of stealing jewellery from her father's wife the first day she had been brought to Brandr Keep. She had denied the false claim, but who was her father and his wife going to believe? The unwanted bastard of a servant, or the son who had grown up at the keep?

Her father's wife had ordered her whipped with a switch and Osbert watched—laughing the entire time.

She'd quickly learned that to avoid punishment for crimes she hadn't committed she needed to be in someone else's company, someone her father would trust to tell the truth. Which was why she had made friends in the kitchen. Who else would he trust if not the people who were preparing the food he put into his belly?

That didn't mean Osbert had stopped tormenting her. Far from it. Her bedding had been smeared with horse dung, her clothes soaked in urine, a comb her father had given her broken into useless bits and a cloth doll her mother had made for her cut up into pieces.

As he grew older he didn't change. He just became meaner, sneakier, more devious than ever. To this day, she still believed that the stable boy who'd been found hanged from a post in a stall had not killed himself.

Not when earlier that same day the boy had made the mistake of making Osbert wait to have his horse saddled. The lad had been nearly done mucking out the stalls and hadn't dropped everything to immediately fulfil Osbert's order.

She'd expected her half-brother to make the boy pay, she'd just not thought he'd go so far as to kill the lad.

Osbert was not to be trusted.

And now he was following her husband.

No.

Avelyn raced out of the chamber and down the stairs to the Great Hall. She stopped the first servant she saw, asking, 'Where is King David?'

The woman nodded towards the small private chamber at the rear of the hall, and warned, 'He is with some of his lords.'

Avelyn didn't care who he was with. She needed his help, now. Nearly running across the hall, she ignored the gasps of those milling about as she pushed by them. Without pausing to knock on the door, she burst into the chamber and dropped to the floor on her knees at the King's feet. She breathlessly pleaded, 'My lord, please. I need your help. It is a matter of Elrik's life or death. Please.'

To her relief, he cleared the chamber with a wave of his hand and then assisted her to her feet, asking, 'What is this about, Lady Avelyn?'

'My half-brother Osbert and his companions just left your courtyard, heading in the same direction as Elrik.'

King David groaned. 'This is not good.'

'Not good? Of course it is not good. Osbert will kill him.'

'That is the last thing you need worry about.' He headed towards the door, motioning her to follow as he explained, 'Elrik blames Brandr for his father's act of treason.'

Avelyn nearly stumbled as she tried to keep up with the King and digest that morsel of information at the same time. 'That is why he hates my father?'

'That and more.'

'And yet he still wed me?'

'Yes. He knows you were not to blame for your father's actions.'

She frowned. Bits and pieces of his words yesterday raced through her mind. 'But I am my father's daughter.'

'Exactly.'

'And my brother showing up…' She let her words trail off. Osbert could unknowingly ruin everything for her. He could so easily make Elrik think she was as deceitful as her father and brother.

'I need to get to his ship.'

The King stopped so suddenly that she ran into him. He grasped her shoulders to steady her, saying, 'That is the perfect solution. I could send word, but you delivering it would go a long way in making him realise that you are not involved in whatever scheme your brother has planned.'

He released her to summon a servant and quietly gave him instructions before turning back to Avelyn to assure her, 'So that is where you are going. I could send one of my men, but who knows if Elrik would believe him or not. As angry as it'll make him, you truly are the best choice to give him warning.'

Leaving the castle, they walked out into the courtyard where three stable hands were readying a horse each. Avelyn groaned.

'Tell me you can ride.'

She grimaced. 'Not well.'

'Then I suggest you hang on tightly.'

Two of his guards ran into the courtyard followed by the servant he had spoken to inside. King David took the items the servant carried and handed Avelyn a cloak. 'You will need this.'

Once she secured the full-length cloak about her shoulders, he gave her two rolled parchments. 'If Elrik's ship has already set sail, make sure you board the very last ship. The other women will be aboard that one. The other ships will be overcrowded with nothing but men. The last ship, Avelyn. Show either one of these to the captain and tell him who you are.' He tapped the wax seal on each one. 'He will recognise my seal and believe you. Trust that he'll find a way to make contact with Elrik.'

'The last ship and show these to the captain.' She repeated his instructions.

He then handed her a pouch. 'Ginger. You may find that you need it for your stomach while at sea.'

She clutched the pouch and the scrolls. 'I don't know how to thank you.'

'Just get to your husband before your brother does.' He assisted her on to the horse. 'I truly want this union to work for the two of you.'

Nobody wanted that more than she did.

'Be safe, Lady Roul. This journey will be fraught with danger, so do whatever he tells you to do. Give your husband no reason to worry for your safety. Now go.'

She hung on to the reins of the horse for dear life and followed the guards out of the courtyard.

* * *

Elrik stood on the deck of the forecastle and watched the other ships follow his away from the docks. One by one they moved into the channel towards the sea.

The first five, including the one he was on, carried arms, food, household goods, horses and guards. The last would transport the women—maids, kitchen helpers, and washer women; along with the tools of their trade. It also carried the camp followers. He'd given that ship over to the command of the oldest and most experienced crew. He knew the captain would not be easily swayed by the lure of a comely lass, but mostly because he knew the crew would get no help from the women.

Sort of like the help he was currently getting from Samuel and Fulke. This voyage would take over a week, nearly a fortnight if the winds were unfavourable, to complete and he wasn't sure how much longer he could endure their silence and glares of censure. Both of them were angry at the way he'd handled Avelyn yesterday. And angrier still that he'd left her behind. How could neither one of them not realise what he'd done? How could they not know it was for the best? Not just for him, but for Avelyn, too.

At Roul Isle she'd be safe under his brothers' protection and he wouldn't have to worry about her.

They'd known him all his life. Didn't they understand how hard it had been to crush her dreams and break her heart the way he had? He'd left much back in that castle. His dignity, honesty and, if he were to be truthful, a piece of himself still lay in shards atop a trestle table in King David's Great Hall.

He'd tried to make amends after the ceremony this morning. But their time together had been brief. Despite what she'd told him, he had no way of knowing if she understood his reasoning, or even if she forgave him for having been such a fool.

Never in his life had he intentionally set out to hurt an innocent person. Never. Did they know so little of him to think he'd willingly done so now? What he'd done, at the King's suggestion, was the hardest thing he'd ever done. So difficult that he'd been unable to go through with it all the way. The sadness in her voice after their wedding had been unbearable. He couldn't leave her like that. He had to try to explain himself. Hopefully, his explanation had been enough.

Fulke climbed the ladder to the forecastle and stood before him. 'I would prefer to sail on another ship.'

Fulke was treading very near his last bit of patience. He was still their commander, their liege, and their friendship could only be tested just so far.

'You will sail on this one.'

'I'd rather not, Elrik.'

'Lord Elrik.' He was tired of his men's mistrust. He might have felt the need to explain his actions to Avelyn, but he was under no obligation to explain anything to his men. If they wanted to act like strangers, so be it. They could address him as such.

'As you wish.' Fulke's jaw tightened, then relaxed. '*Lord Elrik*, you are an ass.'

That comment took Fulke well across the line. Without thought, Elrik slammed his fist into Fulke's jaw. When the man picked himself up off the deck, he ordered, 'Get out of my sight, but stay on this ship.'

Elrik silently watched Fulke climb back down the ladder, wondering if this day could possibly get any worse.

He turned back to watch the fifth ship leave the dock. The sixth and final ship was now taking on the last of the women.

A few of the women were married to guards under his command and had refused to wait until later to join their husbands. Thankfully, his own wife hadn't thought to argue. Since he would not permit children on this voyage, these women were either done with raising children, or hadn't yet conceived.

He'd have preferred not to allow women on this transport at all, but King David had taken that decision away from him.

He still disagreed with the King as nobody knew what they would encounter at this new keep of his.

From what he'd read in Lord Geoffrey's missives to the King, this could very well prove a bloody takeover. It seemed that two neighbouring lords had been promised possession of the lands upon the old Earl's death.

Those promises had no merit. Unlike Roul Isle, the Norman lands were not fully entailed to the Roul family—they were held only by the grace of the King, or at this moment, the Empress Matilda and her husband, Lord Geoffrey, the current Duke of Normandy.

As was her right, the Empress had decided that she needed the eldest Roul to take possession of the title, the lands and the keep, but also to establish a shipyard and wharf at Roul Keep.

So, not only did he need to first secure the area for the Empress and those under his command, he also needed to oversee the construction of docks, warehouses and eventually a shipyard.

The first task was well within his ability. While his younger brother Gregor had seen to everything related to the Roul ships, he'd seen to the protection of Roul Isle, the keep and the day-to-day operations required for the upkeep of the isle and its inhabitants.

The construction of the docks and warehouses wouldn't

prove too difficult—as long as he found a trustworthy master carpenter to oversee the task. While he could use a hammer, saw, adze or a jack plane, he didn't know the first thing about designing a building—at least not one that needed to last more than a couple of years.

Again, when it came time to build a shipyard, he was either going to need to hire a master shipbuilder trustworthy enough to do the job, or drag Gregor into this new venture. Thankfully that was something he wouldn't need to consider for at least a year or more.

For now, he needed to concentrate on two things—getting this transport to Roul and then seeing to the safety of all under his charge, including the women.

His attention was captured by three horses galloping down the wharf at a dangerously fast pace. From their livery, two of the riders were King David's guards. The third slipped from the horse clumsily, almost falling with the effort, and then raced to board the last ship just as the crew had started to pull the plank away and cast off.

The hood of the oversized cloak fell back, permitting long raven locks to fly about the face and shoulders.

No.

Erik shook his head. Surely he was seeing things that weren't there. He peered harder at the woman.

Chapter Ten

Samuel stepped up on to the forecastle deck just as curses that would burn any hardened sailor's ears left Elrik's mouth. He turned to follow the direction of Elrik's stare and laughed. 'Did you expect the Wolf's lady to do anything different?'

'The intention had been to ensure her safety. To keep her from doing just this.'

'That is what you have been doing? You couldn't have explained that to us?'

'It was hard enough without having the two of you try to talk me out of it.'

'Well, I would say your intention fell short.'

'She promised to wait. She knew how important her safety was to me.'

'Perhaps she felt she'd be safer with you.'

Nothing happened at Carlisle without David's knowledge. So, how had she left the castle without the King noticing? What had the man been thinking to permit her to join a group heading into battle?

Worry—something he'd hoped to avoid—settled cold around his heart. Something was wrong. She wasn't here without a reason.

The last ship sent a red cloth up the mast, signalling trouble. Elrik ordered the men to lower the sail of his ship, giving the other vessel time to catch up and pull alongside.

Avelyn accepted the captain's help in climbing to the upper deck of the ship. His surliness hadn't yet fully subsided—he'd not been the least bit pleased when she'd boarded so hastily at the last possible second.

And less pleased when she'd frantically interrupted his orders to the men.

By the time she'd explained who she was and shoved the documents with King David's seal prominent beneath the string holding the rolled parchments closed into his hands, the man's face had taken on a frightening shade of red.

Now that he'd issued new orders to his men and led her to the deck above, he'd stepped back, leaving her to face her husband alone.

She pulled the borrowed cloak tighter around her body to ward off the chill of the breeze whipping across the water. Her stomach churned, but she wasn't certain if that was from the sickening bobbing of the vessel, from knowing Elrik was going to be livid, or fear that her half-brother had already set what plans he had into motion.

When she caught a glimpse of her husband's glare, she gripped the rail with both hands. His eyes blazed and even from this distance she could see that his jaw was clenched. Samuel, standing at his side, looked amused. The lopsided grin curling up one corner of the man's mouth gave her hope that maybe Osbert had yet to make an appearance— perhaps she'd jumped to the wrong conclusion and he wasn't among the men in Elrik's company.

As the ship she was on pulled alongside her husband's, he raised an eyebrow, waiting for her to say something.

Avelyn swallowed and scanned the men standing on the

deck of his ship. To her relief she didn't see Osbert. But that didn't mean he wasn't aboard one of the other ships.

She turned her attention back to Elrik, uncertain how to begin.

Finally, he broke the silence, shouting, 'Is there something you require, Lady Avelyn?'

Oh, yes, as she'd expected, he was angry. It was evident in the furrowed brow, the hard line of his jaw and the dark tone in his voice. She couldn't help but wonder if his touch would still be gentle.

She swallowed, fighting back the urge to be fearful and called out, 'We need to make land.'

'Why?'

'My Lord Roul, I must speak to you.' Suddenly realising that was exactly what she was doing now, she added, 'Privately.'

He shook his head at her response and glanced down at the water, before looking back up at her to ask, 'Have you sprouted wings?'

His nonsensical question wiped away any lingering remnants of fear. He was not as angry as he'd appeared. Granted, it was likely he was very unhappy with her actions, but unhappy or disappointed was a far cry from angry.

She held out her arms and made a point to check beneath each one before lowering them and answering, 'No.'

Samuel looked as if he were ready to burst from laughter, but he kept his mouth firmly closed. Elrik only shook his head and motioned the captain of the ship she'd boarded forward. 'Move your vessel behind mine. We will dock some time tomorrow.'

Tomorrow? Avelyn shook her head. 'No. My lord, this is important.'

'It is too dangerous to swim. So, unless you can fly from that ship to this one, you are going to have to wait.'

She leaned forward to look over the rail of her ship and then to his. It didn't appear that far. She'd learned to swim many years ago as a child. However, that had been in a pond, where her feet could touch the bottom, not in a bottomless ocean. And she hadn't been dressed in a heavy tunic that would likely take on a great deal of weight when wet.

'Avelyn!'

His roar made the man standing next to her flinch. She ceased trying to judge the distance and looked up at her husband.

His hands were tightly clenched on the rail before him. Even Samuel's humour had been replaced with wide-eyed shock as he, too, grasped the rail.

The captain by her side had also grabbed the rail. He muttered, 'Are you daft?'

Elrik pointed at her. She wasn't certain, but it was possible that his hand shook. Before she could decide, he shouted, 'Woman! You will stay aboard that ship until we dock. Do you understand me?'

His disappointment had bloomed into rage. He appeared angry enough that she wasn't at all certain if he touched her right this moment that there would be much gentleness involved.

'Answer me!'

'Yes,' she shouted back, adding, 'my lord.'

Elrik's stare shifted to the still-shaken man next to her. 'She is your responsibility. See to it well. Use a rope if need be.'

He spun around, climbed down the ladder and disappeared beneath the forecastle, leaving Samuel to shake his head at her before also climbing down to follow Elrik.

The captain took hold of her arm. 'My lady, will I need to tie you to the mast like his lordship suggested, or will you refrain from jumping into the water until after you have left my ship?'

She shrugged off his hold. 'I can swim.'

'That does not answer my question.'

'I was simply trying to judge the distance. I wasn't going to jump overboard.'

'Your answer?'

Avelyn glared at him. 'No, you do not need to tie me to the mast. Yes, I will refrain from jumping into the water.'

Elrik dragged a still-shaking hand down his face. This was why he hadn't wanted her along in the first place. He worried about her, more than he found to his liking.

If anything happened to her, King Óláfr and Lord Brandr would not rest until he was planted beneath the cold ground.

He sat heavily on a small stool, barely acknowledging Samuel when he entered the makeshift chamber.

Samuel asked, 'You aren't going to leave her on that ship, are you?'

Elrik nodded. 'Unless you have a way to transfer her to this one safely, while at sea, yes. She wanted to sneak aboard one of my ships without my knowledge and, after she'd been told to wait for my brothers to escort her to Roul, she can spend the night with the other women.'

'Elrik—'

'No.' He cut Samuel off with a short wave of a hand. 'None of the options to get her aboard this ship are safe. I am certainly not going to let her swim. Nor am I going to risk bridging a plank between the ships on choppy water. So, she will stay put. And it is in your best interest to not tell me how to handle my wife.'

Without another word, his man turned and left.

And this was the other reason he hadn't wanted her along. His men were too enamoured with his wife. Jealousy wasn't the issue. He didn't worry that she found them more to her liking, or that either one of them would be disloyal in that manner.

No, the difficulty was that both of them, Samuel and Fulke, had this odd impulsive idea that they were like her older brothers and needed to take care of her, to guard her. That was all well and good, until, like now, when they disagreed with his handling of her or got the notion that they needed to guard her against him. Had he known what King David had been planning, he never would have let her get so friendly with the two of them while they'd been on the road to Carlisle.

As it was, the damage was done. And now that the opportunity for time and distance to lessen their overprotectiveness was gone, he needed somehow to make them understand that even though she was his wife, she was no different than any other woman under his protection. Or he needed to find a way to put their need to protect her to good use. Either way, she was his responsibility, not theirs—it was a responsibility he was not willing to relinquish, not even to them.

Avelyn pulled her cloak tighter around her shoulders and pushed harder into the gap between two full barrels of fresh water. She hoped that as long as the barrels remained full they would continue to provide the stable support that she so desperately needed.

Her stomach churned, making her realise why King David had given her a good-sized pouch of sugared ginger—he'd obviously known the motion of the boat would not settle well with her stomach. Even she was aware that ginger would settle a stomach distress. She'd simply not known that being on the water would cause her to need the sliced root.

She popped another small piece in her mouth and sucked on it slowly as she watched the sun start to set.

Right at this moment, she was truly grateful that he'd left her alone. She'd expected him to be outraged and knew that she would have to find a way to deal with it on the small confines of a ship. But doing so right now, with the roiling of her stomach, would be more than she could endure.

Four women caught her attention as they approached. The smallest of the group asked, 'You are Lord Roul's wife?'

'That I am.'

'Then why are you travelling on this ship instead of on his?'

Avelyn shrugged, then replied, 'It was a last-minute decision. I sought adventure and this voyage seemed a good idea.' It wasn't exactly a lie. It *was* decided at the last possible minute and she was certain it would prove to be quite an adventure—of sorts.

'No. There isn't a lord alive who would permit his lady wife to do something so impulsive. You are his mistress, aren't you?'

The other women laughed as they all sat down around her. The oldest reached out and patted her knee. 'Honey, it is fine, there is no need to lie for our benefit. We understand since it comes with the profession.'

Profession? Ah, Avelyn realised that once again she'd found herself amidst a group of women who plied their trade on their backs.

It didn't matter to her if they believed the truth or not. She wasn't going to be aboard this ship long enough for it to make a difference. So, instead of trying to convince them she was Lady Roul, she only nodded before focusing on the wood deck beneath her.

All four women chuckled. One said, 'She's too shy to have been at this very long.'

Another chimed in, 'Fear not, there are only six of us, seven counting you and five ships full of men. You'll be able to quickly get all the experience you need.'

One woman sighed heavily, before saying, 'Just thinking of all those manly bodies makes me near to fainting.'

'I hear tell their commander is quite a fine-looking man.'

'You mean King David's Wolf?'

'I could never share his bed. I'd be too fearful.'

'Oh, not me. I like them a little dangerous.'

Avelyn's head spun, trying to keep up with the conversation. Her focus bounced from one to another and back to the other so fast, she feared her bag didn't hold enough ginger.

The oldest woman leaned forward and looked from side to side at the other women. 'Hush. This is the commander's woman. She can tell us how he likes to pleasure a lady.'

One of the younger women whined in a way that made Avelyn's eyes widen. What was she going to tell them? That his kiss robbed her of the ability to think? Or that his touch made her feel safe, while causing her to long for something she didn't quite comprehend? Somehow, she didn't think that was going to satisfy their curiosity.

Another one of the women leaned forward to ask, 'Does he use his mouth?'

Avelyn frowned. 'Well, yes, when he kisses me.'

The women giggled, then explained what they'd meant. Fire raced along her cheeks and down her neck. Her reaction only had the women laughing harder.

'She hasn't been with him long enough yet.'

'Oh, honey, we have plenty of time to teach you everything you'll need to know.'

She smiled weakly, nodded and softly said, 'I would welcome the learning.'

While she did want to hear what they could tell her, what she really wanted to do was get up and leave before she perished from embarrassment. But where would she go?

One of the women frowned, asking, 'Did I not just hear that the King's Wolf was recently wed?'

The oldest waved away the question. 'What does being married have to do with anything? Men don't care who the willing body belongs to as long as it'll gain them release.'

No. Avelyn would never believe that her husband was like her father. Never. She couldn't let herself think that.

Elrik jerked awake and wiped a hand across his sweat-soaked brow. This had been the fourth time this night he'd been awakened by the kind of dreams he'd not had since he'd been a young man.

Erotic dreams, not of a faceless woman, or the cook's daughter, but of his wife. He slammed his fist down on to his pallet. Damn her for invading every minute of his day and every second of his night.

He got out of bed, tugged on a tunic and walked barefoot on to the deck to lean his forearms on the side and stare out at the dark, moonlit water. And hoped that maybe this night, the brisk air would cool his heated body.

'Trouble sleeping?' Samuel asked as he joined him.

'No. Not at all. I'm still fast asleep. You are only dreaming.'

'Why don't you just make landfall and go get your bride?'

As if he hadn't thought of doing that countless times already. 'Where would you suggest we make landfall?'

The ships were loaded. They were already low enough in the water that if they sailed into shallow waters they could tear the hull, or become stuck if they ran on to a sandbar. No. They would wait until they could dock.

'Raging at the crew and the men hasn't done much good. Maybe a good marital row will clear your head.'

'Yes, that's exactly what I need to do in front of the crew and men.'

Samuel sighed. 'Elrik, it hasn't even been a full day and the men are already talking. You are only letting their gossip grow unfettered by any amount of truth.'

Even though he didn't want to know, he asked, 'What are they saying?'

'The obvious. You have set her aside. The marriage isn't yet binding. She's travelling with the camp followers because she's a whore.' At Elrik's flinch, he asked, 'Is that enough, or would you like to hear more?'

'That's more than enough. You can stop.'

'You do realise that Fulke and I can only do so much to keep their gossip in check?'

Of course he knew that. He was also well aware that keeping the gossip in check was his job, not theirs.

He didn't want to drag her aboard his ship and make a spectacle out of both of them. That wasn't a way to gain any amount of respect for him or his wife. It wasn't a way to set any sort of example for the new men under his command.

But now that she was his, and she was so close at hand, he wanted her.

'Elrik, she may have disobeyed you, but she isn't a bad woman. She's kind. And even you have to admit that she's brave, albeit foolhardy.'

He snorted. 'She is a bit foolish.'

'How are you not full of yourself just knowing that a woman as lovely as Lady Avelyn, wanted so desperately to be with you that she followed you, into possible danger, against your orders?'

'I hadn't given that any thought. The whole idea of leaving her behind was to keep her safe and to keep her from distracting me. Besides, King David wouldn't have let her leave Carlisle without good reason.'

'Perhaps.' Samuel shrugged. 'While your original idea made perfect sense, even if it was a bit misguided, the fact is, she's here for whatever reason. Short of having her thrown overboard, I don't see how you can change that.'

Elrik straightened. Enough was enough of this conversation. 'I've already given orders to make for the first wharf available to us. In the morning, repeat that order to the captain. I'm going back to bed.'

Samuel nodded. 'I'll see that it's done.'

Chapter Eleven

A long, high-pitched scream tore Avelyn from her sleep. She opened her eyes, then squinted against the brightness of the rising sun. Amazed that she'd finally slept so well, she tossed her cloak aside and rose to find the source of the screaming.

It didn't take long as there were a dozen women gathered around another woman lying on the deck in obvious agony.

'What is wrong?' she asked a woman at the outside of the circle.

'She's in labour and it does not seem to be going well.'

Why would a woman that far along take the risk of making this voyage? What was she thinking? What had her husband been thinking to allow such a foolish move?

Avelyn pushed through the growing crowd. 'Is anyone here a midwife?'

One girl answered, 'The cook has done this before, but she is too sick to leave her pallet.'

Avelyn dug into her pouch of ginger and gave the girl a handful. 'Take these to her and tell her we need her help, sick or not.'

The labouring woman screamed again and it was all

Avelyn could do not to cover her ears at the pain-filled, frightened sound.

She spotted the captain, took a deep breath and marched towards him, knowing what she had to do.

Stopping right in front of him, she said, 'We need to contact Elrik. That woman needs help.'

He looked down his nose at her, curled one side of his mouth and snorted before saying, 'If the woman doesn't survive, she can have a burial at sea, matters not. We will make port when his lordship orders us to.'

Avelyn stiffened her spine, raised her chin and glared up at the man, pleased to see him take a step back and widen his eyes. 'You know full well that I am Lady Roul. In my husband's absence I am giving you an order that you will follow.' In a milder tone, she added, 'Or I will simply jump into the water. That should get his attention.'

There was now another crowd gathering around her and the captain.

The man sputtered, but he turned to shout at the men, 'Man the oars and put your backs into it. Come alongside Lord Elrik's ship.' He pointed at a younger man, ordering, 'Hoist that red flag—again.'

The woman screamed again, making Avelyn shudder. 'Just hurry, please.'

Certain they would quickly catch up to Elrik's ship, she went back to the woman in labour. There was nothing she could do except offer comfort, so she knelt beside the struggling woman and took her hand. 'We are heading for help. Where is your husband?'

'He's…on the first…ship.' Her gasping answer brought Avelyn a measure of relief. Elrik wasn't hard hearted. Surely, she could convince him to permit the man to be with his wife in her time of need.

* * *

Before too long, the captain called out, 'Lady Roul, we are nearly abreast.'

She patted the woman's shoulder and released her hand. 'Soon, we will get you help soon.'

She rose and shook out the skirt of her tunic, not to make it presentable, but to give her a brief moment to gain a small measure of confidence before facing Elrik once again.

The captain escorted her to the ladder leading up to the forecastle and helped her climb up to the deck. She stared across the water at her husband. The wind whipped his silver-streaked hair about his face, his stance—legs spread, fisted hands on hips and that familiar dark scowl—only made her wonder how she'd been blessed to have been given such a fine-looking man. The odd thought made her smile, before she forced the smile from her lips.

He shouted at her, 'Now what?'

'We require a midwife.'

One of the men on the deck of his ship dropped a crate he'd been carrying and rushed to the side. 'Is it Brigit?'

Avelyn nodded. The man gripped the side of the ship so hard his knuckles turned white.

Elrik cursed. 'There is a pregnant woman aboard?'

A scream cut her off, but supplied the answer to his question.

Elrik cursed again.

'My lord...' Avelyn paused, knowing this was probably not the time to ask, but she had no choice, so began again. 'My Lord Roul, can you spare her husband?'

A wicked half-smile curved his lips in a way that made her grasp the side of the ship so she didn't swoon overboard into the sea, before he answered, 'No, Lady Roul, I cannot. But when we make port, I will exchange him for you.'

After having issued what sounded ominously like a warning, he climbed down the ladder and headed towards the crew, pausing only to grab the father-to-be by the back of the neck and drag him along.

She didn't want to hear that conversation. She was too worried about the one she and Elrik would soon be having. It was doubtful there would be many pleasant words spoken between them.

To her relief, the ships changed course almost immediately, and sooner than she'd expected, she could see land. Reaching into her pouch, she pulled out another piece of her dwindling supply of ginger, hoping it would calm her stomach from not the motion of the ship, but from the worries of facing her husband without any distance between them.

The sudden churning of her stomach and the rapid beating of her heart made Avelyn wish she were anywhere else besides standing on the deck of this ship nervously awaiting his arrival.

Elrik, Samuel, Fulke and three other guards were already standing on the wharf as the ship she was on was tied up to a piling.

The other four ships had continued on, not coming into this harbour. She didn't know where they had made landfall, but at least it appeared to be a good-sized town. Hopefully, it was one that had an experienced midwife in residence.

Samuel and Fulke both tipped their heads as they came aboard. One of the guards—the young one Elrik had singled out earlier—raced past her to go to his wife's side. The other two carrying a litter and blankets followed behind the father-to-be.

Elrik jumped down from the plank on to the deck and paused to silently glare down at her. She felt an icy chill race against her—not from the wind, but from his stare that conveyed his anger clear to her soul.

Determined not to let him so easily intimidate her, she stiffened her spine, took a deep breath and returned his glare. He'd been the one who had left her behind. No matter his reasoning, or that he'd apologised, if anyone should be angry it should be her.

His only response was to hike one brow and nod before he went to talk to the captain of this vessel. Had he wanted her to stand tall before his anger, like he'd told her to do in the King's hall? Did he expect her to accept his anger as her due for not following his order to remain behind? She bit her tongue to keep from saying anything she couldn't unsay later.

The men loaded the distressed woman on to the litter and carried her off the ship. As he walked by, Fulke reached out and gently squeezed her fingers before following the others to the wharf.

Elrik finished his conversation with the captain and without a word of acknowledgement stepped up on to the plank that would take him from the ship to the wharf.

Avelyn's heart seemed to skip a beat and she held her breath. He was going to once again leave her behind? But she needed to warn him about Osbert. How was she going to do that if they were on separate vessels?

Her eyes filled and she swiped a hand across them, refusing to shed even a single tear because of a man who so obviously did not want her near at the moment. No. She would not be like her mother, pining for someone she could never truly have at her side.

She turned away, intending to join the group of women who had befriended her yesterday. They might be whores, bawdy and brash, but at least they were kind and not ashamed to have her near.

'Lady Avelyn.' He grabbed her shoulder, preventing her from leaving.

When she stopped to see what Elrik wanted, she was surprised to see that he'd extended his arm, hand out to help her mount the plank.

She looked up at him and he said, 'Come.'

His tone wasn't friendly in the least, but neither was it overly harsh. He sounded more impatient than anything else.

At her hesitation he scanned the ship, then looked back down at her. 'Not here. Not now.'

She, too, glanced at those on this ship and found everyone looking at them. Avelyn agreed, this was not the time nor the place for the discussion they had to have. She reached up and took his hand.

The fingers that closed over hers were warm. His touch filled her with a sense of safety she'd not realised had been missing until this heartbeat.

As he helped her up on to the plank, the women who'd become her friends rushed to the side of the ship to bid her farewell. One called out, 'Don't forget what we taught you.'

Even though she highly doubted she would get the opportunity to put any of their lessons to use, she promised, 'I won't.'

Elrik looked down at her and then over his shoulder at the women before once again giving her that hiked-brow stare she was coming to expect from him.

She said nothing. It wasn't as if she was about to tell him the things the women had described to her. It would be far more embarrassing to confide in him than it had been to hear the lessons from the women in the first place.

After helping her to board his ship, he led her to a makeshift cabin beneath the forecastle and parted the heavy sail cloth to usher her inside. The unfamiliar semi-darkness, his overwhelming presence, the stifling air and their privacy only served to add fuel to her already tightly strung nerves.

She quickly glanced around the cabin, finding little else but a stool, clothes chest, small table and a pallet that seemed to her the largest item in the room besides its owner.

Avelyn clasped her hands together to still their trembling. She hated feeling like a twitchy cat, with every fibre of her being on high alert as if some danger threatened.

From talking with the women, she knew what to expect, she also remembered their claims that pleasure could be found in a man's arms.

But those lessons did nothing to calm her.

Avelyn quickly spun around to bolt from the cabin and ran into an unmovable body blocking her exit.

He grasped her shoulders and she struggled to free herself, crying out, 'Let me go!'

'Stop this.' When she still fought him, he pulled her tightly against his chest and stroked her hair. 'Avelyn, stop. Nobody is going to harm you, least of all me. So, stop this.'

She relaxed enough in his grasp to be able to think. In the time she'd known him, he'd never once offered to physically harm her. She knew that. Deep in her heart she was certain he wouldn't do so now.

Yet, containing the tremors making her knees weak was nearly impossible. She was still afraid, but not of him. She oddly feared what was to come—not so much anything physical that might happen between them, although that did leave her a bit uneasy, she more dreaded the conversation.

How would he react when she told him about Osbert? Would he think she was somehow involved with her half-brother's schemes? Or would he believe her innocent of any wrongdoing?

'I must see to the arrangements for my men and Matthew's wife.' He released her. 'Stay here. Rest. I'll return as quickly as possible.'

She heard him give orders to guard the cabin and peeked out to find Samuel and Fulke positioned on either side of the flap opening.

Her sigh of relief must have caught their attention, because they both looked at her.

Samuel asked, 'Were you expecting someone else to be here?'

She shook her head. 'I wasn't sure, but I am relieved to find the two of you.'

Fulke glowered at her. 'We have better things to do than stand guard over you.'

His expression was far too menacing to be in earnest. She couldn't help but laugh at him. 'And what better *things* might those be?'

Just as she'd expected, his fierce glare eased. He shrugged. 'Aboard this ship, not much.'

'You do realise you disobeyed an order?' Samuel asked.

'For good cause.'

Fulke chimed in, 'Punishment at sea for that disobedience is rather harsh.'

'Will he throw me over the side?' She doubted that would happen, but couldn't envision harsher treatment.

'Worse. A guard would find himself tied to the mast. His back bared and lashed for such defiance.'

Avelyn swayed and grasped the heavy cloth for support. The mere thought of being lashed in such a manner left her dizzy.

Samuel cursed at Fulke, then sought to ease her worries. 'That has happened only one time aboard a Roul ship and Elrik was not the commander, his sire was.

'The young guard lashed was your husband.'

In a near whisper, she asked, 'His father was cruel

enough to do such a thing?' Her own father was unfeeling, but she doubted he'd be so unjust to one of his sons, not even his bastard ones, although it might have done Osbert a world of good.

'The three of us, along with Elrik's younger brother Gregor, pushed the man beyond his patience. And we foolishly did it intentionally,' Fulke admitted.

Samuel added, 'We never expected Elrik to bear the brunt of his rage.'

Curious, she asked, 'What had you done to gain such wrath?'

'None of us wanted to be on that voyage. We didn't agree with the old lord or his companions and had no desire to commit treason against King David.'

She knew her own father had had a hand in that act, but didn't know what he'd done. 'How had that come about?'

The two men looked at each other, obviously hesitant to talk about it. So, she said, 'King David told me that my father had been involved.'

Thankfully, that was enough to start them talking again.

Fulke asked, 'Have you ever witnessed your father talk someone, or a group of men, into doing something?'

'No.' She'd only heard him shout or bluster, but then she'd never been around when he'd spoken to others. She wasn't important enough to have been in attendance.

'Well, Brandr knows how to speak to a group of men in a manner that quickly has them believing that his words were actually their thoughts. After he convinced them that King David was taking property, land and titles from them to hand over to Norman foreigners, it was easy to fire up their thirst for vengeance.'

'It was something to watch.' Samuel added. 'All those old men shouting and acting as if they were twenty years younger, readily able to take on the King's forces without any difficulty.'

'We worried not just for their lives, but for their sanity. It was apparent they'd lost the ability to form any rational thought.'

Fulke explained further, 'When we readied to set sail, we made our displeasure obvious by not helping with the loading of arms, or running of the ship, and by telling all who would listen how foolish the venture was.'

Samuel continued the tale. 'The old lord took about two days of our defiance before he lost his patience and temper. Your father made a comment about how to deal with disobedience aboard ship. Lord Roul was angry enough to take hold of that suggestion and ordered Elrik be stripped and tied to the mast. His brother Gregor tried to reason with their father, but failed.'

'My father suggested the man lash his own son?'

Both men nodded.

She wanted to scream or to sob at the mere thought of such a heartless action. What thoughts must have gone through Elrik's mind?

'I imagine Elrik didn't make it easy for the men to carry out the orders.'

'No.' Samuel smiled wryly. 'One went overboard in full armour and nearly drowned. Another suffered a broken leg to match his broken nose. He still walks with a limp.'

'And while that fight may have been hard to witness…' Fulke paused to rub his forehead before continuing '…it was harder to watch the punishment.'

Samuel, almost under his breath said, 'I would have screamed like a crazed animal, but Elrik never made a sound.'

'He never batted an eye. Didn't even flinch. Just stared at his father while the lead oarsman flayed him.'

Avelyn shivered. *How had he withstood the pain?*

Not just the physical pain, but the mental agony of knowing his father had ordered the punishment at the instigation of another?

Now, knowing the person responsible had been her father, she understood the hatred Elrik felt for the man. What she couldn't understand was how he could have taken her as his wife. How could he as much as look at her without having the urge to see her dead?

Fulke shook his head. 'Less than a fortnight later, he was on the floor at King David's feet, begging for mercy for his father's act of treason.'

Why would he do so for a man who had treated him so cruelly?

'No matter what you do to him, Lady Avelyn, he will remain loyal until he draws his last breath.' Samuel's comment sounded ominously like a warning.

'Me? I have done nothing to him, nor do I have any plans to do so.'

Fulke dipped his head, to say, 'Not all wounds are physical.'

She knew that, but she was taken aback by their certainty that she would seek to harm Elrik. Regardless what anyone thought, she was *not* her father's daughter when it came to Elrik. 'Where is this coming from? I have done nothing. He is my husband, my protector. It would be foolish of me to try to bring him pain or heartache.'

'We have heard that from a woman before, yet the pain was inflicted as cleanly as it would have been with a finely honed knife.'

This was the first time, other than Elrik's offhanded remark in the King's Great Hall, that anyone had mentioned his previous wife. Avelyn stared at Samuel. 'You speak of his first wife?'

The man nodded. 'She went far in creating the man you see now. We will not stand by and let you finish the destruction she started.'

Destruction? 'What did she do? Where is she?'

'No.' Fulke put a hand on Samuel's shoulder. 'That explanation is up to Elrik if he so chooses, not us. Lady Avelyn, just know that no matter how much he may snarl or growl, you are his responsibility and he takes that seriously. He will not turn his back on you, regardless of how the two of you carry on with each other. All we ask is that you not take advantage of his loyalty. We will protect you with our lives, as long as you deal with Elrik fairly.'

A raindrop bounced off the end of her nose. She looked up at the darkening sky and groaned. It was doubtful any amount of ginger would settle her stomach if they were to encounter a storm at sea.

Samuel looked up at the sky. 'Fear not. It's just a passing cloud. Are you hungry?'

'No.' She'd eaten little since leaving Carlisle, but she didn't find the offer of food appealing. Besides, knowing these two, they would bring her every morsel of food on this ship, leaving none for any of the others.

Fulke looked at her and frowned. 'You look tired. Why don't you go back inside and get some rest, sleep while you can? Nobody will disturb you. Elrik will be a while yet and he's the only one who will enter.'

She yawned, giving proof to his observation, then agreed, 'Perhaps I'll do that.'

Avelyn slipped back inside the cabin and looked at the pallet. Even though she'd slept well, after doing so on a hard deck, wedged between two water barrels last night, it appeared inviting. She removed her soft boots and stockings and debated on whether to leave her tunic on. She turned down the fur-lined cover on the pallet to find, what seemed to her, clean sheets beneath. Her tunic was damp and filthy, so she removed it, folded it and placed it on the stool before climbing between the sheets dressed only in her thin chemise.

A sigh escaped as she stretched out and drew the cover over her shoulder. There were many things she needed to think about before speaking with her husband. But surely a short nap wouldn't be out of place, it would help to clear her mind so she could think better.

Elrik ducked through the flap of his dark cabin and dropped a pile of women's clothing on the floor. At least this time she couldn't argue his purchases—she was his wife, so it was his right to purchase anything he wished for her.

Samuel stuck an arm through the flap and handed him a lit lantern. He'd been gone much longer than expected, the sun had set hours ago. But it had taken time to find something for his wife to wear—more time than it had to make arrangements for Matthew, the man's wife, their recently born son and the two trusted, well known to him, Roul guards he'd left with them. He'd made certain to leave them enough coin to cover everything. Once the woman and babe were able to travel, they would all make their way to Roul.

He set the light on the table and stared down at his wife. The woman sleeping in his bed was far more desirable and lovely than the woman he'd envisioned in his dreams.

No matter how lovely she appeared, she'd still wilfully ignored an order. But, dear Lord help him, right now he wanted nothing more than to make her his wife in so much more than name only.

Her hair was tousled, her cheeks pinkened from hours spent beneath the sun, her features were softened with sleep. She'd kicked off the covers and her chemise had caught beneath her body, exposing the length of her legs. He wanted to stroke that length. He wanted to kiss her lips until they were pouty with desire. He wanted to see her eyes flash with all-consuming desire.

And he would.

But not just this moment.

Right now, they needed to talk. Wasn't that why she was here in the first place? She had been the one to claim they needed to talk—in private. Now was as good a time as any.

Quietly undressing, he wondered if she would awaken when he climbed beneath the covers and, if she did, how would she react?

He hung the lantern from a hook on the beam closest to the pallet. Since they weren't at sea, the danger of fire from the lantern falling was not as great. Besides, he wanted to see her face. They hadn't spent enough time together for him to know all that her body was seeking to convey— or hide. But she wasn't skilled enough to hide the expressions of her face and he hoped she never would become adept enough to do so. Maybe if that did happen, by then he would know every inch of her body as well as he knew every line and scar on his own hand.

Elrik slid beneath the covers. She made room for him and when he rolled on to his side to face her, she spooned against him instinctively as if they had been sleeping together like this for years.

With one arm bent beneath his head, he draped his other arm over her waist. He'd almost forgotten what it was like to share a bed with a woman—the warmth of soft curves, a gentle sigh as she eased against him, the silkiness of long untamed tresses tickling his face, her scent invading his senses with each inhale of breath.

He closed his eyes and relaxed against her, savouring the long-forgotten feelings, one part of his mind longing for this moment to last for ever, while another part chided him for such idle whimsy. He'd been fooled once by a woman's gentleness. It wasn't going to happen again.

She curled tighter against him, her soft skin pressing against his groin. His heart thudded hard, he opened his eyes and swallowed a groan.

She tensed, alerting him that she'd awakened. 'Elrik?'

'Are you seeking to ask me a question, or asking if I'm the one in this bed with you?'

'The latter.'

She squirmed against him in her effort to pull her chemise from beneath her. Her innocent movements were making it nearly impossible to control the urge to make her his—now. When she wiggled again, he didn't hold back his groan. He tightened the arm he'd slung over her waist, splayed his fingers across her belly and pressed his groin against her. 'You must stop.'

'But…' She froze, apparently just now noticing that he was naked and ready for much more than talking or sleep. She whispered, 'Oh.'

'Just be still.'

She nodded vigorously in response.

Elrik unbent the arm beneath his head and toyed with a lock of her hair. 'Why are you here?'

When she did nothing but sigh before falling silent, he tugged her hair. 'Are you awake?'

'Yes.'

'Then answer me. Why are you here?'

'Because my husband is here and I need to discuss something with him.'

'Ah, but this husband of yours told you to stay with King

David until your brothers by marriage arrived to take you to Roul Isle.'

'It could not wait.'

'What could be of such importance that you deemed it necessary to disobey an order?'

When she didn't answer, he pulled her tighter against his chest. With his hand on her forehead, he tipped her head back and whispered against her ear, 'There's a price to be paid for disobeying an order.' He lightly grazed his teeth along her neck. 'Especially one meant to have kept you safe.'

She trembled against him, asking, 'Safe? How could I not be safe with the Wolf and his men?'

Frustrated that he couldn't see her face, he released her long enough to adjust the pillows against the side of the ship to use for padding and sat up against them. When she turned over to see what he was doing, he said, 'Come here.'

Avelyn hesitated a heartbeat too long for his liking, so Elrik pulled her up to straddle his legs, facing him.

The candle in the lantern cast a soft glow over them, just enough light to see her wide-eyed stare at his chest. 'You are naked.'

He stroked his thumb along her jawline before threading his fingers through the silkiness of her hair to pull her closer. Against her lips, he whispered, 'Get used to it. Before this night is over you will be as naked as I.'

The sound of her gasp filled the cabin. Her exhaled breath brushed against his face. She parted her lips. To keep her from commenting, Elrik leaned forward to draw her into a kiss.

She moaned softly. Placing her palms against his chest, she leaned closer.

Thankfully, his kiss distracted her enough that she didn't

notice, or perhaps didn't care, when he tugged her chemise free from beneath her knee and slowly slid his palm up the softness of her thigh.

He wanted to go further, do more, but not until this discussion was over. For now, it was enough to know she would gladly accept his touch.

Elrik broke their kiss and fought back a laugh at her groan.

She pushed herself away and looked at him to ask, 'Are you seeking to distract me from my purpose?'

'Yes.'

The light shimmered in her eyes, the line of her mouth was soft from their kiss and he couldn't resist running a fingertip along her lips before lowering his arm.

Still lightly stroking the tender skin beneath his touch, he asked, 'How did you evade King David?'

'I didn't.'

Her near-breathless answer let him know his tactic was working. 'He let you leave?'

'Let me leave? He thought my suggestion was an excellent solution.'

'What needed a solution?'

She started to sway towards him and he grasped one of her shoulders to keep her upright. 'Perhaps you should start at the beginning.'

Avelyn looked away and worried her lower lip between her teeth. Elrik frowned. Something was troubling her greatly.

'Avelyn?'

Her brow furrowed, she stared at him. Ice-blue eyes peered into his with an intensity that took his breath away.

He withdrew his hand from her thigh, to rest his palm against her neck. 'Talk to me, Avelyn. I will carry your troubles willingly, but I cannot do so if I don't know what they are.'

'Do you blame me for anything my father has done to you? Will I be the one who pays the price my father never did? How could you have married me?' Her words came out in a whispered rush.

'Avelyn, what is this? Why would you ask such things?'

She lowered her head, her chin nearly touching her chest. 'My half-brother Osbert has followed you and I trust him not.'

Now he understood why she was so upset and hesitant. 'Did you send him after me?'

'No!' She vigorously shook her head. 'Never. I would never betray you like that.'

He couldn't be certain that would never happen in the future. But he was positive she hadn't done so now. 'Then why this needless worry about paying for your father's wrongdoing?'

'You said if I betrayed you that I would wish we'd never met.'

'And I meant that. But I know without a single doubt that you haven't done so.'

'How? How can you be so certain?'

'Since the day I found you, the few moments you have been out of my sight, Samuel and Fulke have watched you. When would you have conspired with your family? Not after I departed from Carlisle. You were in your chamber when the men and I left the courtyard. Shortly thereafter you were racing down the wharf. I assume you talked with King David before leaving?'

'Yes. He doesn't trust Osbert either and thought the idea of me coming to you with the warning was the best option.'

'Of course he did.' This was likely David's way of ensuring this marriage he had arranged became validated quickly. 'So, there wasn't time for you to have planned anything with your brother, talk to the King and get to the dock before the last ship left.'

She visibly relaxed. Her body melted against him. 'I was so worried.'

'Needlessly.' Elrik wrapped his arms about her. 'What did you think I was going to do?'

'Become angry. Shout at me. Set me aside.'

'I was angry—most of that has vanished.'

'Most?'

'I told you to stay at Carlisle until my brothers arrived and you didn't. So, yes, I was angry.'

Her cheek brushed against his chest as she nodded. 'I know.'

'Shouting at you would be a waste of my breath, since it only upsets you to the point of not listening.'

He kissed the top of her head. 'And setting you aside is not what I have in mind for you this night, or any other. But first, we need to discover if your brother is on one of these ships.'

'He isn't on the one with the women.'

'No, he wouldn't be. I made sure I knew every crew member on the ship came from Roul.'

'And I didn't see him on this one either.'

'Ah, that's what you were looking for so intently yesterday when you studied the men on the ship before telling me what you wanted.'

'Yes.'

'So, he could be on one of the other four.'

A shiver rippled down her spine. He chased it with his hand, soothing it away. 'Avelyn, you are out of his reach for now.'

'I am not worried about me.'

Elrik laughed. 'You worry about me?'

'You don't know him.' She pushed herself up away from his chest. 'He is evil.'

'So is his father.'

'True, but Osbert is sly and without any honour.'

And she thought her father had any honour? Not wanting to discuss Brandr, he didn't make any comment. Instead, he asked, 'Was he travelling alone?'

'No. There were five other men with him in the court-yard.'

'He's on the original third or fourth ship.'

'How do you know that?'

'Because six men claiming to be from King David arrived late. Since I didn't know them and neither did any of the men on my ship, I split them up, assigning half of them to each of those two ships.'

'You don't think they will try to sway your crews like my father did yours?'

'Ah, more of the bits and pieces you've been told.'

'Yes.'

'No, I doubt they have your father's ability to rouse men to go along with what scheme your brother has planned. Besides, the captains of those ships are King David's men and will keep them in line.'

She folded her hands in front of her and looked down at them. 'So, if they disobey an order, they'll be punished.'

He frowned at the nervousness once again evident in her trembling voice. 'Yes.'

'Do I need to be punished for disobeying you by leaving Carlisle?'

Punish her? Did she think him that vile? He reached out to touch her chin, tipping her head up, he asked, 'Where is this coming from?'

Her eyes filled with tears. 'Elrik, I am sorry for what my father had done to you.'

What her father had done to him... They were no longer talking about his father's act of treason. And he had the awful feeling someone had opened their mouth about something that had horribly frightened his wife.

Chapter Twelve

'Avelyn, we need to put a few things to rest.' He patted the spot next to him. 'Come here.'

She moved off his lap to sit next to him and he slung his arm across her shoulders to pull her closer. 'There isn't anything you can't tell me, nothing you can't ask me.'

Her strange sound of disbelief—something between a huff and a snort—made him laugh, but he waited for her to respond.

'What if it angers you?'

'Then I get angry. I am not a saint, but I have never harmed a woman and I am not going to start doing so with my own wife. What do you fear I'll do?'

'My father—'

'I am nothing like your father.' If she feared setting off his rage, this was a good way to do so. This act of talking was not going to be easy. He had attacked fortified keeps with more ease than this. He took a breath to steady his temper. 'No, I am not like your father. In the time you have known me, what have I done to make you think such a thing?'

She leaned away to look up at him, one brow arched high.

He had lost his temper and threatened to kill her father

in King David's chamber, but that was different. That was man to man. He reworded his question. 'To you, Avelyn. What have I done to you?'

'Nothing.'

'What do you think I'll do?'

She shrugged.

Elrik closed his eyes a moment, then looked down at her. 'If we are to make any kind of peace between us, you need to talk to me. I can't guess at your thoughts. I swear to you, nothing you say is going to change the fact that we are wed, nor will your words make me strike out at you. Talk to me, tell me what weighs so heavily on your mind.'

'Did my father talk yours into going against King David?'

'Yes, he did. Brandr managed to convince many of the older men to band together in an act of treason that had no chance of success.'

'And you became caught up in it, too?'

'My plan had been to make my father see reason. I failed miserably.'

'So, when their attempt was thwarted, you paid the price.'

He'd already told her this. She had to be bringing it up again for a reason. 'Yes, Gregor and I offered ourselves in our father's place. King David required all four of us—Edan and Rory included when they came of age—to serve him exclusively in exchange for our father's life.'

'How could you have done so mere days after your father had been so...so cruel to you?'

Elrik knew two men who were going to pay heavily for having told her of this. 'Do you think that's what I'm going to do to you for not staying at Carlisle?'

He glanced down at her, but she was staring at her lap. Elrik wondered for a heartbeat if what he was about to do would help or hurt her worries. Never before had there been a reason to put on such a display, especially for a woman, but right now, she needed something. Since his words weren't working, the only thing he could think of was to show her.

He leaned forward so she could see his back. 'Avelyn, look at me.'

Her gasp seemed to echo in the confines of the makeshift chamber. Glancing over his shoulder, he saw horror and pain etched on her face. Her hand paused inches from his back. 'They are just scars, that is all.'

A shiver rippled down his spine at her tentative light touch. 'I am so sorry.'

The choked tone of her hushed voice fell against his heart. The feathery brush made him long to gather her close and chase away the guilt she bore for something not her fault.

'You have nothing for which to be sorry.'

'I am sorry for the part my father played in this mistreatment.'

Elrik leaned back against the pillows, admitting, 'In all honesty, it had been a long time coming.'

'How…?' Her voice caught, but she swallowed and then tried again. 'How did you bear it?'

'Little dove, my father and I were at odds from the time I learned to walk. The older I got, the more I tested his patience. I was able to bear it, because I knew doing so would serve to enrage him more. I wasn't about to let him break me. I'd not give him, or Brandr, that satisfaction.'

She pulled free of the arm he'd slung over her shoulders and threw herself against his chest. 'Oh, Elrik, I am so sorry. I would never hurt you in so horrible a manner. I swear I will never betray you. I will never seek to harm you or your heart in any way. Never. I swear it.'

What the hell had those two said to her? Of course, she wouldn't ever harm him like that...he narrowed his eyes. She would never seek to harm him *or his heart* in any way. *His heart.* Now why would she have said that? They wouldn't have... No. He felt as if someone had just punched him in the stomach. He knew two high-ranking guards who were going to find themselves at the working end of an oar come morning.

Whether he wanted to or not, he needed to put a stop to this before it went any further. 'Just what exactly did Samuel and Fulke tell you?'

Avelyn sat up slowly and looked into his eyes. He didn't appear angry, at least she didn't think so. Impatient? No, it was something else. Something she'd not seen before and couldn't yet define.

Ask whatever she wanted... Did she want to know about his first wife? She'd got the impression that he'd cared deeply for her. What if the woman had hurt him so badly that he could never let himself care for her in the same way? Would she be able to live with his answer? Or would it be harder not to know?

He placed a hand against her cheek. 'Ask what you will, but I'll not lie, Avelyn. So be certain you truly wish to know.'

She took a deep breath before saying, 'I know you were wed before. And while, yes, I am curious, I am more concerned with our marriage, with us and our tomorrows, than I am about your past. I fear the answer will prove more than I can bear. So, I have only one question for you, one thing I want to know above all else.' She leaned forward, her hands splayed across his chest to softly ask, 'Lord Elrik, are we well and truly wed?'

The lantern's light glimmered in his eyes. A smile played at one corner of his mouth and before she knew what he was planning, he pulled her into an embrace that nearly took her breath away and he then kissed away all her concerns about something so small as breathing.

He rolled her on to her back, coming over her. Propping up on his elbows, he broke their kiss. 'Yes, Avelyn, we are well and truly wed. I paid for the honour with five Roul ships that I could ill afford losing. King David has the signed documents in his possession. One set will go to my brothers on Roul Isle. You'll not be rid of this old, ugly, grizzled warrior so easily.'

His comment caught her off guard and she glanced up to see him roll his eyes. She lifted a brow, trying to imitate him and yet doubting if she looked as fierce as doing so made him appear, but determined to give him back a measure of his teasing. 'You are not old and far from ugly. I found Richard with his unblemished face much less attractive than my grizzled husband.'

'Ah, but Richard is so much prettier.'

She shook her head. 'You know little about women. His prettiness belies his inexperience. He obviously is not man enough to see to my safety. Besides, who is to say I wish to rid myself of the Lord Wolf?' She grazed his arm with the tips of her fingernails. 'At least not before I've tasted more of his kisses.'

His eyes widened before he warned, 'Be careful what you start, little dove, your talons are no match for my fangs.'

Avelyn laughed at his silliness. This was what she'd wanted from a husband. Someone who would talk with her and laugh with her—not at her.

'Avelyn, you did not ask, but I am more than willing to set your mind at ease.'

When she parted her lips to tell him that his explanation was not necessary, he stopped her words by sliding his tongue along her lower lip until she shivered, then kissed away her comment.

Too soon he stopped. 'When it comes to my first wife...' He frowned and stared at the side of the ship a moment before returning his gaze to her. 'Muriel and I met once before our marriage. I was young, she was older, more experienced and easily had me believing we were deeply in love. I soon learned how wrong I'd been and how easily she had lied. By then we were already wed, so there was nothing I could do about the huge errors in judgement that had been made by myself and King David.'

Avelyn swallowed, trying to still the sudden queasiness of her stomach. 'How do you know our marriage wasn't also an error?'

'There is no way for anyone to know for certain. But, Avelyn, neither of us went into this marriage with any thoughts of love.'

'True.' She didn't love him, at least she didn't think these emotions washing over her were love. And he held no love for her. She wondered what he did feel for her.

'What happened to her?'

'We had only been wed a few months and I returned to Roul Isle from a mission for the King to find her in a fit of rage because she'd just discovered she was carrying a child.'

'Rage?' Why would anyone be outraged at finding out they were pregnant?

'Yes. Carrying my child—the Wolf's child—was not something she desired. Muriel claimed it would be born with fangs and probably kill her.'

The woman's mind was unsettled. Avelyn kept that thought to herself.

'I thought I had calmed her worries and believed all was well. When I came back from the next mission for the

King, she was dying. She'd taken some root concoction to rid herself of the babe and ingested too much.'

'Oh, Elrik, that must have been terrible for you.'

'No. What was terrible was her deathbed confession. She feared me, hated me because I was nothing but a lowly beast and truly believed I'd implanted the devil's spawn in her.'

'She'd lost her wits.' Avelyn slapped a hand over her mouth. She hadn't meant to say that aloud.

'Yes, fear will do that to a person.'

'She was unstable long before you wed her. Elrik, you are not a monster to be feared.'

'You are the only woman to think that.'

Then other women were blind. 'It is sad that your first marriage ended so badly, since you had obviously looked forward to it. It is easy to understand why this time you had no desire for another wife.'

He stroked the line of her jaw, ending his touch with a tap on the end of her nose. 'That isn't quite true. I wanted you as my wife, but not until later when this business with Roul Keep was settled.'

Avelyn still didn't understand why he wanted her, Brandr's daughter, as his wife, but this moment was not the time to sort it out. Her emotions were all jumbled simply by their closeness. Thinking clearly was impossible when the heat of his body covered hers.

He nudged her chin up with his own. 'But, little dove, I find that I could easily get used to having you around.'

She forced a smile, hoping he didn't see any lingering signs of worry.

'And I need never fear your lies, because you are truly bad at hiding anything.' Elrik brushed his lips briefly across hers. 'It is a waste of time to worry over whether this marriage was a mistake or not. It is done.'

His logic did nothing to banish her concerns. 'You could set me aside.'

'Yes. I could.' He smoothed away her frown with the pad of his thumb. 'But if I did so, Avelyn, how would I ever discover what makes you shiver?' As if on command, she shivered at his touch trailing along her neck.

'And how would I ever know what brings a sigh to your lips?' He kissed her—thoroughly—his tongue sliding along hers, tracing the line of her lips and catching her sigh as he broke the kiss.

'I would never be able to hear you gasp with wonder at building desire.' Elrik moved slightly off her to stroke along the edge of her chemise while tugging at the tie with his teeth. Once untied, he slipped the worn fabric down her arm, freeing a breast. The cool air was quickly chased away by his caress.

Instinctively she raised a hand to cover herself, but was stopped by what sounded like a low growl before he dipped his head and drew the tip into his mouth. She gasped with surprise at the heat of his tongue.

Barely lifting his head, he asked, 'And how would I ever hear you moan softly for more?'

So intensely focused on the sudden flurry of fluttering wings in her stomach at the feel of his mouth on her, she never noticed that he'd moved his hand beneath the skirt of her chemise until his calloused palm slid up her thigh.

He'd so easily made her shiver, sigh and then gasp. A small part of her feared what he would do to make her moan. Yet, she welcomed the discovery with a tingling of anticipation racing down her spine.

She closed her eyes and held her breath, waiting... wondering... Only to notice that he'd stopped his slow, tantalising ascent.

Against her ear, he asked, 'Are you hiding, or are you still here?'

Avelyn turned her face towards the heat of his breath to look at him. Her heart drummed faster at the intense shimmer in his darkening gaze. She swallowed hard, surprised by the sudden dryness of her mouth and answered truthfully, 'I don't know what to expect.'

He pulled his hand from beneath her chemise to stroke her cheek with the back of his fingers. 'I would hope not. Avelyn, I'll not have you frightened or cowering beneath my touch, so I must ask, do you wish to be my wife in my bed?'

Startled, she blinked. 'Are you giving me the choice?'

His deep chuckle took her breath away. 'This is not something I want to do *to* you. I would rather do it *with* you since it is much more enjoyable when the act is shared willingly.'

While his chuckle had stolen her breath, his answer made her tremble with a need she didn't quite understand. All she knew for certain was that she longed for more of his touch, for his kiss. Is that what he wanted, too? To be certain, she hesitantly asked, 'And if I say no?'

'I will leave you be.'

As he sat up and started to move away, she grasped his am, stopping him. 'No, Elrik, do not leave me be. I know not what you have awakened, but I will not rest if you go.'

He looked down at her. 'Do you trust me?'

'Why would I not? You have asked for my participation when you had every right to simply take.'

'Ah, but this night I want to be certain you are willing. I need to hear the words from your lips.'

'Yes. I am willing.'

He ran a finger along the edge of her chemise, trailing a

warmth against her skin. 'You do understand your partici-pation will mean that this needs to be removed.'

She slowly nodded, trying to ignore the heat flooding her cheeks and neck.

Elrik slid the garment off her shoulder as easily as he had earlier to the other side, then moved to kneel between her legs.

Avelyn couldn't stop her body from shaking as he ever so slowly eased the garment to her waist. She pulled her arms free to cross them over her breasts.

'Don't.' His tone deepened. 'Your embarrassment will soon ease.'

He leaned forward to cup a breast with each hand. Drop-ping a kiss first on the top curve of one and then the other, he said, 'Besides, I want to see what five ships have gained me.'

The half-smile and creases at the corner of his eyes let her know he was but teasing her. She laughingly asked, 'Isn't this how you purchase a horse?'

'Actually...' he paused to work his lips up to her neck '... I wouldn't be purchasing a horse...' he grazed the line of her jaw to her ear with his teeth '...the stable master would.' His lips teased the rim of her ear. 'Do you know what he would do?'

Avelyn was having a hard enough time trying to breathe let alone answer senseless questions. Between the pound-ing of her heart and the heat flooding her veins, the best she could do was to answer, 'Hmmm?'

Elrik pushed himself up and gently parted her eyelids. 'He'd make certain there were no signs of blindness.'

He then parted her lips and peered inside her mouth. 'He would judge this horse's age to be...around nineteen to perhaps twenty-five.'

'Twenty-five!' She nipped at his fingers.

'Oh, a biter. Need to keep an eye on this one.'

He pressed his fingers along both sides of her head and neck. 'No lumps or outward signs of pain.'

Moving on to her arms, he checked her elbows and shoulders before tracking his touch down her chest to smooth his palms over her belly—pushing the chemise down at the same time. 'A little thin, but not too skinny, and definitely no bulging or bloat.'

He tickled her side and she bit her lips to keep from laughing until she could stand it no longer. She squirmed beneath him, trying to push his hands away.

When tears of laughter trailed down the side of her face, he relented and stroked her hips, whispering, 'Yes, well formed for bearing little ones.'

Avelyn was not thrilled at hearing she'd be a good brood mare.

He reached back to grasp her ankle and pull it up on to his shoulder. 'Hooves seem fine.'

'Stop it!' She tried unsuccessfully to pull her foot from his tickling hold.

He worked his way up from her ankle. 'Fetlock, hock, stifle all feel sturdy.'

The further up her leg his touch travelled, the faster her heart beat until it seemed to drum loud and strong in her ears.

He'd been teasing her to keep her distracted and calm. She knew that and greatly appreciated his thoughtful, albeit silly, method.

But now that his warm, strong hand stroked the back of her thigh, her distraction ended abruptly.

Now she noticed that her chemise was bunched into a thick rope just above her hips. The chill of the night air raced across her breasts, pebbling her nipples.

His fingertips brushed the short curls between her

thighs, causing the skin over her belly to quiver and drawing a gasp from her lips.

Elrik's darkly seductive stare held her still. 'Are you very certain of this, Avelyn?'

She paused, letting the quick waves of ice and fire wash over her, then answered, 'Oh, yes.'

He grasped the rolled fabric of her chemise with both hands and pulled it down over her hips. Avelyn lifted her foot off his shoulder to assist him, but he grasped her ankle, stopping her. 'Let me.'

Once he'd freed that leg, he slid the chemise off her other leg and tossed the garment on to the floor.

Instead of coming over her as she'd expected, he turned his focus back to her leg. But this time, his teasing fingers were followed by his lips. From her ankle, pausing halfway to pay attention to the soft skin behind her knee, before working his way up to where the back of her thigh met the roundness of her bottom.

He touched only her leg, yet her entire being had fallen under the spell he seemed to weave around her.

She felt the racing of her heart not just as it beat wildly inside her chest, but in the steady drumming along the side of her neck and the building pulse low in her belly.

Her breasts seemed heavier and peaked as if begging for his touch, for the friction of his calloused palms and the warmth of his mouth.

Avelyn's cheeks heated at her thoughts and she closed her eyes, seeking to shut out the visions forming in her mind.

Once again, Elrik's touch stilled until she reopened her eyes. 'Avelyn, don't seek to hide from whatever is besetting you. Be it good or bad, I am here. Share it with me.'

She didn't think the fire burning her face could possibly get any hotter. 'I don't know what spell you've woven. I can't put it into words.'

'I don't need to hear your words when I can easily read them in your eyes, or in the way your body reacts, whether you pull away.' He stroked the bottom of her foot and she instantly sought to tug free.

'Or whether you lean into the touch.' His fingers crept back up her leg, lingering behind her knee, and she found herself more than willing to let that caress continue.

'There is no spell, Avelyn. You know exactly what is happening here. I am learning every inch of my wife's body. Discovering what she likes and what she doesn't, while I seduce her and tease her until she begs for an end to the torment robbing her of the ability to think.'

She'd been wrong—it was quite possible for the fire burning her cheeks to grow hotter. To banish the dryness, she ran her tongue along her lips, then asked, 'And when will I learn every inch of my husband's body?'

His eyes widened a moment, before he tilted his head and frowned. 'Is that what you want?'

She nodded. 'As much as I am thoroughly enjoying your exploration, I, too, am curious to learn about the husband with whom I will share a bed.'

He hesitated and she feared she'd somehow displeased him. 'Elrik, I am sorry if—'

His laugh stopped her apology. 'No. Do not ever be sorry for something you want to do in our bed. I was but trying to decide if I'll be able to withstand your touch without dying.'

It was her turn to laugh. 'I vow I'll not use my talons on your ever-so-delicate skin.'

He sighed and lowered her leg. 'As long as you promise to be gentle. This is my first time after all.'

She laughed again at his silliness. 'My Lord Roul, I do not believe you for one heart beat.'

He winged a brow. 'It takes a brave woman to pet a wolf and you are the first one I've met willing to risk so much.'

He unfolded his legs, stretching them out on either side of her and moving further back on the pallet. Avelyn sat up. 'I find it hard to believe any woman wouldn't want to touch someone as magnificent as this Wolf.'

'Ah, yes, magnificently battle scarred.'

She stared at him, wondering who he spoke about so poorly. How could anyone not see what she did when she gazed upon him?

He was a fine specimen of a man—muscular limbs peppered with near-black hair that her fingers itched to touch.

A well-formed chest tapering to a narrower waist—her perusal froze.

One of the women on the other ship had stated that men were oddly made. Another claimed they were made to fit a woman so completely that the couple became one.

Avelyn wet her lips. The second woman appeared to be correct...maybe.

His deep laugh barely registered and when his finger touched beneath her chin, she flinched with surprise and looked up at him.

'When you stare at a man as if you wish to devour him, it will always be his manhood that responds first. It can't be helped.'

She shook her head, clearing away her concerns. He wouldn't have asked her to trust him if he thought he was only going to end up hurting her.

She rose up on to her knees and straddled one of his thighs. He closed his eyes while she smoothed the lines across his forehead and brushed the silky hair from his face. Even the strands of silver were soft.

She trailed a fingertip down his nose, pausing to retrace a crooked bump.

Elrik shrugged. 'Gregor took offence to something I said.'

Continuing her exploration, she was surprised at the softness of his lips and more so at the way he shivered when she retraced them with the tip of her tongue. Her own shiver was not a surprise in the least. The more she touched him, the faster her heart pounded.

The stubble covering his face, the square edge of his chin and the line of his jaw were far from soft.

When she caressed the edge of his ear, he pulled away, but had no complaint at having her stroke the side of his neck. And when she tasted his neck with her lips and tongue, a low rumbling groan rewarded her action. That deep throaty sound did as much to send fire rushing through her veins as his touch on her thigh had.

His shoulders were broad, leaving her certain that he could bear whatever weight was placed up them. Whether it be the weight of his armour, or that of troubles.

She smoothed her hands across his shoulders and down his arms. A laugh escaped at his antics when he flexed his muscles. She'd seen the bulge of his muscles before and was not surprised by the solid hardness that was impossible for her to squeeze, even with both hands.

Her hands drifted over to his chest where she traced more than a few white scars. Some were thin, likely nothing more than nicks from the tip of a sword or knife. But two were long, jagged and wide enough to have been much more than simple nicks.

'This one.' She touched one just beneath the middle of one collar bone. 'How did you survive it?'

Again, he shrugged. 'It slipped right past anything I required to live, I suppose. Hurt like hell and it took a long time for me to gain strength back in that arm, but it didn't threaten my life.'

She leaned forward to place a kiss on the wicked-looking scar. 'You were lucky.'

'No, Avelyn. I am luckier this day, this moment than at any other time I can remember.'

Rising up on her knees to press against his chest, she teased at the corner of his lips with her tongue. 'How so?'

He wrapped both arms about her, holding her tightly, to whisper hoarsely against her ear, 'Forgive me. But this exploration of yours is over. I ache for you.'

She laughed softly, her tone just as hoarse and shaking as his had been. 'And I for you.'

'Hold tight.'

She slung her arms around his neck only a second before he rose up on his knees, and then dropped her on to her back. Freeing his arms from beneath her, he slid down her body. His hands caressing her breasts were no longer gentle or teasing, a gasp caught in her throat, escaping as a moan when he covered one tip with his mouth.

He slid slightly off her and smoothed a palm down her belly, over the patch of curls to stroke down one thigh and back up the other, coming to rest between her thighs. She drew in a ragged breath, wondering if he could feel the maddening pulse against his palm.

His first stroke made her jump, but the weight of his leg slung over one of hers kept her in place. She curled the fingers of one hand in his hair while the other grasped at his arm. 'Elrik... I don't...'

Whatever she'd been about to say was forgotten when he released her breast and pushed himself further down her body to replace the hand teasing at her core with his lips and tongue.

While she'd been embarrassed before, now she was horrified, but when she tried to move away, he held her in place with a firm hand on her belly. She was positive, certain she would die…if he stopped.

She felt his intimate caress in nearly every part of her body. Her scalp tingled, heart raced. She shivered from the streak of ice racing down her spine. Her thighs trembled from the building heat.

When she gave into the sensations washing over her, he relaxed his hand on her stomach and reached up to tease a peaked nipple. Her eyes widened as all the wondrous sensations raced to centre beneath his tongue.

She grabbed his shoulders, gasping, 'Elrik…please.' Avelyn had only a vague idea of what she begged for, but she knew without a single doubt that he could ease this frantic pulsing of her body.

He slid one finger inside her, stroking, teasing her even more until she was unable to make any coherent sound other than a higher-pitched whine as her body started to rapidly contract beneath his touch.

She closed her eyes and bit her lips to hold back the shout she wanted to release. He was instantly there, above her, whispering, 'I've got you.'

When she felt him entering her, filling her, she moaned and wrapped her legs around his to hang on.

Where was the pain she'd heard whispers of? Or the disgust and shame her mother had often warned about? What about the boredom, the waiting for it simply to be over which some of the women had spoken of?

Instead of pain, she felt a sense of being…complete. An overwhelming emotion that she wished not to look at too closely washed over her for the husband holding her close. This was far from boring, her heart beat so hard, so fast that it was nearly impossible to catch her breath, yet she wished for it not to end too soon.

No one had spoken of this dizzying spinning of her

head. Nor had they once mentioned feeling more alive than she'd ever before experienced; the joy of it brought tears to her eyes.

Avelyn gasped at the increased sense of spinning out of control. Elrik caressed the back of her head and held her face against his shoulder. 'Let the wave crest around you. You are safe.'

His tone was gravelly, rough, and his body trembled against hers. Just as she reached a height she didn't think she could return from, she felt as though she were falling and bit his shoulder to keep from crying out.

He stiffened and groaned against her ear, making her wonder if he'd experienced the same feelings, emotions that she had.

Once he stilled and his breathing calmed, he rolled on to his back, bringing her atop of him. 'I don't want to crush you beneath me.'

Avelyn sighed. 'I wouldn't notice, or care.'

She felt the silent laugh shaking in his chest and closed her eyes, wishing this moment could last a lifetime.

When she opened her eyes, the cabin was awash in darkness. She lay on her back, Elrik next to her on his stomach with one arm slung across her waist.

While the closeness was nice, her legs were cold and she wanted to pull the cover over them. But when she tried to move, he rolled on to his side, tightened his hold around her and pulled her hard against his chest.

Unwilling to awaken him, she curled her arm over his and settled into the embrace to give herself over to the beckoning call of sleep.

Chapter Thirteen

Elrik stepped out of his cabin and into the brilliant light of midday, squinting against the glare of the sunshine.

'Well, you are still alive.'

He ignored Samuel's comment and climbed the ladder up to the deck of the forecastle, motioning over his shoulder for the man to join him.

Fulke remained in place guarding the door to the cabin, while Samuel climbed the ladder to join Elrik at the railing.

'Haven't seen much of you these last three days.'

Elrik leaned his forearms on the railing and stared out over the water. 'Anything gone awry while I saw to my new bride?'

'Not a thing.'

'Then my absence caused no trouble.'

'No. Although from your surliness I would guess something is troubling you.'

Elrik slowly turned his head to glare at Samuel. 'Care to explain why you found it needful to tell my wife anything about my past?'

His man took two steps further down the railing, putting him well out of reach. 'It seemed the reasonable thing to do at the time.'

Elrik stood up and moved away from the railing, putting more distance between them. 'It seemed reasonable for you to frighten Avelyn?'

'The intent wasn't to frighten her. It was to explain why you sometimes act the way you do.'

'And to what? Warn her not to hurt my tender feelings?'

Samuel's eyes widened briefly. 'She told you that?'

'No. She said nothing of the sort. You just did.' Elrik stormed closer, stopping when he was toe to toe with the man. 'I've no need, or desire, to be coddled by anyone, least of all my wife. What right did you have to say anything to her?'

'Nearly thirty years of friendship.' Samuel held his ground. 'And over seven years of watching you hold yourself back from any personal involvement with a woman. If any of us needs to be wed, it is you.'

'Me?' Elrik shook his head. 'You are daft.'

'Of the three of us, you are the only one who needs to protect and care for someone smaller and weaker.'

'It is my duty.'

'No. It is your desire. You need it as much as you do the air you breathe.'

'Ack.'

When he turned away, Samuel said, 'Tell me you are not more content now than you have been in a very long time.'

'Content?' Elrik turned back. 'After three days in bed with my wife I would call it exhausted.'

'Well, that's one way to avoid the issue.'

'There is nothing to avoid. Did you and Fulke enjoy your time on the oars?'

Samuel snorted. 'You made your displeasure fairly obvious.'

'That was the intent.'

Samuel turned to stare out over the water. 'Have you

given much thought to what you're going to do with her half-brother and his companions?'

Elrik joined him. 'Did you get the ships back into their original order?'

'Yesterday.'

'Good. Now we just need to identify all six of them.'

'Will Lady Avelyn help with that?'

'Other than pointing out her brother, I'm not sure she'd know the others. But I don't want to involve her unless there is no other choice.'

'Do you think she knows what he's planning?'

'No. Not at all.' He had never thought that. 'I simply don't want to put her in the position to choose between her family and her husband.'

Samuel stared at him. 'There wouldn't be a choice for her. She'd side with you.'

'I know. But I'm trying to keep an eye to her future. What if something were to happen to me and she needed her family's assistance?'

'Speaking of her future, how are you going to protect her after we land?'

'I've yet to figure out how to do that, control her brother and take over Roul at the same time. Short of putting her back on the ship with the women and sending them away, I am not certain what else to do.'

'That might be the best course of action.'

'I can't send a lone ship of women all the way back to King David and I have no certain allies in Normandy. So, where do you suggest I send them?'

When Samuel offered nothing more than a shrug, Elrik added, 'I thought about having them go just off shore. But for how long? While subduing Brandr's son and his companions should be easily accomplished, this taking possession of Roul could require nothing more than a few days with little or no fighting, or it could be weeks of battle.' He didn't give voice to the third option—they could be met by overwhelming forces and die—because every man went into battle with that knowledge.

'It is not like you to over worry things so much, Elrik.'

He sighed. 'A hazard of having a wife and a ship of women to protect.'

'Better you than me. I would set them up in a camp and be done with it.'

'Unfortunately, that's most likely what will happen.' Although, until they were all safely behind Roul's walls, he wouldn't be done with it.

'There is little time to consider what needs to be done.'

Samuel agreed. 'And with no head winds the last few days, we'll make landfall tomorrow morning.'

'Since there is nothing to be done until then, I'm going to take a bucket bath. You and Fulke see if the two of you can figure out a way for Avelyn to have a bath. Our method isn't going to work for her.'

Without waiting for a response, he climbed back down the ladder and headed to the other end of the ship where he took off his low-cut boots, stockings, shirt and braies. Once naked, Elrik dumped two buckets of cold water over his head, letting it sluice down his body. Someone handed him a small pot of soap and a rag.

He scrubbed and rinsed the soap off, then nabbed a drying cloth from one of the men.

An eerie sense of being watched crept up his spine. The laughter coming from his men along with their nods towards his cabin let him know who was watching him. He didn't need to turn around to know that Avelyn peered out at him.

With his back to her, he took his time wiping the water from his body and hair. He dropped the drying cloth, then bent to retrieve his braies. After stepping into them and securing the tie, he turned around and slowly stretched before running both of his hands through his hair to slick it back.

Avelyn's half-closed eyes and parted lips gained more than a few suggestive comments from the men. Elrik knew he'd provided the crew with more entertainment than he'd intended.

He glared at them, quelling their amusement, and asked, 'Do none of you have anything to do?'

The group quickly broke up. He grabbed the rest of his clothes and headed for the cabin.

She didn't move until he was within reach. Curling her fingers into the waist of his braies, Avelyn tugged him through the opening of the makeshift door and into her arms.

He laughed and tossed his clothes to the floor. 'Something you want, my lady?'

She pulled at the tie to his braies. 'Yes. You.'

The time they'd spent inside this cabin had done much to alleviate any shred of her embarrassment with him. He sighed heavily. 'Where has my shy, timid wife gone?'

She paused to lean back and look up at him. He was well aware that she did so to judge his mood. How long would it take for her to know instantly if he was serious, or just teasing her?

Finally smiling, she placed her palm over his obvious erection and answered, 'I fear that dying at least a thousand little deaths in your arms may have killed her.'

The soft laugh building in his chest wouldn't be contained. As it escaped he drew her into an embrace. 'You do realise the men will talk.'

She feathered tiny kisses against his chest. 'I am sure they have already been talking.'

'Elrik?'

Fulke's call from outside the door drew his attention. He released Avelyn slowly, his touch lingering to stroke down her arm. He promised, 'I'll not forget where we were.'

As he approached the door, he called out, 'What?'

'You wanted a bath for the lady?'

Avelyn pushed past him to tear open the heavy flap. 'Yes!'

Fulke and Samuel carried in a large wooden barrel that had been lined with sailcloth and placed it in the centre of the room.

'This is the best we could find on short notice. It is mostly watertight.'

'Mostly?' Elrik looked into the barrel, noting the steam rising from the hot water already inside.

'Once the water hits the halfway mark it starts to leak.'

Samuel added, 'That's all the hot water available. If you want more it will take some time.'

Avelyn was already taking off her soft boots. 'That is plenty.'

Knowing she wasn't about to wait for her bath, Elrik waved the men out of the cabin. 'Go. Thank you. Leave a few buckets of water by the door and I'll grab them.'

By the time he turned away from the door, Avelyn had already stripped down to her chemise. He dumped two buckets of cold water into the barrel and tested the water to make certain she wasn't going to climb into a scalding bath in her haste.

He set the buckets back outside the door, grabbed another one, then came back to see her stepping out of the chemise that was pooled on the floor.

'Wife, you are robbing me of my fun.'

She tossed her hair that was now free of a braid. 'Husband, you cannot blame me if you are too slow.'

He laughed at her quip as he set the bucket by the barrel and picked her clothing up from the floor to hang on a peg next to his tunic.

'Elrik, a hand, please.'

She stood at the side of the barrel, waiting for him to help her into the water.

He stared at her, wondering how he'd been so blessed. Not only did her lusty appetite match his, she was the loveliest woman he'd ever seen.

Her hips were nicely rounded and soft, providing a perfect place to grasp when he wanted to hold her still. And while her breasts were small, he had an inkling that the first time she bore a child they would fill out to be as soft and rounded as her hips.

'Elrik!'

Impatient, she shouted and waved her hand to beckon him closer.

He grabbed the small wooden stool and slowly, taking as much time as possible, joined her at the side of the barrel.

She narrowed her eyes, then moved close enough to slide her breasts against his chest.

When he did nothing but look down at her, she leaned harder against him, making a point to press her body suggestively against his groin.

Elrik winged a brow, then leaned around her to drop the stool into the water before delivering a quick tap to her bottom.

Avelyn jumped back. 'You hit me.'

He slung one arm behind her knees and the other across her back to lift her off her feet. 'I did no such thing.'

She wrapped her arms around his neck. 'Then what would you call it?'

'Gaining your attention.' Elrik kissed the end of her nose and lowered her into the water.

She leaned her head back against the rim of the barrel, closed her eyes and sighed. 'This is nice. Thank you.'

Standing behind her, Elrik traced the line of her throat. 'Lift your head.'

He scooped up a goblet full of water and dumped it over her head.

Avelyn sputtered. 'A warning would have been welcome.'

He reached down to refill the goblet, then paused with it above her head, long enough to say, 'Warning.'

She pushed her dripping hair out of her eyes. 'Do you have nothing else to do?'

'Yes.'

'Then feel free to go about doing it.'

He stepped away from the barrel. 'I forgot the soap.'

He retrieved a chunk from a small chest against the wall and returned to get it wet before rubbing it against her scalp.

'Elrik! Stop it.' She snatched the soap away and dropped it in the water. Reaching up to feel the mass of soap on the back of her head, she groaned. 'You have no idea how long it will take to rinse that out.'

His lips twitched. Actually, he was well aware of how long it would take. That had been the whole idea. They had this day left to them and he was going to make the most of it. Even if it meant acting the fool.

He cupped a hand to scoop up water and work it through the thick soap, repeating the process until the lather was thin enough to work through the length of her hair. Once satisfied the long thick rope of hair was clean, he used his fingertips to massage tiny circles against her scalp.

When she sighed, relaxing into his touch, he worked the tightness from the back of her neck and shoulders.

Again, using the goblet, he took his time rinsing her hair before fishing around for the soap.

She looked about the cabin. 'Is there a rag or wash cloth?'

He ignored her question, not wanting anything between his touch and her skin. Elrik ran his soapy hands over her back before pressing his fingertips down, then back up the length of her spine.

Avelyn arched her back beneath his touch, moaning.

Moving to the side of the barrel, he lifted her arm.

'You do know I can do this myself?'

'And what fun would that be?' he asked while soaping each of her fingers.

She leaned back against the barrel, her head tipped back against the rim. 'Who am I to deny you your fun?'

Running his hands slowly up her arms, he laughed softly. 'You couldn't stop me if you tried.'

She only nodded in response.

He went to the other side and repeated his actions with her other arm, set on memorising every inch of her body with his hands and fingers.

Stepping back, he debated…then tapped her knee. 'Lift your leg.'

It took a little work in the confines of the barrel, but she managed to prop her leg up on the rim.

He started with her foot, noting her frown as she twitched beneath his touch and moved quickly up her ankle and calf. He slowed his hands at her knee, making certain the soft skin behind was well washed.

Her frown relaxed and her fingers gripping the sides of the barrel made him smile. She might be sitting there quietly as if nothing was out of sorts, but he knew she found this leisurely bath anything but relaxing or soothing.

With both hands, he stroked and kneaded his way up her thigh, then slipped a hand up to glide over the curve of her hip.

He tapped her other knee. 'This one.'

He repeated the same process and by the time he'd finished, she was trembling and his heart thudded as he bent her leg to put it back down into the barrel.

Working the soap between his hands, he stood in front of her and stared down. Her eyes were closed, lips parted, nipples peaked and he could see the pulse tapping a steady beat beneath the skin of her neck. The erection pushing against the inside of his braies and the pounding of his heart inside his chest meant he wasn't any calmer than she.

He wondered who would call an end to this play first. Hopefully, neither of them. There was no way of knowing if they would ever have such a carefree time again. Why did that knowledge suddenly make his chest ache as if he'd lost something important to him?

He leaned over and ran his hands over her shoulders, then across her collar bone before sliding his palms slowly lower.

Avelyn's eyes opened. She held his gaze a moment, then frowned. Grasping his wrist, she asked, 'What is wrong?'

'Wrong?' He palmed a breast and teased the nipple with his thumb. 'Nothing is wrong. I am but bathing my wife.'

'There is no shimmer in your gaze. It is as if you are sad.' She sat up to stroke his cheek. 'You look at me as if you'll never see me again.'

'Don't be so fanciful.' He turned his head away from her touch. 'You are seeing things that aren't there.'

'Elrik, please. If you have plans to set me aside soon, tell me now. Let me savour what time is left to me without the burden of worrying when that time will come.'

He cursed beneath his breath and slid his hands beneath her arms to pull her up from the stool. Holding her close to his chest, he ignored the water pouring on to the floor. 'Avelyn, cease this worrying about being set aside. I will never do such a thing. I swear to you, while I have breath in my body, I will never forsake you.'

She clung to his shoulders. 'Then tell me what is wrong.'

The tremor in her voice made his stomach clench. How had she learned to discern his moods so quickly? 'We make landfall tomorrow. I do not know if, or when, we will ever be able to again share the carefree time we've had these last few days.'

She sighed. 'But we still have today and tonight?'

'Yes.'

'Then why are we wasting such precious time with a bath?'

Chapter Fourteen

Avelyn reached out in her sleep to find nothing but an empty space where her husband should have been. She came fully awake with a start, terrified that she'd slept through his leaving and sat up, calling, 'Elrik?'

She heard heavily booted footsteps cross the floor of the cabin, the tell-tale jingle of spurs and the clinking of chainmail. 'Here.'

The cabin was bathed in semi-darkness, the only light a small candle in the lantern sitting on the floor by his clothes chest. 'Has the sun even risen?'

'Just.'

She frowned at his harsh tone of voice, knowing that Lord Elrik of Roul had taken the place of her teasing husband. He had to have been up a while, because he was almost fully dressed for battle. She wondered who had assisted him into the mail while she slept. 'Did you get any sleep?'

'Enough.' He pulled his long sword belt and scabbard from the chest and secured the belt round his body.

'Have we made landfall?'

'Soon.'

Avelyn knew he was preoccupied, but his one-word answers served only to make her more worried.

Samuel entered the cabin, carrying a sword that he extended to Elrik. 'As sharp as can be.'

Avelyn pulled the covers up to her chin.

'Beg pardon, my lady, I didn't know you were awake,' Samuel apologised, then pulled two daggers from the back of his belt and handed them to Elrik, who slid one into a smaller scabbard hanging from his belt and the other into the top of a boot.

She now knew who had helped dress her husband and she was taken aback by the oddly sudden flare of jealousy flooding through her.

Samuel pulled two leather straps from the chest and wrapped them crosswise over Elrik's chest and back, before sliding two short swords into the leather-wrapped sheaths resting against his back.

Elrik reached over his shoulder. 'Higher.'

After shortening the straps and making certain the buckles were tight, Samuel stepped back.

This time when Elrik reached over each shoulder, he easily pulled a weapon free.

When he turned to look at her, Avelyn gasped. She'd spent four years in her father's keep. She'd seen men ready themselves for battle numerous times. But never had she seen a more frightening vision.

Samuel picked up Elrik's mailed gloves, head covering and metal helm, then left, saying, 'I'll leave you two alone.'

Elrik said nothing; he simply spread his arms. Without hesitation, Avelyn tossed aside the cover and nearly flew across the cabin to rush into his hard embrace.

He tried to pull her away, but she clung to him. 'Avelyn, you'll hurt yourself.'

'I don't care.' She looked up at him. 'Kiss me.'

He pulled her up against his chest. 'That was the plan.'

Thankfully, his hold was tight, otherwise Avelyn was

certain she would faint from the myriad of emotions overwhelming her. One after another—lust, need and longing—built at the sweep of his tongue across hers. Only to be followed by loss, sadness and fear. A cry caught in her throat. He could be killed. This could be the last time she tasted his kiss.

Elrik groaned and lifted his lips a breath away to whisper, 'Stop, Avelyn. Don't do this.'

Before she could respond, he swept her away once again.

Too soon he lowered her to her feet and broke their kiss. 'The men will be in here soon. You need to get dressed.'

Struck with the urgent need to tell him what she felt for him, she said, 'Elrik, I—'

'No.' He placed a finger over her lips to stop her from speaking. 'Do not.'

When she closed her lips, he said, 'I know what you think you feel. But it is only because you are afraid. Save your words for later, when all is settled and you are not beset by needless fear.'

He swiped his thumbs beneath her eyes to wipe away tears she didn't know had started to fall. 'Now, get dressed.'

She reluctantly moved away to pull her clothes off the clothes peg and tossed on her chemise and overgown.

Elrik pushed her trembling fingers aside and tied her laces before wrapping her belt low on her hips. He handed her her stockings and soft boots and waited until she sat down and donned them before putting a comb through her hair.

She patiently sat still, enjoying the brush of his fingers against her neck as he fumbled with making a long braid that fell down her back.

Finished, he kissed the top of her head before calling out for Samuel and Fulke to enter.

The two men came into the cabin. Neither man was

dressed for battle, their solemn expressions mirroring each other.

Avelyn rose and looked from them, to her husband. 'Elrik?'

He pulled a scroll from the chest and handed it to Samuel. 'If anything should happen, this will ensure everything I own falls to Avelyn unimpeded. Everything.'

She gasped, speechless.

At his nod, both men knelt—before her.

'See to her safety as you would mine. Be as loyal to her as you have been to me.'

They both swore to do so.

He stared at her. 'Treat them well, Avelyn.'

Avelyn looked from the men to her husband, her mind working furiously to comprehend what had just happened.

The two men rose and stood before her—waiting. However, she had no idea what they waited for.

The weight of his action settled cold around her heart. She stared at her husband. 'You cannot leave them with me. Elrik, who will protect your back? Who will warn of coming danger?'

He reached up over his shoulder and tapped a short sword. 'My back is protected. There are dozens of men to keep their eyes and ears attuned for danger.'

'Elrik, no.'

'It is done, Avelyn. These men are now yours.'

'What about Osbert?' He didn't realise how dangerous and unpredictable her half-brother might prove to be.

'You need not worry about Osbert. Why do you think I chose these guards for you?'

'No. Not for me, Elrik. For you—if his plan is to go after one of us, it will be you, not me. Had his plans centred on me, he would have stayed at Carlisle.'

'I am well able to handle your half-brother. This is not open for debate.'

Fear set her legs trembling. But from the stern look on his face and the furrowed brow, he wasn't going to change his mind for her—not about this.

She turned to Samuel and Fulke. 'Talk sense into him.'

Fulke shrugged. 'Do you think we haven't already tried?'

Samuel said, 'Can you not see that your safety is more important than his own? There is nothing any of us can say that will sway him. My lady, do not make this harder for everyone than it already is.'

'Enough.' Elrik pulled her into his embrace. Holding her close for a moment, he kissed her forehead, then relaxed his hold. 'You have nothing to fear, Avelyn. Edan and Rory will welcome you on Roul Isle if need be.'

'I don't want Edan, Rory, or Roul Isle. I want you.'

'You talk as though my death is already set when what you need to be doing is planning for the future. There is an entire keep that will need people to run it. And bed-chambers that will need to be filled with children. Avelyn, instead of thinking about my death, think about the hard work it will entail creating all those children.'

She laughed at his silliness, grateful that he'd taken the time to tease her.

'The three of you will have much to keep you busy. Lord Geoffrey, or one of his men, will meet me when we make landfall. An area will be set aside for you to make camp for yourselves, the women and the few men I leave behind to guard the camp.' He tipped her head so he could stare down at her. 'You are in charge, Avelyn. I will send word to you.'

She was in charge? Had he lost the ability to think clearly? She shook her head. 'No. I cannot be in charge.'

One brow lifted. 'There is no choice. These people will

look to me, or to you. As I won't be here, it will fall to you to make decisions.'

Her stomach rolled. She had never been in charge of anything, except making the decision to run away and that hadn't turned out so well. 'Elrik, put one of the men in your place.'

'Listen to me.' He frowned. 'I know everything is happening quickly. Remember, you are a king's great-grand-daughter. You are the wife of a baron. You need to start acting as such without delay.'

'But...' Her words trailed off. She didn't want to put her new worries on him. One way or another, she would have to work out how to deal with these fears on her own.

'If you need anything important, send me word. I'll see that an answer is returned quickly.'

They'd never discussed her learning—or lack of learning to read or write. She lowered her voice. 'I cannot.'

He studied her a moment before saying, 'We can remedy your father's lack of preparing you for this life, later. Both of your men can read and write. Samuel better than Fulke.'

It seemed wrong that the men who would answer to her were better suited for this task than she would ever become.

'Avelyn, do not worry so. Like you did at David's court, show them no fear. How you act, and how you appear, will go further than what you do, or do not, know. Act as if you know what you are doing. If you ask someone to do something and they ignore you, bark that request as an order—it will be followed. If it's not, you have men to correct that problem.'

'I am not certain I can get my voice quite as low as yours.'

He shrugged. 'Just don't screech and you'll be fine. Little dove, make certain to keep Samuel and Fulke close. Otherwise, I will worry and I've enough to do without having to be concerned for your welfare. Do you understand me?'

She nodded.

Without warning, he pulled her hard against his chest again and rested his cheek against her head. 'Be safe, Wife. Be strong. Be brave.'

He released her just as abruptly and left the cabin. She looked at Samuel and Fulke. 'You just stand there? Someone needs to help him with the rest of his armour and see that he gets safely to Lord Geoffrey.' When neither of them moved, she waved a hand towards the door. 'If one of you doesn't, I will.'

Samuel nodded, turned and left. Fulke remained. The last thing she wanted right this moment was anyone standing around watching her. She had every intention of having a good cry now, so that she wouldn't need to do so later when there would be more than enough work to be done and she would be surrounded by people expecting her to be strong.

'Does the sight of a woman's tears bother you?'

His eyes widened as if horrified by the mere mention of tears.

'I am going to throw myself on my pallet and cry until I can no longer do so. You might want to leave.'

He headed for the door at a near run, saying, 'I'll be right outside.'

Avelyn pushed the hair that had slipped free from her braid off her face. She surveyed the section of the camp they'd set up from her spot atop a small hill. In the waning light of the day, it appeared peaceful and inviting.

She hadn't received word from Elrik until late in the morning, so they'd all worked extra hard to unload the supplies they would need from the ships. The women and the small squad of guards assigned to the camp had all worked together without any major difficulties. She'd only had to call on Fulke's assistance once to end a dispute between two of the men. It had been immediately apparent that they'd been fighting over one of the women and she didn't want to put herself in the middle of that argument.

When she'd first stepped off the ship, it had been oddly comforting to find Little Lady saddled and waiting between Samuel and Fulke's horses. At least she didn't have to become accustomed to riding a new horse.

The area Lord Geoffrey had given them to use wasn't too far from where they'd made landfall and he'd also given them the use of two carts with draft horses, so transporting the supplies hadn't been too difficult.

In truth, the hardest thing for her all day thus far had been trying to decide where to set up the tents. The only experience she had came from the days she'd been on the road with Elrik and the men. She didn't want the cook fires too close to the trees for fear of stray embers starting a fire. But the denseness of the trees would provide additional shelter from rain. On the other hand, the same denseness would provide too much cover for anyone wishing to attack the camp.

It had been rather nerve racking to stand there trying to make up her mind with everyone looking at her expectantly. Samuel had come to her rescue by circling the area on his horse and bringing it to a stop in the middle of where he'd just ridden.

That's where the fire was built and the tents set up forming a half-circle on the side away from the woods.

So far, four tents had been erected—one for the camp women, one for the wives, another for the cook, her helpers and supplies, and the fourth for her. The men would make do with pallets on the ground near the fire tonight. She prayed it wouldn't rain. Tomorrow they would set up the remaining three tents for the men and the rest of the arms and supplies.

'You did a good job.'

Avelyn nearly jumped from the hill. She spun around and shouted, 'Don't do that! What are you doing here?' Then she took Elrik's hand, admitting, 'I am glad to see you.'

He released her hand to sling his arm over her shoulder and pull her next to his side. 'We spent the day poring over maps and details. Since I knew you were close, I didn't see why I should sleep alone this night.'

'When do you set out for Roul?'

'At first light.'

She gazed up at him. 'You look tired.'

'No. I'm more impatient than anything else. Just sitting around and talking about what needs to be done seems a waste to me.'

'Does Lord Geoffrey think it will be difficult to gain control of Roul?'

'He managed to get one of the neighbouring lords to see reason. So, we only have the other one to convince.' He nodded towards the camp. 'How did you get so much accomplished?'

She smiled at the ease in which he'd changed the direction of their conversation. 'Other than one fight that Fulke had to break apart, all of the women and guards worked together. Did you find Osbert?'

Elrik's laugh sounded downright evil. 'Oh, yes, I did. Found him and his five companions. They are currently polishing chainmail while under close watch.'

'You should have had them confined to a secure cell somewhere.'

'That might happen soon enough. But not until they give me cause, Avelyn. I can't just toss men into a cell without reason.'

'So, you will wait until he kills someone?'

'As closely as he is being watched, he won't get the chance.'

Little Lady walked over from where she'd been nibbling on some grass to push her nose into Elrik's back. He reached behind him and grabbed her reins. 'What do you want?'

Avelyn pulled some apple slices from the pouch hanging from her belt and handed them to him. 'Probably this.'

'You are going to ruin a good horse.'

'How so?'

'By giving her whatever she wants whenever she wants it.' He held his hand out flat and let the animal have the slices.

'You mean like you are? She deserves a treat for the work she did this day.' Avelyn stared up at the darkening sky. 'By the way, why is she here?'

'I wasn't about to leave her in King David's stable for you to ride off on.'

'Ah.'

'Why did you think she was here?'

'Nothing, never mind.'

He nudged her with his shoulder. 'Tell me.'

'I'd had some silly notion that perhaps you'd hoped I would join you.'

'For the horse?'

She nodded and followed his line of teasing. 'Yes, for the horse.'

'Something to keep in mind should I need you to travel somewhere you wish not to go. I'll just be sure to bring Little Lady along.'

'Perhaps by then I'll have chosen a different horse.'

'Where are Samuel and Fulke?'

She wrinkled her nose. 'They both needed bathing and

I didn't think it necessary that I went with them, so I sent them off to the stream.'

'They don't shirk their duty that easily. I have to assume you told them you'd stay in camp, but instead of doing so you came up here, in the open, alone?'

Avelyn nodded towards the camp. 'There are four guards, right there, watching.'

'None of them look like Samuel or Fulke to me.'

'No. They don't. I think they might be younger.'

'With less experience.'

Avelyn flinched at his harsh tone. He wasn't teasing her, he was angry. When she tried to step away, he tightened his hold on her shoulder to keep her at his side.

'I thought I told you to keep Samuel and Fulke nearby at all times.'

'You did.'

'And in the span of one day you decided to ignore my advice?'

'Advice? It was more like an order.'

Realising her mistake by admitting that she knew it had been an order, she quickly shut her mouth.

'That's worse. You understood it as an order and intentionally ignored it.'

Avelyn remained silent. What could she say?

'Would you care to explain your reasoning for willingly placing yourself in danger?'

'Did you not tell me that I was in charge? And that I was to be brave and strong?'

'I'll not argue this with you, Avelyn. There is a difference between brave and foolish.' He swung his arm out sweeping the area between the camp and this hill. 'You are unarmed. And if your father did not bother to ensure you could read, write, or even ride a horse, I am certain you were never instructed on the use of any weapon.'

When again she remained silent, he asked, 'Am I right?'

'Yes.'

'While I have no qualms rescuing a maiden in need, it would be quite hard to do if I were not here and worse if you'd put yourself in harm's way after being told not to do so.'

'It appears so peaceful here, I did not think there would be any danger.'

'A snake hides in the soft, lush grass for a reason.'

She couldn't argue that logic. Avelyn turned towards him and rested her palm on his chest. 'I am sorry, Elrik.'

'I don't care if you are sorry or not. Don't do it again. See to the camp, see to the household duties of Roul when we gain possession. All else is under my control and you will follow my orders. Understood?'

She tamped back the urge to bristle at his high hand-edness. This was not what she'd wanted from a husband. She'd never wanted someone who would control her, order her about—she'd wanted someone to be her partner, sharing in all things.

But to keep him from having to be concerned about her well-being, she answered, 'Yes, I understand.'

He grasped her chin and stroked his thumb across her lip. 'Liar. For now, Avelyn, do as I ask. We can renegotiate later.'

That he knew the direction of her thoughts made her smile. 'Are you hungry?'

'Not at all.'

'Tired?'

He grabbed the reins of both horses, saying, 'No. But I would like to stretch out in a tent and share a goblet or two of wine alone with my wife'

'Is that all?'

He took her hand and started towards the camp. 'We will see where the night leads us.'

Chapter Fifteen

'Stop. Stop. Please, stop,' Avelyn whispered between clenched teeth.

Fulke rose from his seat on a log next to her. 'We are just trying to help.'

'I know.' She tossed the stick she had been using to crudely draw letters in the dirt at their feet into the bushes behind them. 'I am too stupid to learn.'

'Stop that.' Samuel retrieved the stick. 'You, my lady, are not stupid. Frustrated because of Elrik's absence, but not stupid.' He handed the writing implement back to her. 'Now try it again.'

Fulke cleared her previous scratches from the dirt with his foot, then tapped the area with the toe of his boot, ordering, 'Your name.'

She didn't want to write her name, or learn letters and numbers. She wanted to touch her husband, hear his voice, feel his strong arms pulling her close. It had been three long unending weeks since any of those things had happened.

Yes, he'd sent missives daily. Short, brief letters describing what he'd done that day. Letters that contained nothing of a personal nature because he knew Samuel or Fulke would be reading them to her.

If she ever wanted that to change, she needed to focus on these lessons. Bending to the task at hand, she drew the letters of her name.

Before she could complete her fifth try, a loud commotion broke out in the camp. It sounded as if quite a few of the men were fighting. 'Go.' She rose, waving Samuel and Fulke ahead. When they hesitated, she said, 'I will be right behind you.'

'Avelyn.'

She froze in place, unwilling to look towards the voice calling her name. It couldn't be. How could it? Elrik had him under guard.

'Avelyn.'

Closing her eyes, she fought with the need to cry out for Samuel or Fulke. They were needed in the camp. She could deal with this distraction on her own. She was no longer a child who could be easily cowed.

Slowly she turned around to scan the bushes between her and the stream.

A head popped up from between two of the larger bushes. 'Avelyn, here.'

Checking behind her, to make certain no one was watching, she went towards the bushes. 'What are you doing here, Osbert?'

When she was close enough, he grasped her wrist and tugged her along upstream from where the laundry was done.

'Why are you here? Did your father send you?' she asked once they'd stopped and he released her.

'*My* father? Don't you mean *our* father?'

'That man is dead to me.'

'Of course, he is, especially now since you snagged not only our great-grandfather's interest, but that of King David and your titled husband. You no longer require his assistance to survive.'

'I never required his assistance.' As far as she was concerned, she would have been better off without it.

'Blame your mother for that. Had she not had proof that you were indeed a Brandr, he never would have come to the village.'

He was talking about her grandmother's ring. The one she'd safely stowed inside Elrik's clothing chest back in their tent. If she'd had it around her neck right now, she would gladly give it to Osbert in hopes that he would then leave her alone.

'You always were the lucky one.'

Lucky? She stared at her half-brother, recognising his whining tone of voice for what it was—unwarranted jealousy. This boy, two years her senior, had always acted like a petulant child, pouting and railing until he got his way and turning vicious when he didn't.

When he'd been fostered out to a neighbouring lord last year she'd hoped she'd seen the last of him.

Once again, her hopes had been in vain.

'What do you want?'

'Oh, come now, don't sound so vexed. Surely you aren't still angry over childish pranks?'

'Childish pranks?' Avelyn heard her higher pitch and stopped to swallow. The last thing she wanted to do was to let him think he had the upper hand, or that he was still capable of making her so angry that she lost the ability to think.

She repeated her previous question. 'What do you want?'

'Since you seem to have gained such lofty connections, I thought you could easily find me a place.'

'A place?' She knew that for the lie it was. Even if what he said were true, why would she do anything for him? Why would he assume she'd even be willing to do so? 'I thought you and your companions had a place cleaning armour.'

'So, you knew I was here all along.'

'Of course. And so does my husband.'

From the slight widening of his eyes it seemed that information took him by surprise. She laughed at him. 'You are not dealing with servants or villagers who you can torment at will. King David's Wolf will not be so easily controlled.'

'Perhaps. But just like servants and villagers he can bleed.'

She took a step towards him. 'One scratch and I swear, Osbert, I will take your life without remorse.'

'And I can promise you, should that happen, Father will skin you alive.'

He could try, but he would only get to her through Elrik and she doubted that would ever happen. 'Are you here on his orders?'

'That's none of your concern. The only thing you need to worry about is finding me a position in Roul's household.'

The last thing she would do was find him a position in any household where she resided. 'Mucking stalls, perhaps?'

His already thin lips tightened, nearly disappearing as he took a step towards her.

A year ago, she would have cowered beneath his threatening move. But that was before she'd run away, before she'd become the Wolf's wife and before she'd become the Lady of Roul. He was not going to threaten her any longer.

Avelyn stared at him, unflinching. 'You had a place with Lord Westfall. Why are you not there now?'

'His youngest daughter and I fell in love, but Westfall disagreed with the idea of our betrothal.'

Westfall's daughter either lacked the ability to see and reason, or Osbert was lying again.

Her half-brother shrugged. 'He caught us kissing in the stable and, to make herself look innocent, she cried rape, so I was thrown from his keep.'

Cried rape? That was the reason he'd been sent away last year. Two of her father's maids *cried rape* and from the way they'd been beaten she'd believed it had happened. But they'd been ordered away like her mother had been and, soon after, Osbert was sent to foster with Westfall.

'Instead of returning to Father, I thought since you and I have so much in common you'd be more than happy to find me a place.'

He truly didn't believe that he was fooling her, did he? He was here for some other reason and she was certain that was to bring harm to her and Elrik.

'So much in common? What exactly do we have in common?'

'We are both Brandr bastards.'

'So?' It was not as if anyone could tell by looking at them. Their father was dark and built like a barrel. She'd always been told that she looked like her grandmother, with dark hair and ice-blue eyes. This boy was so fair he appeared sickly, thin with no muscle and had ginger-coloured hair.

'We were raised in the same household and have the same temperament.'

Had she been prone to cursing she'd have done so. 'You were raised at the keep from birth. I didn't even know who my father was until a few years ago. As for having the same temperament...no, not at all.'

He stepped even closer, putting him nearly on top of her, then reached out to stroke her hair.

Before she could back away, Osbert pulled her into an unwelcome embrace. 'Come, Sister, let us set aside childhood mistakes.'

He was laughing. She heard it. Felt it shaking against her chest.

The feeling that he was up to something, seeking once again to bring her harm, flooded her. At the same moment, the exact same heartbeat, Avelyn felt someone watching them. Not just someone, but she felt her husband's hard stare boring a hole through her back.

Shoving at Osbert with all her might, she shouted, 'You did this on purpose!'

She spun around to see Elrik riding towards the bridge to cross the rapidly moving stream. He would not make it to her in time to keep Osbert from doing her harm.

Her half-brother laughed. 'What is wrong, dear Sister?'

Avelyn fisted her hands and turned back to him. 'How long had you planned this? Will you not be happy until you have taken all from me?'

'No. I won't. How does it feel to have something you held dear stripped from your hands? How do you think I felt when Father brought you into my home? And now that you of all people gained the attention of our great-grandfather is more than I am willing to bear.'

He grabbed her, his deadly intention clear in his wild-eyed stare. 'Twice I have sought your death, only to be thwarted. I'll not fail again.'

Unwilling to die at the hands of this snake, and with her own deadly intention firmly in place, Avelyn raised her knee hard and fast, slamming it into his groin. As he fell to the ground, she ran for the road that would lead her to Elrik.

Near blinded by tears, she managed to make out the form of him and his horse as the sound of pounding hooves raced towards her.

Elrik brought the horse to a stop, reached down to grab a handful of her gown and hauled her up against his chest.

Holding her tightly with one arm, he asked, 'You are un-harmed?'

Unable to speak, she nodded.

He kept her against his chest as he rode into camp and lowered her to the ground. She stumbled and fell at Sam-uel and Fulke's feet.

Before she could utter a word, Elrik slipped from his horse and pulled her up from the ground.

'What—?' Fulke's question fell silent at the dark look on Elrik's face.

She knew by his rage-filled expression that he'd misun-derstood what he'd seen with Osbert, just as her half-brother had expected. Avelyn threw herself against his chest. 'Elrik, please, listen to me.'

He shook his head one time and dragged her into their tent where he pulled himself free of her hold and let her fall to the floor.

She wanted to curl into a ball and cry, but knew that somehow, she had to make him understand what he'd wit-nessed.

'Elrik—'

'Close your mouth.'

Avelyn shivered. Never had she seen his eyes so dark, or his expression so bleak.

'Like a blind fool, I could have come to love you.'

Those few words, spoken with such sadness and loath-ing, settled like ice around her heart. With one unwanted embrace Osbert had taken all she held dear, all she had hoped for, all she had ever dreamed of having in this life.

No.

Avelyn pulled herself to her feet. She was not about to let this happen, not without a fight. And this marriage, this man was worth fighting for. No one in her family was going to destroy her, or her future.

He might be angry. He would probably shout and might say things he didn't mean. He could very well break her heart, but he would not physically hurt her.

She grasped his wrist, hanging on for dear life when he tried to shake free. 'Elrik, listen to me.'

He stared past her, through her, at the side of the tent as if she weren't there. Did he think it would be that easy to ignore her? No matter how much she wanted to cry in fear and frustration, it would gain her nothing. But she was certain that rage would get his attention.

Without releasing his wrist, she moved into his line of vision. 'I thought Wolves were smart and cunning. Ruthless hunters who measured every move. When did you lose the ability to see beyond what was before you? Has Lord Geoffrey somehow turned my Wolf into a pet dog?'

She was shocked at the words coming out of her mouth, but at least he was now staring at her instead of through her. It was a start.

'You know how much I hate my father and how I despise my half-brother. You claim to be able to see through my lies. Then clear your sight enough to see me now, Roul. Tell me if I lie. Osbert, a selfish, arrogant tyrant, fooled you on purpose and, like any good fool, you believed his actions were true. Worse, without any proof, you believe I have plotted and planned with him against you.'

One dark eyebrow arched and it took every ounce of willpower she possessed not to smile. 'You can hate me all you desire. I never wanted your love. But I have not betrayed you and, for that, I expect to be treated with honour.'

He twisted his arm, breaking free of her hold and grabbed a handful of hair at the back of her head to pull her closer. For a brief moment Avelyn wondered if maybe she'd gone too far.

With his mouth a breath away from hers, he asked, 'A pet dog?'

No amount of self-control could have stopped her relieved laugh from escaping. But he silenced it with a harsh kiss that quickly turned demanding and hungry.

Avelyn clung to him, groaning at the chainmail that kept her from curling her fingers into his shoulders.

He relaxed his hold and lifted his lips from hers. 'Woman, one of these days you will get yourself killed.'

'Perhaps. But not at your hands.' From his kiss maybe, but at least she would die with a sigh of pleasure.

Elrik turned and walked out of the tent. For one heartbeat she feared he was leaving, but her worry dissolved when she heard him barking orders at Samuel and Fulke. Then, just as abruptly, he came back into their tent.

Stripping off his sword belt, he asked, 'Why was your brother here?'

'I think that is my question for you. How did he escape your guards' watchful eyes?'

'Since both of them were found dead, hanging from a tree, I'd say that aided in his escape.' He pulled his tunic over his head and dropped it on the floor.

Avelyn gasped. Not again. Her heart ached at the memories flooding her mind. The stable boy's mother had been inconsolable when she'd been informed of her son's death. The families of these men would likely be just as distraught. It would be one thing to learn their beloved had perished in battle, that might be expected, but to learn they'd been murdered would be nearly impossible for them to understand.

Elrik looked down and frowned. 'What is troubling you?'

She took a breath to still her trembling. 'It is not the first time Osbert has so heartlessly killed another.'

'It will be the last.' He tossed the coiffe down on top of his tunic and reached for the laces of his armour.

Avelyn batted his fingers away and started to unlace his hauberk. 'No tears will be shed for him.'

She tugged at the lacings running down the back of his armour and, noting a few mangled dents in some of the links, asked, 'How are you?'

'A few nicks. Otherwise my body is whole. Why have I once again found you without your guards?'

She'd expected him to target in on that sooner or later, so his quick change of subject didn't surprise her. 'They had just left. I was on my way to join them when Osbert showed up.' Avelyn pushed at his shoulder. 'Lean over.'

'And you couldn't call them back to your side?'

'They were attending to a fight back at camp, so, no.' She tugged at his hauberk, trying to move it up to his shoulders.

'Likely one started by Osbert's friends as a distraction.' He shrugged the mail from his body and let it pool into a pile on the floor. Then straightened with a sigh. 'I haven't been free of that armour for five days. Thank you.'

Once she'd divested him of his mailed leg coverings and quilted shirt, she circled him, checking to assure herself that he was indeed whole. Coming back to stand before him, she poked his chest with a finger. 'You have been but a day's ride away, yet I have not seen you for three weeks.' She poked him again. 'What explanation do you have for that?'

His crooked half-smile made her want to scream. She hadn't intended to amuse him.

He reached for her, asking, 'Did you miss me?'

Miss him? Only every moment of every day. But telling him that would give away the fact that she had begun to feel more for him than even she found comfortable and she wasn't yet willing to do that. Avelyn spun away. 'No.'

'I wrote to you daily.'

'Oh, yes. Tender words detailing how much ground had been covered, the level of resistance met in the villages and how much closer you were to securing Roul Keep. Words any woman would cherish.'

Avelyn clamped her lips closed to stop the words flowing from her mouth. What was wrong with her? He had done nothing to upset or confuse her in this manner. Yet she was both and becoming more upset with each passing heartbeat. For no good reason.

He hadn't lost his temper. He'd listened to her and had believed her about Osbert. He was whole, unharmed by any recent battle. She should be relieved. Why then did she find herself fighting back tears? What caused this tightness in her throat? And why did she feel as if her heart were breaking over nothing?

Elrik paused. Slowly turning, confused by her clipped tone of voice, he watched her busy herself with gathering his clothing. That finished, she started arranging and re-arranging items on the small table in the corner. He tipped his head, noting the stiffness of her back and slight tremor of her hands. Mostly he noticed the way she was pointedly ignoring him.

'I wanted to tell you how much I longed to kiss your lips. And that the nights were far too cold without the warmth of your body pressed against me. Or how I wanted to caress the softness of your breasts and taste the sweetness of your heat. But mostly I wanted to tell you how much I ached to make you cry out with release as you pressed your talons into my back.'

'Now you are talking nonsense.'

She hadn't turned around, but he heard what sounded like a sniffle. 'Avelyn, I tire of waiting. Come here.'

Her arms wrapped around him and she buried her face against his chest before he could draw another breath.

His lips against her ear, he whispered, 'It isn't nonsense if it's the truth. The only reason I didn't write those things was because I didn't think you wanted to provide Samuel and Fulke with that much amusement.'

'Elrik. Stop talking.'

He lifted his head and blinked. The sudden dampness on the front of his shirt, the broken shaking of her voice made it clear she was crying. Why? He hadn't done anything, or said anything he could think of to cause her to be this upset.

'Avelyn, talk to me.'

'No.' She tipped her head back and reached up a hand to draw his face closer. 'Talking is not what I want.'

For the first time, his wife kissed him. Her lips worked across his, her tongue slid against his. There was no doubt about who was initiating this and he had no complaint— for now he would let her have her way. He was curious to see how far she would go alone. He wondered how long would it take for her to realise this was much better when both of them participated.

Cool fingers slipped beneath his shirt to stroke down his chest and against his belly before deftly releasing the tie of his braies. Curiosity dimmed as she wrapped her fingers around his hard length.

He held back a groan of disappointment when she released him too soon and issued a frustrated groan of her own.

'Elrik.'

Lifting her with one arm and hanging on to his loose braies with the other, he strode to their bed. It didn't take long for both of them to tumble naked on to the pallet.

Elrik pulled her beneath him to bury his face against her neck. He just lay there, supporting most of his weight on his forearms, relaxing atop the softness of her body and savouring the scent that was distinctly her.

This was what he had really missed—the little things—
the sound of her voice, the tone of her laugh, the lilt of her
teasing. The way she would roll her eyes when he tried to
torment her, or her breathless sigh after a kiss.

How had this happened in such a short amount of time?
Steadily, bit by bit. He'd come to listen for her voice and her
laugh on their way to Carlisle. Aboard the ship he'd found
himself teasingly tormenting her just to see her eyes narrow in exasperation and to hear her voice change when she
teased him back.

He lifted his head to look down at her, asking again,
'Did you miss me?'

Avelyn trailed her fingertips across his back. 'I missed
this.'

Raising up, he entered her slowly. 'This?'

Her eyes fluttered closed. 'Oh, yes.'

He wanted more than that. She could miss physical contact with any man she was married to whether she cared for
him or not. He wanted her to have longed for him—all of
him. As agonising as it was, he stopped moving until she
once again returned his gaze.

'And you, Elrik. Yes, I missed you.'

Chapter Sixteen

Avelyn awoke and squinted against the sunlight streaming into the tent. She frowned in confusion until her mind slowly came awake, too.

They'd spent the last many hours in bed oblivious of the afternoon, evening, night and rising of the sun slipping by.

If she were to marry dozens of different men, all of them added together could not come close to providing the excitement, or fulfilment Elrik did. Her cheeks burned just thinking about the way they'd so passionately passed the hours.

There were obvious benefits to being wed. However, no matter how much she enjoyed the time they spent together in bed, that was nothing upon which to base a marriage.

She'd wanted a husband she could call friend. Did she have that with Elrik? In a way, yes.

He walked into the tent, fully dressed in his armour, except for his gloves and head covering, and closed the flap behind him. She stared at him and couldn't stop herself from sighing.

The sound caught his attention, he looked at her. 'What are you doing?'

'Thinking.'

His dark eyebrows disappeared beneath the hair hanging over his forehead. 'I am uncertain if I like that or not.'

She laughed. Yes. She considered him a friend. They could tease and jest with each other.

He crossed to the pallet to extend a hand, helping her up from the bed. 'What are you thinking about?'

'You. Me.' She glanced over her shoulder at the pallet. 'And other things.'

His laugh rumbled up his chest. 'Thinking about those other things could get you in trouble.'

She leaned against him. 'I've recently learned that I rather enjoy that sort of trouble.'

He swung her round so her back rested against his chest, then curled both of his arms tightly about her body to hold her close and whispered against her ear, 'I need to find you another name. Little Dove doesn't suit one who purrs and stretches like a satisfied cat.'

Avelyn ignored the burning of her face to respond, 'Thankfully I don't have the same problem since you growl just like a wolf.'

Cupping one breast, he groaned. 'This next day will feel like years.'

'You have plenty to keep you busy.'

'And all the while I'll be distracted with thoughts that will make wearing this armour unbearable.'

She reached up to stroke his cheek. 'You have only yourself to blame for the direction of your thoughts.'

'If you remember correctly, you will discover that you were the one who urged me on in some of those directions.'

She trembled against him. 'The act of remembering would not be wise with you standing so near.'

'Ah, but I am fully clothed.'

'I seem to recall you shedding all of your clothing yesterday with a little help.'

'And caught hell for my mistreatment of the armour this morning from a churlish squire.'

'My big, strong, brave wolf fears a puny squire?'

'I seem to have taught him too well.' He nipped her earlobe. 'Be careful, or I will send you to deal with him.'

Her returning quip got lost in the air when he stroked a palm down her belly. She grabbed his wrist. 'Elrik, no. Do not leave me in a state of need when I have much to do, too.'

'I hadn't planned on leaving you needing.'

Thankfully, he let her pull his arm back up to her waist. 'Now that you've tried to distract me, did they find Osbert?'

He released her. 'Get dressed, we'll talk while we eat.'

Apparently, the answer would be no, they hadn't. Otherwise his playful mood wouldn't have ended so abruptly. She bent to retrieve her chemise from the floor, which gained her a quick pinch on her bottom.

She jumped and swung around to point towards the tent's flap. 'Go away, Elrik.'

He sat down on the stool, trailing his half-closed gaze from her toes to the top of her head. 'I will be leaving soon enough. Right now, I plan on enjoying the view before me.'

Avelyn walked over to a small chest, nabbing her stockings and gown as she walked by them and placed them on the nearby table along with her chemise. She looked over her shoulder at her husband.

'Now what are you doing?'

'You wanted a view.'

She picked up one stocking and drew it over her foot. Placing her foot atop the chest, she slowly smoothed the stocking up her leg, then, as if unsatisfied with the fit, rolled it back down to her ankle and once again smoothed it up her leg, taking her time to get it on right.

She glanced in Elrik's direction and smiled at the purely evil grin starting to tug at the Wolf's lips.

She then repeated the whole process with the other stocking.

'Tell me, Little Dove, what makes you think playing with fire is wise?'

Avelyn laughed at the roughness of his voice, then dropped her chemise over her head. 'You wanted a view. I was only trying to help.'

'My innocent little wife is certainly a fast learner.'

His tone had changed. She looked at him. He didn't appear angry, but his frown was not an indication of amusement. 'What are you saying?'

He shook his head. 'Nothing, Avelyn. I am not saying anything.'

'You sounded as if you were accusing me of something.'

'I wasn't accusing you of anything other than being a fast learner.'

Did he think someone other than just him was giving her lessons? She paused. No. Now she was reading things into his words that perhaps weren't there. She tugged on her gown. Again, confusion was clouding her thoughts. What was it about him that made her forget how to reason?

Elrik rose to come to her side. He pushed her hands away. 'Let me.' Lacing up her gown, he asked, 'What do you think I am accusing you of doing?'

She shook her head.

'Avelyn, I know you haven't been with another man. I also know you rarely visit the women's tent.'

How did he *know* these things? Were Samuel and Fulke there to guard her, or watch her?

With a finger beneath her chin, he turned her gaze to his. 'Do not do this.'

'Do what?'

'Do not imagine words I have not said. Do not twist things I do say into something I never meant.'

'How do you *know* what I do in this camp when you aren't here?'

'Now you think I have spies watching you?'

'Samuel and Fulke were your men.'

'And now they are yours. I chose them for the simple fact that I knew they would be loyal to you. Yes, they have been my friends since childhood, but, Avelyn, unless you are in grave danger, or dire need, they are not going to come running to me.'

'Then how do you *know* what has been happening in this camp?'

'It doesn't require a great deal of deceit on my part to know what goes on in my absence. All I have to do is listen. Who talks about you? The cook and her helpers. The laundress and her helpers. The wives of the men. Everyone.'

'Everyone?'

'Yes. It is obvious from listening to them that you spend more time in their company than anywhere else. That is what I do. As David's Wolf, I was tasked with finding things and people. To do that I needed to listen and to watch with a keener sense than most. As careful as you were when you ran away, you left a trail for me to follow. Rumours of a black-haired wench and people who sought to hide those rumours led me straight to you. I will always see more, and hear more, than most other men you know. I cannot help that. I will always know when you are upset, angry, happy, sad, or wanting. I will know by the tone of your voice, the stance of your body, the rhythm of your breath. And I know that right now you refuse to meet my gaze and you hold yourself away, not because you are afraid or angry, but because you are undecided—uncertain about something.'

'I apologise. I…' She grew silent, not knowing what to say. He was right. She was uncertain. About him and her, them. Before she could stop herself, she looked at him and said, 'I don't want to care for you. I never wanted anything more than a friend.'

He stepped back as if shoved by an unseen hand. 'We are married.'

His tone held an undercurrent of sadness. She hadn't meant to hurt him. This was what she wanted to avoid. But since she'd already said too much, she had to find a way to explain herself. 'Neither of us wed for something as petty or useless as love. Both of us know what kind of pain it causes. I don't want it, Elrik. I don't want to care for you in a way that will bring me nothing but heartache.'

'Avelyn, do you seek to separate us over something you cannot control? If I died in battle today, would you grieve my loss?'

She gasped as agony washed over her at just the thought. 'Greatly. I would miss you terribly.'

'What would you miss?'

What would she miss? His touch, the sound of his voice, his laugh. The shimmering warmth of his gaze. His sigh of contentment and moan of satisfaction. 'I would miss you— all of you. Everything about you.'

He approached her to gather her close. 'I will gain possession of Roul before the sun sets this day. You and the others will be joining me at our keep tomorrow.'

'So soon?'

'Yes. That soon. Do not send me away wondering if you will still be here when I return.'

'I would not do that to you.' She shook her head. 'Elrik, I will not run away from you. If I were to ever leave…it would be with your knowledge.'

'Your hesitation tells me that you have given this no thought.'

'Not until this moment, no, I haven't.' She leaned against him, sighing as his arms came around her. 'Elrik, my mind is in conflict with these feelings I don't understand. I don't know what to think any more.'

'Then stop thinking. Stop tearing everything apart to look at it so closely.' He kissed the top of her head. 'Listen to the feelings instead.'

'No. My mother wasted her entire life pining over someone she could never have instead of realising that he'd never been hers to begin with. Had she thought with her head instead of letting feelings rule her, she might not have died bitter, lonely and sad.'

'You are not your mother. I am most assuredly not Brandr. I am not someone you could never have—I am someone you already do have. For just a day or two, a very short time, try not to *think* about me, or this marriage of ours.'

'I don't know if I can do that.'

'Of course, you can. You do it by instinct when you are angry or afraid. You don't think about it—you react. That's all I ask you try. Close your eyes and let your heart lead you. Just for a short time.'

'This coming from a man who mere weeks ago claimed that he wished not to wed anyone? A man who believed not in love or tender feelings?'

He laughed softly. 'I know little about love or tender feelings. All I do know is that when I am with you, I have no desire to be anywhere else.'

'I feel the same way, but I don't understand why.'

He grasped her shoulders and pulled her away. 'That is what you need to stop doing. What difference does *why* make? Who cares why? It simply is the way it is. What else do you need to know?'

She frowned, trying unsuccessfully to sort it out, then placed a hand on his chest. 'For right now, I need know nothing else.'

'Good. Now, let us eat and discuss your half-brother with Samuel and Fulke, so we can get this day over.'

Soon, too soon, she watched him ride away leaving Samuel and Fulke standing at her side. She'd tried so hard to make Elrik take his men with him. With Osbert still out there, he needed the extra protection more than she.

But he'd flatly refused, quickly becoming angry enough to order her to stop begging. All she could do now was hope and pray that Osbert was as unsuccessful in killing her husband as he had been trying to kill her.

Hope, pray and pace.

And pace she did. Nothing held her attention. Every little sound—pans clanging together, the scrape of blades being sharpened, the clink of a guard's chainmail—had her ready to jump out of her skin until she wanted to do nothing more than scream.

By the time the evening meal came around, she was so sick with worry that nothing the cook tried to tempt her into eating looked, sounded or smelled appealing. It wasn't food she craved—it was the sound of Elrik's voice.

She didn't care if it was the deep rumble of his laugh, or the cold harshness of anger—she simply needed to know he was safe and sound.

Heavy footsteps behind her made her glance over her shoulder. Samuel and Fulke stopped alongside. 'I like this not.'

She looked up at Fulke. 'And you think I do?'

'He said the fighting was all but over and that the only thing left to do was to send this trespasser and his followers out of the keep.'

Samuel only repeated what Elrik had told all of them earlier.

'Then perhaps one, or both, of you need to go find out what is happening to cause this delay.'

They both looked at her and shook their heads. Fulke said, 'He would kill us if we left you.'

'Who do you answer to? Him, or me?'

'You,' they answered in unison.

'Well, what are you waiting for then?'

Fulke tipped his head towards the horses, telling Samuel, 'You go. I'll keep guard.'

Saddling up his horse quickly with the help of a younger lad, Samuel rode out of camp.

Avelyn's stomach still knotted with the sense that something was wrong. She couldn't shake the trepidation, this odd knowing, that danger chased her husband.

'Lady Avelyn!'

The pounding of hooves and a strange voice shouting her name sent her running to the middle of the camp. Fulke followed, a string of curses leaving his mouth in a loud rush.

Elrik's squire jerked the reins of his horse, bringing the lathered animal to a rearing stop. Three other men, guards, followed suit. Fulke grabbed her arm, pulling her out of the beasts' paths.

Out of breath, filthy and blood-spattered, the squire fell to his knees at her feet, gasping, 'My lady.'

Unable to still the shaking of her legs, Avelyn dropped to the ground and grasped his shoulders. 'You are injured.'

'Not…my…blood.'

Her head spun. She knew whose blood splattered his tunic before he said, 'Lord Elrik… My lady…he…'

'No. No. No.' Avelyn rose to stagger backwards away from the blood, away from what her eyes saw and her heart felt.

No. She refused to accept what her gut was telling her. He was *not* dead.

They'd come too far. He'd risked too much for him to have perished now.

More horses thundered into the camp. She turned to see the men, but her vision failed her. Clouded by her fear, they were nothing more than blurry, unrecognisable forms.

A whine, a high-pitched moan rang in her ears, blocking out the voices around her.

Without warning, a strong pair of arms pulled her forcefully against a hard chest. Links of chainmail bit into her cheek. She struggled against the near-brutal hold until she was lifted from her feet and a low, rumbling growl brushed hot against her ear.

Relief at the menacing sound collided with rage and she beat her fists uselessly against his back. 'Damn you, Elrik.'

'And you said you couldn't let your heart lead you.'

'So, you let me believe the worst, just as a test?'

'God, no, woman. I lost a race back to camp is all. Seems my squire is a bit lighter in the saddle than I.'

'Don't ever do that again.'

'Lose a race?'

He'd intentionally misunderstood. She glared at him. 'Put me down.'

When he lowered her to the ground, she scolded, 'You knew I was waiting for you. You knew I would be worried. Don't you ever put me through that again. Ever. Do you hear me?'

He reached out and brushed his thumb and a finger beneath her eyes, then held his hand up to study them and said, 'These can't possibly be tears. If they were, I would have to wonder if perhaps you may have let yourself care for me.'

She spun around and took one step away before he grasped her wrist. 'Come, I'll tease you no more.'

'Liar.' She leaned against his chest.

'Probably.' He ran a hand through her hair to tilt her head back. 'Are you ready to go for a ride?'

'Where?'

'Roul.' He tossed his nasal helmet to a nearby page and pushed the mail head covering back to rest against his neck.

'Elrik, the sun has begun to set. It will soon be—you are bleeding!'

'It is nothing.'

'Nothing?' She swiped a finger across his brow. 'Feels like blood to me.' Taking his hand, she led him over to a stool and pushed him down, asking, 'How did this happen?'

He snorted.

She snorted back at him, adding, 'That is not an answer.'

Before he could say anything, her heart skipped a beat. 'It was not Osbert, was it?'

'No. He nor his companions have been seen.'

'Then how?'

'The fool who tried to take Roul thought challenging me to a fight would somehow be a wise move.'

Avelyn motioned to one of the women who brought her a cloth and a bucket of water. She wiped the drying blood from his brow and tsked. 'That'll leave a scar. What did he hit you with?'

'His helmet.'

'And you let him?'

'It's not as if I was expecting him to ram his head into my face.'

'And where is this fool now?'

'Safely imprisoned in one of the Duke's cells. He is no longer my problem.'

She dipped the cloth back into the water and wrung it out before lifting it towards him again. He caught her hand, stopping her. 'Are you finished?'

'This should be stitched closed.'

'Can you ply a needle?'

'I can.' She laughed. 'However, it will be far from pretty.'

'Heaven forbid you mar this lovely visage.'

'It is a very handsome visage and I would prefer it not be used as a cloth for sewing practice.'

'I will make you a deal. We go to Roul now and if it is still bleeding when we arrive, you and Samuel can argue over who can do a cleaner stitch.'

She heard Samuel's chortle from behind her. He tapped her on the shoulder. 'My lady?'

When she turned around, he handed her the reins to a saddled Little Lady.

'Elrik, it will soon be dark, can we not wait until morning?'

'No. The men can carry torches to light our way through the forest. Once we crest the top of the hill, the moon will provide enough light. I want to spend this night in our keep, Avelyn. Under a roof and in a bed.'

A bed. She smiled at the idea of sleeping with him in a real bed instead of a pallet and nodded. 'Then by all means, Roul it is.'

Chapter Seventeen

Once through the dark forest, they rode up a hill. Elrik stopped at the top and waved an arm, saying, 'From here, north to the sea, and from the crumbling Roman wall on the east, to the other side of the forest on the west are the borders of Roul.'

Avelyn followed the sweep of his arm, realising that the area covered so much land, that even in the broad light of day she would not be able see those borders. Samuel's low whistle caught her attention and she looked in the direction of his stare.

Far off in the distance four towers rose towards the sky. She could see pinpricks of flickering light—torches meant to light the entrance, perhaps. Her desperate grip on the cantle of her saddle was the only thing that kept her seated. 'That can't be Roul Keep.'

Elrik chuckled. 'No.'

Relief flooded her.

'Those are the barbican towers on the outer wall.'

The relief disappeared, leaving her weak and near dizzy. 'Elrik…' She let her words trail off, uncertain what to say and more uncertain what her place would be in something that large…that grand.

He looked down at her and smiled. 'I'm told that these lands have been held by the Roul family for three generations. They have had the time and the wealth to fortify and enlarge Roul. A strong arm is needed to hold this land for Normandy. I swore to the Duke that I was that man. Do you think I was wrong?'

Avelyn swallowed. She couldn't argue his strength, or his determination. He was obviously able to command, his men followed him without question. 'No. You were not wrong.'

He nodded. 'We are wasting time.'

As they rode down the hill and across the open grassy field, Elrik explained, 'The forests are full of old-growth trees that will supply the lumber for the wharf and ship building.' He glanced at Samuel and Fulke. 'We will do the same as we do on Roul Isle and only utilise sections of the forests at a time, replanting what is taken.'

At her frown, Fulke said, 'Otherwise we would soon run out of trees.'

'You can't see them from here, but there are wheat fields and pastures for sheep closer to the coast. The mill is within the walls, as is the town.'

Avelyn asked, 'There is no village outside the walls?'

'Not any longer. There had been a small one, also near the coast, but it was overrun by those who threatened to take unlawful possession of Roul.'

'Where do the villagers live now?'

'Lord Geoffrey provided tents that we erected in the outer bailey.'

A fine solution for now, but Avelyn knew that eventually those people would begin to chafe living so enclosed.

'Do you plan to rebuild the village?'

'I've already spoken with the elders and tomorrow they will gather men to start clearing out the rubble.'

Yes. He would be a good lord for Roul.

The clouds parted, letting the full light of the moon shine down, and Avelyn stared in shock at the sight before her. Behind the tall towers of the wall, a keep appeared, reaching towards the sky and dwarfing the stone towers.

'And that is Roul. It began as a Roman fort centuries past on a rocky area that juts out into the sea. The base is actually part of the rock cliff, doing away with the need for a surrounding wall. Instead, the outer and inner walls form a half-circle around the keep from one edge of the sheer cliff coast to the other.'

'It is a castle.'

Elrik nodded. 'That is what I first thought also. Lord Geoffrey said it was built that tall so that seeing out over the water is possible while still being able to keep watch beyond the walls.'

'How many bedchambers are there?'

'Bedchambers?'

She nodded. He had told her that she needed to fill the bedchambers with children and she wanted to know just how many they were talking about.

'I haven't yet been through the entire keep, but from what I remember, there are eight, maybe nine bedchambers.'

She gasped. 'My lord, the first thing we are going to do is discuss that renegotiation you mentioned.'

At first, he frowned, but soon his confusion cleared and he burst out laughing. 'I suppose we could keep a couple of the chambers free of children and use them for visitors instead.'

Her sigh of relief would have been humorous had they not arrived at the main gate tower. The portcullis was lowered to prevent entry. Eight men guarded the entrance—four on each tower.

Elrik looked up at the men and shouted, 'Open this gate.'

An older guard nodded to the others and within moments she heard the scraping groan of the iron gate being winched up.

Elrik waved her forward. 'Shall we?'

They rode side by side under the gate. She noted the grille above them, spanning the width and length of the twin gate towers. The guards peered down at her through the openings. Thankfully they were only curious and not attempting to toss rocks, hot oil, or arrows down at her as they would in a time of defence.

Once inside the outer yard, the first thing she noticed was that it was overcrowded with people and animals. She saw the tents that had been erected for those who had been forced from their homes. There was nothing worse than losing one's home—especially when it was all you had. Thankfully they would begin rebuilding the village soon.

The next thing she noticed was a gathering of mounted guards, a dozen perhaps, all dressed in mail with tunics of black trimmed in silver.

She looked at Elrik.

He nodded. 'From Roul Isle and King David.'

As they approached, the guards split into two single file rows, one on each side of the well-worn path leading to the inner wall. The men at the head of each line acknowledged Elrik by tapping their fist to their chest and then waving the line forward.

The main gate was open. No guards appeared on either of the towers. Without stopping, they rode beneath another iron grate, larger than the one at the outer wall. This wall was higher and wide enough for them to ride four abreast.

Once inside the inner bailey, she understood why the outer yard had been so crowded—the only signs of life here were stable hands and pages who ran forward to take charge of the horses and the guards. There had to be at least fifty men standing in tight formation, shoulder to shoulder, four deep.

Some of them she recognised as guards from the ships, others were unfamiliar to her. None of them wore the black and silver of Roul. The men who had ridden from the camp with her, Elrik, Samuel and Fulke dismounted and joined the formation.

The twelve guards who'd joined them at the inner bailey, the ones who were Elrik's men by the colours of their tunics, moved their horses into a single line behind her and Elrik.

Her husband urged his horse forward and slowly paced the horse before the formation of men. Samuel and Fulke moved in to flank her.

Elrik stopped his horse to face the men. 'If any of you wish to end your service to Roul, do so now.'

Not one man moved.

'Those who remain take note. I will say this only once.' He swung his arm in her direction and beckoned her forward. When she moved to his side, he said, 'This is Lady Avelyn of Roul, my wife, and you will be as loyal to her as you are to me.'

After the men all nodded their acceptance of his order, he looked over his shoulder. 'Sir Daniel, they are yours. Get these walls guarded.'

An older, grey-haired man behind them dismounted, shouting, 'Yes, my lord, gladly.' Before he'd taken two steps, he started barking orders for the protection of the keep.

Four boys ran forward to gather the reins to their horses. Samuel and Fulke slid off their animals and watched the guards set about their tasks.

When Elrik came to her side to reach up and help her from Little Lady, she asked, 'What are you going to do with the two of them?'

He set her on her feet and looked around. 'Who?'

'Samuel and Fulke. They will soon grow tired of following me around, if they haven't already. Elrik, they need to be useful.'

'Have they complained?'

'Of course not. You know they won't.'

'They are your men, Avelyn.'

'They would be better served as yours.'

With a deep frown, he asked, 'Do you never grow tired of this discussion? You know how it will end.'

'I fear some day it will end with the two of them leaving Roul.'

'Then I suggest you find them something useful to do.' He slung an arm across her lower back, pulling her closer as they walked. 'Just make certain the useful something includes keeping you safe.'

Avelyn didn't think she was the one who needed to be kept safe, but she held her tongue, fearing that just mentioning Osbert would somehow make him appear.

One of the guards she didn't recognise handed Elrik a lit torch before he led her up the stairs to the entrance door of the keep. She wrinkled her nose. 'I would have expected the door to be…larger.'

He laughed and shoved the tall, thick, iron-banded door open and ushered her into a small disarming room where she stood in open-mouthed shock.

'What were you saying about the door?'

The twin doors before them had to be at least two men high and each one was just as wide. They were studded with iron points and triple banded to keep the slabs of wood held tight.

He warned, 'You are not going to be happy with what's behind those doors.'

'Why?'

'It reeks worse than any un-mucked-out stable. The rushes are mouldy, rotted, and I couldn't begin to guess what lives in them.'

'There is a nice, clean tent back at camp.'

He shouldered one of the doors open and waved her through. 'No. We'll make do.'

The stench was so strong it burned her eyes as it wafted through the open door. Avelyn took a step back to catch her breath. 'Oh, my.'

He picked up the hem of her gown and held it to her face. 'Hold this. It's better up in the lord's chamber.'

They crossed the Great Hall quickly and nearly ran up the stairs leading to the upper floor.

Without slowing their pace, Elrik led her down a long corridor to a chamber at the far end. Once inside, he slammed the door closed behind them and stuck the torch in one of the wall sconces. He found another torch, lit that and placed it in the sconce on the other side of the room.

Thankfully, the room didn't reek with rot, instead it held a lingering closed smell as if it hadn't been used in a long time. Avelyn crossed the chamber to lean into the tall, narrow recessed window and tore the coverings free to let the night breeze in. The thin skins were so brittle they broke apart in her hand.

She turned around to survey the large chamber. The flickering light was too dim to see into the raised alcove at the side of the room, but she was easily able to tell that the rest of the chamber was sparsely furnished.

There was one chair with a small side table against the wall near the windows, two chests—a large curtained bed took up most of the space. The curtains hanging in tatters and the bare mattress made the bed look less than inviting.

Avelyn slapped the palm of her hand hard atop the mattress, relieved the action didn't send anything scurrying for safety and more relieved to find the mattress bag was stuffed with dried grass instead of straw. She could see to having the stuffing replaced later, but at least for now straw would not be poking at them while they slept.

She opened a small chest at the foot of the bed and waved towards a larger one against the wall near the door, telling Elrik, 'You check that one for bedclothes and I'll go through this one.'

Their search came up empty.

She dropped the lid of the chest and wiped the dust from her hands on the skirt of her gown. 'While you work at getting your armour off, I'm going to go check the other bedchambers for bedclothes.'

Elrik frowned. 'That doesn't sound like a good plan.'

'You and I are the only ones inside this keep, what could happen?' She headed towards the door.

'You will not leave this level.'

Even though he hadn't asked a question, she answered, 'No. I swear I will stay up on this level.' She grasped the door latch.

'And you will scream if you need me.'

'Yes. I will be within earshot should anything happen.' She opened the door.

'Avelyn?'

Now what? She turned to find him holding out a lit torch. Avelyn took the torch. 'Yes, I suppose that will help.'

She stepped out into the corridor and quickly grabbed the hem of her gown to hold it against her face to ward off the stench as she headed for the closest bedchamber.

Finding nothing in that room, she went to the next one only to find the same there—empty chests.

Finally, around the corner of the corridor, in the fourth chamber, her search produced a pillow and a couple of sheets, which she grabbed and headed towards the fifth one. As she reached to open the door to that room, she heard a noise and felt the hairs on the back of her neck rise. Before she could call out for Elrik, a sharp point was pressed against her neck.

'Now, sister of mine, we have all the time and privacy we need.'

It had taken her too long to check the other chambers for bedclothes. Elrik grasped the hilt of his sword still hanging from the belt wrapped low around his waist and headed towards the door.

A noise…hesitant footsteps from at least three men floated in from the corridor. Finally. He pulled a short sword from the cross scabbard on his back and a dagger from the top of his boot and flattened his back against the wall near the door.

The first man hit the floor with a heavy thud, his last breath nothing but a gurgle from the deep slice across his throat. The second one staggered, gasping as he clawed at the dagger planted in his chest, until he, too, fell heavily to the floor, his gasps now silent.

Elrik held out his sword and turned to face the third man.

Shocked to find himself at the point of a sword and his companions dead, he scrambled backwards quickly, stumbling in his haste.

Elrik saw the danger and reached out to grab the man's wrist, but his fingers closed over air—the stumbling fool had fallen hard against the wooden rail, breaking it beneath him, and he fell to the hard floor in the Great Hall, landing with his head at an unnatural angle.

Quickly checking to be sure none of the other men was near, Elrik gripped his sword tighter and headed down the corridor. There were still three men out there—one of whom was Avelyn's half-brother. Now that the cur was close at hand, he would end this tonight.

As he rounded the corner, he heard voices. One high pitched and accusing. He assumed that had to be Osbert. The other voice, stronger and steady, was undoubtedly his wife.

Again, placing his back to a wall for added protection in lieu of his guards' blades, he silently crept towards the voices.

Avelyn asked, 'What do you plan to do?'

Osbert removed the tip of the dagger from her neck and moved to stand in front of her, his weapon still ready, pointed at her chest. 'My men are now securing your husband. When they have completed that task, we will join them.'

His twisted smile set her heart to racing. 'I will knot a rope about his neck, throw the free end over a sturdy beam and haul him from his feet. You will watch as he dies slowly, legs kicking, fighting uselessly with each precious breath he has left.'

Every fibre of her being wanted to scream. But she held her tongue, knowing her show of fear would only inflame Osbert's determination to make her and Elrik suffer. That wasn't going to happen. She just needed to give Elrik time to get away from Osbert's men and come to her aid. Surely she could do that much on her own. So, instead, she swallowed her fear, tamped down her sense of right and wrong, and lied, 'Thank God.'

Osbert jerked his head back and narrowed his eyes. 'A few days ago, you acted as if you cared for this man you wed.'

'That was only because I feared his men were near.'

'You had sent them away, to deal with the fight my men had started in the camp.'

'Ah, but Lord Roul has me closely watched at all times. One or both of them could have returned at any moment.'

'He has you watched? Why?'

Her brother's nasally, whining voice made her head pound, making it doubly difficult to quickly come up with lies to spew. 'I am a Brandr, am I not? Do you think Roul married his enemy's daughter by choice? Osbert, even I know that you are smarter than to believe he would do so.'

The man preened at her praise. His wild, darting gaze stilled and he puffed up his chest. 'He was forced to wed you.'

'Of course he was. As I was him. Do you truly think I wanted to wed someone as beastly and dangerous as King David's Wolf?' She made a show of shivering as if in disgust. 'Just the thought of that animal touching me makes me sick.'

'But I have seen you laugh with him as the two of you entered his tent.'

She made a show of rolling her eyes and lifted her arms, palms out as if begging him to understand. 'I am his wife. He can do with me as he wills. Since I had no desire to die at his filthy hands, what choice did I have but to pretend I cared for him? I knew that eventually you or Father would come to rescue me from this horror.'

He lowered his blade. 'I am here now.'

'I know and I am indebted for ever.'

Osbert stepped closer, resting his hands on her shoulders. He sighed heavily. 'Unfortunately, Father has ordered me to kill you, too.'

Avelyn spun away. 'Why?'

He shrugged. 'And to get that ring.'

'That's what all of this is about? A ring?'

'The ring was my idea. I may need to prove I am related to King Óláfr, too. So possessing it will go a long way to having the proof at hand.'

'I don't have the ring any more.'

'Ah, but I am certain you can lure its location from your husband before he dies.'

'And you think that tyrant will tell me anything?'

Faster than she thought possible, Osbert lunged for her. She turned to escape, but he was quicker. Wrapping an arm about her neck, he jerked her against his chest. With a laugh he dragged the sharp point of his dagger down her cheek. 'Just a taste of what is to come.'

Pain filled her eyes with tears. She clawed at his forearm. 'Let me go.'

To her shocked surprise, he did. His gasp blew against her ear. His arm fell away from her neck. Cool air rushed in between her back and his chest. And then she heard the thud behind her.

Slowly turning around, Avelyn stared down at the floor where Osbert lay dying at her feet. She lifted her gaze and stared into the cold, dead gaze of her husband.

He said nothing. Just stared at her. Hatred and hurt were the only emotions shimmering from his gaze. He'd heard every lie she had told Osbert.

And he'd believed them.

A hand grasped weakly at the hem of her gown and she knelt down by Osbert. To her consternation, she felt a deep sorrow, maybe for the loving brother she never had, when she should have felt nothing but relief that he would never harm another.

She shook her head. 'You never should have come here.'

He gasped for breath, then said, 'Father...will...kill... you.' His head rolled to the side and she knew he was gone.

When she rose, the doorway was empty. Elrik had left.

Chapter Eighteen

Avelyn paused in the open door to their bedchamber. Elrik stared out of the window with his back to her. His sword lay on the floor near the entrance to the alcove. Two pools of blood on the floor of the chamber identified where the bodies she'd seen the guards carrying towards the stairs had died.

A dagger was next to one pool. A short sword by the other. For him to have taken down two men so close to each other, without gaining a scratch, must have been something to witness.

Not turning around, he asked, 'Is he dead?'

'Yes,' she said, skirting the blood when she stepped into the room. She wondered where to start. 'Elrik, I—'

He shook his head, stopping her explanation. 'No. Don't.'

His tone held no trace of anger, so she knew that seeking to enrage him would do nothing. She didn't enjoy it, usually ended up with a pounding head, but at least she could deal with his rage. But this…this was the voice of a man who had been hurt, deeply.

And she'd been the one to inadvertently cause that pain. She hated Osbert and what he'd caused her to do. But she hated herself more. Never had she wanted to hurt her wolf. Never.

He turned away from the window and then crossed the chamber to retrieve his sword from the floor. After tossing the weapon on the bed, he grabbed the chair and dragged it nearer the torchlight while motioning her over. 'Sit.'

Samuel walked into the chamber. 'Here are the things you asked—what the hell happened?'

He stared at her. 'Lady Avelyn?'

Elrik took the bucket of water and cloths from Samuel's hands and knelt on the floor alongside of her. 'This might hurt.'

He placed one rag against her cheek and held it while dropping another into the water. 'Avelyn, this is going to need to be sewn closed and it's not going to be pleasant.'

Just the pressure of the cloth against her cheek was less than pleasant. She shivered. 'Are you certain?'

'On both counts, yes.' He replaced the rag he'd been holding with the wet one. 'How do you want to proceed?'

'How bad is it?'

Fulke entered. He dropped the saddle bag he'd carried into the chamber, looked at her, swore and took a step back.

If it was enough to make Fulke step away, she didn't want to know just how badly Osbert had cut her. She blinked back tears. 'Elrik.'

He grasped her shoulder. 'My sewing skills are good only as a last resort on a battlefield or aboard a ship. Samuel has a deft hand with a needle, or I can summon one of the women.'

'Samuel.'

'Good. But you will need to keep still for him and already you are pulling away from my touch.'

She took a deep breath, trying to stop her limbs from trembling. 'Then hold me. Hold me tight.'

He rose to lift her in his arms, take her place on the chair and hold her on his lap. With her good cheek resting against his shoulder, Avelyn tucked her legs beneath the arm of the chair. If this hurt as much as she feared, she didn't want to kick anyone.

Samuel rooted through the saddle bag.

At Elrik's nod, Fulke moved a stool next to the chair, sitting so close that his own legs pinned hers in place.

She looked up at Elrik as his arms came around her. 'With any luck I'll pass out.'

He agreed. 'That is my hope, too, Little Dove. Close your eyes.'

His lips pressed lightly to her forehead and he covered her eyes with a hand, holding her head firmly against his shoulder.

When she heard Samuel's footsteps return to the chair, Elrik wrapped his other arm over hers and curved his fingers around her shoulder. At the same time, Fulke took her hands between his.

A wet rag dabbed against her cheek. Even though Samuel's touch was surprisingly gentle, she flinched.

Elrik softly said, 'Shh. We've got you. I've got you, Avelyn.'

She felt the heat of her tears as they pooled beneath the hand covering her eyes. 'Elrik, I am sorry.'

'No more than I.'

As if he couldn't tell by her tears and trembling, she admitted, 'I am afraid.'

'I know. It is all right to feel fear at the thought of pain. Just know you are safe. It will be over soon.'

He rested his cheek against her head. 'I think tomorrow we'll get as many hands as possible working on cleaning out the Great Hall.'

Fulke chuckled. 'If you think the hall is bad, you need to step inside the stable. I feel sorry for the horses.'

'Then gather some of the older boys to get started on them first thing in the morning.'

She heard splashing as Samuel dropped his rag into the bucket, then dabbed at her cheek some more. This time she didn't flinch.

Fulke squeezed her hands briefly. 'How long do you think it'll take to put this keep to rights?'

'I would like to have it habitable within a week if possible.' Elrik's heart beat hard against her side. But it was steady and lent her a measure of comfort.

'That might be expecting a little more than what's possible.'

She knew that their conversation was meant to distract her. Avelyn relaxed against Elrik's chest. In truth, their deep voices were starting to lull her to sleep.

She was tired. It was late, well past the time she normally would have sought her bed.

'After the Great Hall, I suppose the kitchens should be seen to next.'

A sharp poke sent a wave of pain rolling through her face and down her spine. Avelyn tensed. Elrik's hold tightened, as did Fulke's.

She felt a whine start in her throat.

Another sharp poke took her breath away. Her husband hadn't lied. This was not pleasant in the least.

Like an injured animal, she struggled to fight against the pain, but Elrik and Fulke held her secure, preventing her from thrashing. The building whine escaped.

Elrik's lips pressed against her forehead. 'Sweeting, I am so sorry.'

Samuel poked the needle into her cheek again—

Elrik breathed a heavy sigh of relief and relaxed his

hold around her arms as Avelyn's body went limp on his lap. Thankfully she'd passed out. He glanced up at Samuel. 'Hurry. Get it over with.'

Fulke released her hands and sat up straighter on the stool with a weak, shaking laugh. 'I thought for certain she'd remain alert the whole time.'

Samuel's fingers stopped trembling and he sped up his task. 'At least the cur didn't cut her all the way through. Still, it's going to leave one nasty scar.'

'I doubt if she will care.' Although Elrik knew that every time he looked at her, he would remember the one time he had let her down. The one time he should have been at her side, he hadn't been and she'd paid the price for that hesitation.

Fulke asked, 'How did this happen?'

'Osbert took her by surprise while three of his men came for me.'

'Why was she alone to begin with?'

He heard the censure in Fulke's tone. Not only did he understand it, he agreed. 'A mistake. One that I cannot undo. I had finally gained control of the keep and thought us safe.'

'So that leaves two more men to find?'

'Yes.'

Samuel glanced at Fulke, then turned his attention to Elrik. 'If you think you can stand guard, once we are done here the two of us will hunt them down.'

Elrik narrowed his eyes to glare at Samuel. 'If you think I don't take full responsibility for this, you are wrong.'

'I simply cannot understand how it could have taken you so long to cut down three men to get to your wife in time to protect her.'

Not long ago he'd been concerned that these two had been acting like overprotective brothers. Now they sounded like outraged fathers.

It hadn't taken him long to dispatch the three men. He had rushed to her, but had hesitated outside the door to the chamber where Osbert had taken Avelyn because he'd heard the words she'd said to her half-brother about him.

Words that he knew were nothing but lies, spoken to save her life and stall long enough for him to get there. Mere words that had fallen across his ears like freezing rain and slammed against his chest as if he'd walked in front of a stallion lashing out with his hooves during a battle.

Ever since he'd given his life over to King David, he'd heard many things said about him. Things that would have sent other men into a rage. His first wife had called him terrible things as she'd lay dying. His own father had often told him how useless he was and what a traitor to the family he'd turned out to be.

And those meaningless words had bounced off him like a tiny pebble, sometimes without any more notice than he would give to a gnat.

But when she'd spoken those words, those lies, he'd realised in that instant just how much he loved her. The searing pain her words caused wouldn't have been possible had he not already lost his heart to his wife.

And he'd hesitated. One heartbeat too long.

For that, he'd never forgive himself.

Samuel cut the thread and stepped back. 'It will do. Might not be pretty, but the stitches will hold until it mends.'

'Good. Thank you. Now if you will get me some clean water and rags, and perhaps find some covers for the bed, both of you can go hunting.'

When they left the chamber, he rose enough to readjust Avelyn on his lap and then settled back down on to the chair. She turned her face into his chest and raised an arm, to curl her fingers over his shoulder.

From the light evenness of her breathing, she was sleeping deeply. He couldn't help but wonder what her thoughts would be upon awakening. Obviously, her first thought would go to the pain she'd feel, but that pain would most likely fire her anger, disgust, if not hate towards him.

How many times had he taken her to task for not being with her guards? How many times had he worried about her safety?

Yet, it had taken only one time for him to relax his guard for her to be harmed. Had he hesitated one more heartbeat, she would be dead.

Elrik closed his eyes. He couldn't remember ever having felt this worthless in his entire life. What good was he if he couldn't protect his wife in their keep?

The men re-entered the chamber. Fulke placed a pile of bedclothes on the mattress. Samuel put the bucket of water and the rags by the chair before retrieving the saddlebag. 'Do you require anything else?'

'No. Go.'

Fulke nodded. 'We won't return until we have both men.'

'You will keep an eye on her?' Samuel asked from the doorway.

He doubted if either of them would ever let him forget what his lapse had cost Avelyn. 'Go.'

Avelyn rolled over, her cheek pressing into the softness of a pillow hurt so badly it made her stomach churn. She pushed herself up on the bed and looked around the semi-dark chamber, frowning.

The last thing she remembered was sitting on Elrik's lap while Samuel worked on her cheek. She must have passed out just as she'd hoped would happen. But that didn't explain how she was now in a bed that had been made up with sheets, covers and pillows, or how she was without any clothing.

She glanced over the edge of the bed and saw her gown soaking in a bucket of bloody water. Reaching her hand up, she gingerly touched her cheek. From feeling the stitches, Osbert had dragged the tip of his blade from almost the top of her ear, angling down towards the corner of her mouth. Thankfully the cut had been across the meaty part of her cheek and not across her jawbone where he could have caused more damage.

She knew it would leave a scar and didn't care. She also doubted if her wolf husband would care either. At least she hoped he didn't.

'What are you doing up?'

Avelyn jumped at Elrik's voice as he soundlessly walked into the chamber.

'From the dwindling sunlight, I'd say I have slept the day away.'

He joined her on the bed, sitting with his back against the wall behind them and his legs stretched out before him. 'It was long night, so I expected you to sleep through until tomorrow morning.'

She looked at him, studying the dullness that had settled in his normally glimmering eyes and the flat line of his mouth. 'We should talk.'

'Not now. We will, but not yet.'

'You are...' She paused. He wasn't angry. More...sad. Hurt. 'I am sorry, Elrik.'

He pulled her alongside him, with his arm around her to hold her close. 'Hush, Avelyn.'

She couldn't let this linger between them. He had to know she'd been lying to Osbert. 'But—'

'No.' The sudden sharpness of his tone stopped her from speaking. 'You are injured and need to rest, to heal. And I am in no mood to talk about anything. Just rest and be still.'

Uncertain how to react, she turned on to her side, resting half across his chest with an arm draped over his waist. The steady beat of his heart soothed her. Soon, she relaxed against the warmth of his body and closed her eyes.

When she'd thought about being married, of having a husband, she'd always longed for a friend, someone to share things with, to laugh with, someone who would treat her fairly. Love had never been a consideration. That elusive emotion had seemed useless and unwanted.

But with each lie she'd spewed to Osbert she'd realised just how much she'd fallen in love with King David's Wolf.

How had this happened? Had her heart known this all along? Was that why she'd been so confused and uncertain of late? Angry one moment and filled with an overwhelming need to hold him, touch him, or just see him, the next moment?

This wasn't what she'd wanted. What good were these conflicting emotions if they added nothing of value to her day?

Ah, but they did add value to her day. He added value to her day. He encouraged her to be brave, to be strong, to take on tasks she never would have imagined doing before. And she did all those things, for him. Doing something for another was the value added to her day that had been missing her whole life.

Avelyn sniffed back a threatening tear. Another thing she didn't like about this loss of control—she found herself near tears over nothing every time she turned around and she didn't like it at all.

Elrik reached over to brush his thumb beneath her eyes. She felt his chest rise and fall with a sigh. 'Go to sleep, Avelyn. All is well. Just sleep.'

He held her close, stroking her arm, smoothing a hand over her hair and back until again he heard her light, even breathing.

For once her tears hadn't upset or confused him. He knew she was going to be emotional for a while. Her face was going to bother her for days to come and once the pain ceased, the healing cut would be uncomfortable as it pulled and pinched. Her brother had attacked her and been killed in front of her. While she swore that she hated Osbert, he had still been her half-brother. The way she'd knelt at his side when he'd died showed that she'd felt something more than hate for him.

Added to the things that would prick away at her emotions was his refusal to talk about what had happened. They would, but not until he knew for certain that he would be able to fully control the wide range of feelings racing back and forth in his mind.

He didn't want to become angry. It wasn't her fault that he was uneasy with the notion that she held his heart. That whole idea was…terrifying to him. The thought that he was no longer in control of what he felt made him feel… vulnerable…as if he were willingly leaving himself open for more pain than he wished to experience.

It would be easier, less frightening, to stand in the middle of a melee without armour or weapons.

He had brought this on himself. Had he argued harder with King David about holding off on this marriage, or waited to leave for Normandy after she'd been on her way to Roul Isle, they wouldn't now be in this position.

She stirred against him, snuggling closer to his warmth. She had come to trust him with little effort, instinctively knowing he would provide whatever it was she sought— simple warmth, fulfilment of passion, and, except for the one time when she truly needed him, she looked to him for protection. Reaching over to grasp the covers, he pulled them over her.

Elrik shook his head. Who was he seeking to fool? He

could imagine all the ways he could have avoided this and think of all the reasons it was not what he wanted, but he knew that he'd have it no other way.

She'd worried more than once that he would set her aside. He would never do so. How could he when her smile was the light in his day and her soft moans at his touch were the brightness in his night? She was the reason his heart beat.

'My lady?'

Avelyn thought she heard someone speaking to her, but she was distracted, and it sounded as if the voice came through a thick, murky fog.

'Lady Avelyn?'

She looked down to find one of the men standing beneath her perch on the ladder propped up against the side wall in the Great Hall.

'Yes?'

'My lady, I can do that.'

A quick glance up at the repaired railing on the floor above made her aware Elrik was once again watching her.

Which explained why a guard was offering to help with housekeeping chores.

The last five days had been…odd. If he wasn't watching her, then Samuel and Fulke were. She hadn't been alone once.

If danger still lurked nearby in the form of Osbert and his men, she would be able to understand their watchfulness. But the last two men had been found dead in the forest, likely killed by Osbert before he'd attacked her, so with that threat gone, why this need to keep her under such close guard?

When she'd asked Elrik about it, he had changed the subject. Between that and the fact that they had yet to discuss what had happened, she was becoming more worried each day.

Something was different. He held her through the night, but that was all, simply held her close, never once trying to so much as kiss her. And during the day, he was…polite. Watchful and polite. There had been no teasing, no talking about anything of a personal nature. He treated her just as he would an acquaintance.

It was as if he were intentionally seeking to distance himself.

Even now, with his ever-present stare upon her, there was nothing of warmth in his gaze. He watched her in the same manner he would anyone under his protection.

And it was beginning to frighten her.

She tore her gaze away from the piercing stare to hand the guard the old shield she'd just removed from its hanger on the wall and then climbed down the ladder.

Wiping her grimy hands on the skirt of the old gown she'd borrowed from the laundress, she said, 'I was just going to take these down, scrub them and put them back up.'

The guard shrugged. 'I should be able to do that.'

She wasn't going to argue with him since running up and down the ladder was something he'd be better at doing than she. 'Thank you. I appreciate the help.'

With another glance up at the railing, she left the man to his task and headed for the stairs.

A commotion at the entryway drew her attention. Samuel and Fulke followed as she went to see what, or who, was causing trouble.

Two men were arguing with the guards about giving up their weapons. Their raised voices gave more of an indication about their displeasure than their words.

She stood in the open doorway to ask, 'Is there a problem here?'

One of the men smiled. 'Obviously, you are Elrik's Lady.'

'Obviously?'

The other man answered, 'Your tone says Lady of the Keep.'

She narrowed her gaze to study them a moment. 'Ah. Like the silver strands in your dark hair say Roul.'

'Yes, his brothers.'

The slightly taller one added, 'I hope you don't mind if we only stay this one night.'

'Why would I mind?'

'I wasn't certain if you would be ready to leave that quickly or not.'

The floor beneath her feet moved. She felt as though she stood on the top of a cresting wave—one that was ready to break upon a rocky shore.

Samuel nearly growled. 'Your brother is above.'

She swallowed and glanced behind her, up at the railing to find Elrik once again returning her stare. She forced her attention back to his brothers. 'If you will excuse me.' Then pushed past them and raced out into the bailey. She couldn't breathe and needed air.

Avelyn wandered over to the well and sat on a bench. She closed her eyes and leaned her forehead against the hard stone. The air brushed against her cheek, cooling the heat of anger and lessening the rage born of despair.

He was going to set her aside without even telling her. How could she have been so foolish to let herself fall in love?

The urge to race back inside and up the stairs to throw herself at his feet and beg him to let her stay nearly overwhelmed her.

No.

She would not. She couldn't live the rest of her life wondering if he'd let her remain only because he felt obligated to do so. She didn't want his pity. Didn't want to be nothing more than an obligation, a responsibility he had no choice but to bear.

She spun the gold band on her left ring finger, wondering if she should leave it for Elrik, or keep it as a reminder of their brief time together. With a groan, she pushed away from the well. She needed to find the will, the strength to stiffen her spine and hold her head up, at least until she was far enough out to sea where she could grieve in peace.

Chapter Nineteen

Avelyn carefully used yet another one of the sharpened quills Samuel had prepared for her and dipped it in the ink horn to finish writing a letter to leave for Elrik.

She had secreted herself away in an unused chamber, taking along the small box Fulke had given her to store the few writing materials she had, a candle and holder for light, and a cover for the bed. Those items she would leave behind, taking with her only what she knew were hers—the dark gown she'd purchased with a kiss and her grandmother's ring.

Avelyn twirled the gold band on her finger. This wasn't really hers. It belonged to Elrik's family. She slipped it off, ignoring the twisting of her stomach and rapid thudding of her heart, and placed it on the table. She would leave it near the parchment for him to find.

After thinking about it for hours, she knew she couldn't face her husband. She couldn't talk to him, couldn't bring herself to even ask why he was sending her away.

She didn't want to know the answers, fearing they would hurt more than not knowing. The only thing she wished to know right at this moment was when this need to cry would stop.

And when this pain would ease.

But she'd sworn to him that she would never leave without letting him know. So, now it was time to put the writing she'd been practising and learning to use. It might be difficult for Elrik to read what she wrote. If so, he could have Samuel or Fulke read it—they were familiar with her fumbling attempts.

She needed him to know that he was loved, that he held her heart and that she knew no matter how sorry she was, she would never be able to take away the terrible hurt she had caused him with her words to Osbert.

She hadn't meant them. They had all been lies. Lies that had saved her life, but had taken away what she held most dear—him.

Her hand ached from the effort of writing the missive. A glance out of the window told her she'd been at this for hours. The sun had nearly set.

And now that her letter was written, she stared at it, wondering how to sign.

Finally, she wrote.

I hope to remain your Little Dove.

It was the best she knew how to do. Maybe some day in the future, she could write him a better note that one of his brothers could bring to him.

Her breath caught on a sob. She let the quill fall from her hand and ran to the bed where she pulled the cover over her, hoping to drown out the sound of her crying.

Elrik's hands shook as he read the missive again for the third time. *What had he done?*

His brothers' arrival couldn't have come at a worse time. He had looked for her all afternoon and evening. Finally, unable to locate his wife, he'd asked Samuel where she might have gone. The man nearly bit his head off when he had replied that she'd gone to Roul Isle just like Elrik wanted.

The row he'd had with not just Samuel but also with Fulke had provided more entertainment for those inside the keep than he ever could have imagined.

The three of them had shouted at each other. His brother Rory had grabbed Fulke when the man had raised his fist ready to go to blows for Lady Avelyn's honour, while Edan had physically placed his body between Samuel and Elrik to keep them from getting close enough to do each other harm.

At first, Elrik didn't understand their anger, but when Samuel had told him that Edan had asked Avelyn if she could be ready to leave tomorrow, everything became clear.

She thought his brothers were there to take her to Roul Isle. And that was true, to a point. They were there because of the missive they'd been sent right after the wedding. Since they hadn't found Avelyn at Carlisle, they'd likely come to Roul Keep to see what was happening. And knowing King David, Elrik knew he'd not explained Avelyn's absence from his castle.

Neither of them had been on Roul Isle when the second missive arrived ordering them to ignore the first, as their service in this matter was no longer needed.

After discovering what had been said, he'd torn through this keep like a man possessed looking for her. He had to find her. Had to explain that Rory and Edan were not here to take her away from him.

Had to tell her that he hadn't been ignoring her these last five days, he'd been giving her time to heal, time to calm her emotions before they talked. That was all. How could he have been so witless?

Finally, fearing she'd run away, he'd rechecked the upper

chambers just to be certain and found her in the smallest one at the far end of the back corridor.

She was buried under the covers and, from the fitfulness of her sleep, he knew she had cried until exhaustion overtook her.

Then he'd seen the quill, ink horn, and her wedding ring. Curious, he'd stuck his torch in the sconce near the little table, picked up the ring and sat down to see what was written on the page.

To his shock and pride, his wife had learned to read and write. While the writing itself was hard to decipher, the words were simple and they'd come from her heart. The heart he'd unintentionally broken so thoroughly.

He stared at Avelyn and frowned. He would cherish this note always, but the fact that she intended to leave it for him to find, instead of coming to him directly, meant she didn't trust him enough yet to talk to him...just as he had yet to find himself able to talk to her.

That had to be changed. But she was going to creep out of here tomorrow and make her way to Edan's ship.

Elrik's lips twitched with the beginning of a smile. He put the missive exactly where he'd found it, placed the ring back on the table, took the torch from the wall sconce and stood over her a moment before quietly leaving the chamber.

She shivered in the damp morning air. This ride to the ship had been the longest, and most silent, she'd ever experienced.

Samuel and Fulke hadn't spoken one word to break the silence. They didn't appear angry, just withdrawn, quiet and there wasn't anything she could do about that.

When the ships came into view, her hands shook at what she was going to do and she laughed softly at her sudden nervousness. It wasn't as if she'd never run away or been alone before. Why was it suddenly making her worrisome now?

Samuel helped her dismount and she turned to Little Lady to stroke the horse's nose and place a kiss between the big, dark eyes. 'I will miss you.'

A squire took the reins, saying, 'She will be well cared for, my lady.'

Avelyn nodded in reply and turned to board the ship.

One of Elrik's brothers waited for her at the flap to the sailcloth covering of the makeshift cabin beneath the forecastle. 'Lady Avelyn. Sister.' He took her hand. 'I am Edan. If you require anything, please let me know.' He held the flap open and dropped it closed behind her.

She heard Samuel and Fulke take up their positions on either side of the flap and was thankful for their protection on this voyage. At least she wouldn't be completely alone amidst nothing but strangers.

The sound of men's heavy footsteps boarding the ship let her know that the crew and some guards had joined them. Soon they would be underway.

Her stomach clenched. She didn't want to go, but she was too much of a coward to face her husband. She couldn't find the words to tell him how sorry she was, how guilty she felt, for hurting him. She tightly closed her eyes to fight back tears. Certain she had control of her emotions, she opened her eyes and glanced around the small cabin she would be calling home for the next several days. It was essentially the same as the one on Elrik's ship—pallet, stool, small table and a chest.

She opened the lid to the chest to find her bags had already been placed inside along with men's clothes that probably belonged to Edan.

Orders to cast off were shouted and she felt the ship

lurch as it moved slowly away from the dock. She took off her heavy cloak and hung it on a hook before stretching out on the pallet.

She curled her fingers and slammed a fist against the pallet. No. She was not going to cry. What good would it do her?

Yet there was no other explanation for the moisture running from her eyes. She rolled on to her side, burying the uninjured side of her face into the pillow, curled into a tight ball, clenched her jaw, and sniffed.

'Damn you, Elrik,' she whispered brokenly into the empty cabin.

A hand stroked her hair. 'I was damned the moment I met you, Little Dove.'

She gasped and froze. Was she now imagining things?

The hand grasping her shoulder was far too solid to be an imagining. 'We need to talk.'

She rolled over on to her back and stared up at him in shock. And if she were to be honest, a small measure of hope flared to life. 'What are you doing here?'

'I am trying to discover which one of us has enough courage to say what needs to be said between us.'

Courage? Avelyn frowned. What would take more courage—telling him she loved him so, or that she was willing to leave because she knew that was what he wanted? 'You sent me away.'

'I did no such thing, Avelyn. My brothers had not received the second set of orders telling them they would not be needed. They arrived only because of a mistake with communication. There has been too much of that lately.'

'How so?'

He moved over her on the pallet and stretched out alongside her, before explaining. 'I have left you alone these last five or so days because I believed you needed time to come to terms with what had occurred between you and Osbert, and to accept his death, when I could have simply asked if you needed time or not.'

'I came to terms with his death the moment he thudded to the floor. It might be a sin, but his loss meant nothing to me.'

'And you could have told me that, had I asked. But I didn't. Just like now, you chose to run away instead of coming to me to discover why my brothers had arrived.'

'I was so afraid of the answer I would hear if I did come to you.'

'As I was afraid to tell you what your words to Osbert did to me.'

'Elrik, I never meant to hurt you.' She shivered, unable to forget the words she had spoken, the lies that had hurt him so.

'I know that. I knew you had lied to save your life and to stall for time.' Gently touching the angry wound on her cheek, he said, 'This happened because of me.'

'You didn't take a knife to my face.'

'No. I only hesitated long enough for Osbert to do the deed.' He clasped her hands between his. 'Yes, your words hurt. I was taken aback by the pain they caused. But in that moment, I realised that those lies wouldn't have hurt had I not already placed my heart in your hands.'

Her breath caught at his admission. She had realised the same thing, at the same moment. But could she tell him that? Did she have the courage to place her heart in his hands, knowing that she could one day find herself alone like her mother had?

Elrik remained silent, waiting to see if she could bring herself to trust him enough not to hurt her. She'd already put the words on parchment, but she didn't know that he'd read her letter and he wasn't going to tell her until she gave voice to her feelings.

Finally, she looked into his gaze, admitting, 'As I spoke each lie I, too, understood why they were so hard to say. I knew it was because I loved you so dearly.'

He smiled and shook his head. 'For two people who claim to love each other, we certainly do seem to fumble with it.'

'Perhaps because it isn't familiar to either of us.'

'I suppose that will take time and we'll have plenty of it these next few weeks.'

'Where are we going?'

'First, we'll head to Roul Isle to drop off Edan. After that wherever you want to go, Avelyn.'

'We have a keep that needs our attention.'

'The keep is going nowhere. We, the two of us, are more important to me than that keep. And it is imperative that you come to understand just how much you can trust me, Avelyn. There is nothing you can't tell me, nothing. Good or bad, I need you to always know you can talk to me.'

He'd told her that before and, while she had believed him, she hadn't wanted to put his words to the test with her feelings for him. They had been too new, too…tender… fragile to expose them to possible danger.

He reached under the corner of the pallet and brought her hand up towards her face. 'You forgot something back at Roul.'

Elrik slipped her wedding band on her finger, tipped her head up and gently kissed her lips. With his lips a breath away from hers, he said, 'Wife, I need you to know that you own my heart and my soul. I love you with every breath I take, today and always.'

As he repeated the words she'd put on the parchment for him to find, Avelyn felt the warmth of his love wash over her, bringing with it the sense that she would always find safety in his arms, no matter what. She rested a palm on his chest over the beating of his heart. 'My Wolf, I return that love and I swear to always hold your heart and soul gently.'

* * * * *

If you enjoyed this story check out these other great reads by Denise Lynn

AT THE WARRIOR'S MERCY
THE WARRIOR'S WINTER BRIDE
PREGNANT BY THE WARRIOR